WOLF

THE FRACTURED FAIRYTALES SERIES

J. A. WYNTERS

Editing by: Dear Jane Editing

Cover design: Jennifer Demeter; The Dust Jacket Designs

Interior Formatting: Dawn Lucous, Yours Truly Book Services

To Wolf

I would follow you blindly into the woods.

PRESENT DAY

Wolf

The music drills into my skull. My head falls back, and I stare at a black spot in the ceiling that's not covered with lights. The club is as full as ever, everyone is out for a good time. The air is drenched with the scent of alcohol and pheromones, and some tight ass blonde has been giving me *fuck me* eyes for the last two hours.

I'm on edge tonight. I feel like a marionette whose strings are pulled too tightly and I just can't shake it off. Everything feels too stiff, too rigid, sitting just out of place.

The blonde walks past me again and the tip of her tongue slips out gliding along her bottom lip. My cock twitches and now, there's another part of me that's tight and sore.

Fuck it.

I throw her my trademark smile and bring the two-way radio to my lips, "Rob, could you come to my position? I have a possible code twenty-two." I step off my podium.

A few smirks spread around the room. I ignore them. I've been in this game long enough to know none of the guys would talk, especially not if they want to keep working for me.

I thought I would enjoy filling a shift, re-live the old days, but I hate it. It takes me back to the beginning when we were just setting up, getting fucked around and beaten on. Hunter and I started our security business five years ago. We started small. Securing local clubs, staring at doors and asses for years. Over time we hired and trained bodies, now we own one of the largest and most formidable security firms in London.

Three years ago, we decided to make the shift to private protection. Celebrities and wannabies who need bodyguards to babysit them. It's easier on the body and the pay cheques are higher. Still, the security business is thriving, so we won't stop the club security. So when we're short, Hunter and I still have to fill in the gaps, which means, for tonight, I 'm stuck here.

Guess I'm going to have to find a way to pass the time.

I jut my chin and walk towards the back entrance, knowing blondie is following me. I hope she had a good time cause after I'm done with her, she won't be allowed to stay much longer. I'll get one of the guys to remove her for being intoxicated. I never double dip and I don't need a broken-hearted chick skulking around me all night giving me hate stares. I've learned from my first few mistakes. We all have. Now we protect ourselves.

The boys will look out for me. They always do. In a world of uncertainty, of this one thing I can always be sure.

I spot Bella, the manager. Her gaze boomerangs from the blonde trailing behind me, to my face. I wink, nod, and keep walking. She's been shooting me desperate looks all night. Last time I worked this club, I had her bent over her desk with my cock pumping inside her and the cops knocking on the door demanding CCTV footage of a fight from the night before. I've been staying out of her way and hope by the end of the night she'll finally get the idea.

I lead blondie to the back door where Dean keeps a straight face and lets us out. She's already clawing at me and I grab her wrist to keep her from touching my cock. I can't let the cameras catch me doing this, despite everything, I have a reputation to uphold— squeaky clean and always doing the right thing— it's how we've managed to climb the ladder so quickly. And how Hunter and I can now work out of an office while the guys have to do the grunt work.

Getting a few blow jobs during a shift is one thing, getting caught is another. I won't let any girl jeopardise what I've worked so hard for.

I yank her out of the club. Fresh air hits my lungs, the bite of crisp air coats my skin and cools me down. I pull her into the dead camera zone and wait for the door to close, muting the music as it does.

The alley glistens. The rain's washed away the sour smell of piss and a few puddles lay scattered among the cobblestones like dark mirrors, beckoning me to look into them and see the monster I am.

I grab the blonde and slam her back into the brick wall, she lets out a gentle giggle and her eyes grow bigger as they rake over me.

"You're pretty," I say dipping my head just a little. She's not, but that's the kind of shit girls want to hear.

She grabs my chin and pulls my head up so that I can look into her eyes, "My name is Jenny."

I nod like it matters, letting the name slip away like all the Samanthas and Karens and Mias that came before her. I smile like I give a shit and pin her body to the wall with mine.

"Are you sober?" I kiss her cheek as I ask.

"Sober enough to know what I want."

"What do you want, baby?" I whisper against her ear.

"You." Desperation clings to her breathy words.

I smirk. Tension cramps in my neck. Maybe it's the full moon making me edgy. But then she pushes up on her tiptoes and sucks on my lips. The kiss is sloppy, and greedy, and will later fade into a bank of unmemorable moments. But right now, all I need is a warm body and a tight hole.

I rip away from her mouth and my hands find her breasts, she moans a little as I curl my hands around them and squeeze through all the fabric of her dress and bra. Under normal circumstances, I would give them more attention but tonight I'm on a clock and she has an expiration date.

I grip her dress and tug it upwards exposing a black lacy thong that's more string than fabric.

Perfect.

Her lips brush my neck and she looks up at me, "You're not taking me home?"

"Here's better baby, plus I have to go back to work. Maybe after..." I won't, but she doesn't know that. The lie gives them hope and butters them up. I *never* take anyone home, it's the one rule I never compromise on.

I sink down to her neck and let my teeth graze the skin, her disappointed moan turns into a needy one. She tastes like salty sweat and leaves a lingering flavour of bitter perfume on my tongue.

It feels all wrong.

Everything about her, about this. I'm too many shades of sober for this. I'm about to pull away when her hands rip at my zip and wrap around my cock. She lets out a small gasp and gives it a gentle tug. Any thoughts of leaving vanish.

Fuck it, I might as well try to get rid of some of the tension.

I fish a condom from my back pocket and lower my pants just enough to expose my ass and cock, shrug her hands off and sheath myself. She looks at me like a hungry girl with a very big appetite and I almost regret not just asking her to suck me off instead.

I pull at her dress, grab her ass and with as much grace as a giraffe on skates, she leaps up and wraps herself around my waist. I grab her lacy number, yank it to one side, then slam into her in a violent harsh movement.

She sucks in a sharp breath like she wasn't expecting me, then buries her head in my neck and holds on.

I drive into her and she moans against my skin, "Jesus, you feel so good."

"So do you, baby." I breathe out as I quicken my pace, I want to finish and get back to work.

"Say my name, Jenny."

I don't think about it, I'm halfway there, "Jenny," I growl as her fingers dig into my shoulders and I piston into her. Her body grinds against the bricks, and even though I'm trying to hold her away from it I know it's tearing at her back and shoulders.

I quicken my pace feeling the familiar sensation in my ball sack, the tightness in my back and the edge of relief, she moans like an alley cat and scratches my skin.

She pushes against me, her body slapping against mine till she mewls and cries out and her pussy squeezes so intensely I come hard and fast leaning us both against the wall as my knees wobble. I suck in a few deep breaths and let the tension seep from my body just as I knew it would.

I slip her off me, and she slumps dreamily against the building, she gives me a dopey smile and tries to pull in for a kiss, I turn my head and her lips land on my cheeks.

"That was amazing," she coos in a wistful voice and I shudder, knowing what she wants.

"Yeah, it was great thanks, baby."

"Jenny." She looks at me and smiles serenely as she fixes her dress.

"Yeah, Jenny." I'm already tucking my shirt back into my dress pants and step away from her. I know I can get to the door in a few strides, and her constant obsession with me using her name is starting to give me a creepy vibe.

"When do you finish your shift?" She reaches for my hand and tries to lace her fingers through mine. I pull away.

I sigh, she obviously didn't get the memo that this was a one-time deal, but she will in a sec. "Not till closing time."

"Should I wait for you?"

"Nah, I'll have to do paperwork and I'm carpooling with one of the guys. This was really… nice though, thanks."

She steps closer, her face twitches for a second then corrects, "Are you sure?"

"Yeah, work you know…" I run a hand through my hair and step back unease sinking into me.

"Oh, okay," she closes the distance between us again, "Let me give you my number."

"Sure," I hand her my phone knowing I'll delete it as soon as I'm inside. She leans against me as she inserts her number, and I swear she's trying to smell me.

What the hell?

She hands it back, "I've put it under Jenny."

"Jenny, got it," I wink and pocket my phone. Her crazy is starting to slither to the surface and I need to get away from her.

"Call me when your shift is done?" She looks at me with big, hopeful doe eyes.

"Are you staying in the city tonight?"

"Just moved here a few weeks ago," she says in her thick Brummie accent.

Damn.

"Great, maybe I can drop by later…" I won't.

Her face breaks into a chilling smile, "I'll see you inside then."

"Sure." She won't.

I don't wait for more conversation 'cause I know where it's going, I've had plenty of these and they all end the same.

I pound on the door and Dean cracks it open. I slip inside then he slams it shut behind me. She'll come in through the front door and hang around giving me looks for the next twenty minutes. After that, I'll get one of the guys to remove her for being too drunk.

When I step back up on the podium to finish my shift, I don't feel a tiny bit guilty. But I do feel the tension creep back around me, bringing with it a familiar, angry emptiness that's been festering for almost ten years.

Bella glares at me again, and for a second, I think she might be worth another round—till a cute brunette passes by me and gives me her best *fuck me* eyes.

I draw in a long breath and reach for my radio, "Hey Rob, I'm going to need you to come back and cover me again, I have a possible code twenty-two."

2

Red

There is an endless list of events in my life that should have left me bitter and jaded. But if I had to choose my top three, they would go something like this:

1. Losing almost everyone I love.
2. Anything to do with Shaw Bennett, AKA–Wolf.
3. Being twenty-five, broke, and going through another breakup.

So, what do all these things have to do with one another? They mean I have to grovel.

Again.

To the only person who might be willing to help. My annoying older brother who is going to preach all the 'I told you so's' I don't want to hear.

Now, I'll have to endure the fact that Hunter will talk down to me in his condescending big brother voice and try to parent me. It's laughable given how fucked up his life choices are, but right now, in this moment, I have no other options.

Not now when I'm standing on the street with my suitcase, my phone, and a tear-streaked face.

I'm such an idiot.

How I didn't see this one coming is beyond me. Dave is an asshole. Another one in a long list that I seem to attract. It's like I'm a magnet for them—they can't keep away, and I keep letting them in just to get hurt again and again.

Then there's Hunter, who always picks up the pieces. I cringe as the phone rings and my heart sinks.

This isn't going to be pretty.

"Red?" His groggy voice strains through the phone, and I realise I must have woken him. Shit, I forgot about the time difference. "What's wrong? Why are you calling me at … four in the morning?"

"You were right," I croak, barely holding myself together.

"I'm going to need some more information here sis," he already sounds pissed.

"Dave is an asshole."

He hisses and sucks in a deep breath and I expect a hiding, instead he clears his throat and mumbles something before he asks, "Are you hurt?"

"No. Just … you know … sad." I swallow a whimper that tries to escape and wipe my face for the hundredth time.

"Are you okay?"

"Well, I'm in a foreign country, homeless, broke, and jobless … so not great."

He exhales. It's harsh and sharp and followed by a too-long silence.

"Hunter?"

"Hang on." His blanket muffles and there's a static buzz with a few gentle thuds in the background, a door opens and closes.

His voice is clearer than before, "Right, now we can talk."

"Because before?"

"Now, I have more privacy."

"You have company?" My stomach churns a little thinking about it, and I push that thought far, far into the depths of my mind where it perishes.

I feel his smirk across the ocean, then he starts, "We're talking about your life choices, not mine. I told you not to go with him."

"Yes, you did. You were right, I was wrong and all that jazz. Can we just skip to the part where you bail me out and we can both move on?" I bristle because I'm not in the mood. I've just discovered the man I travelled halfway across the world with is fucking married. *With children.* I may never be in the mood again.

I visualise Hunter shaking his head or rubbing a hand over his face. Knowing my older brother, he's doing both.

"I'm not sending you money again Red."

"But—"

"No! If you want help, you're just going to have to come live with us for a while."

Us.

"No."

"It's a three-bedroom ..." he prattles on as if he didn't hear me object.

"—Hunter!"

He lets out a long breath, and when he speaks, he leaves no more room for arguments, "Red, this is non-negotiable. You will come and live here. You will get a job, and you will get your shit together."

"Or?"

"Or? There is no *or*, but if you need time to think about it, you can call me back when you've worked out you have no other options."

"Wait," I call out and chew on my lower lip weighing my

alternatives. He's right I have none. "Fine," it's a whinny mutter, "what do you want me to do?"

"Where are you now?"

"Outside our, *his* house." I correct and my breath hitches in my throat. I pretend to clear it and he pretends like he can't hear how much I'm hurting.

"Get to a coffee shop and grab a hot drink."

"I have no money."

"You will in ten minutes. Go now, have a coffee, wait for my call."

"Okay." I grab the handle of my suitcase and look up at the darkening skies.

"And Red?"

"Yeah?"

"Don't spill anything on anyone." He hangs up before I can swear at him.

Ten seconds later my phone pings with an alert from my bank. Brother dearest has come through with some cash. Guess I can forgive him for his little jab.

3

Red

The waitress places the steaming cup of coffee in front of me with shaking hands. It spills into the coaster and she apologises profusely. Her drab hair falls about her, and she grabs some serviettes and shoves them in my face in way of further apology.

I smile briefly and accept her peace offering, then tuck a serviette under the mug. The brown liquid seeps into the paper and stains it. It feels like life is sending me a message in the form of spillage. I look up trying not to dwell on the time I've wasted here with Dave.

Light rain patters on the window and I bite down the sob trying to erupt from me. I haven't grieved the end of our relationship yet, but I'm not out of town, and not nearly far enough to feel like it's actually over.

I sip the rich coffee and let it scald my festering insides. I need it to burn away the anger and resentment and betrayal.

The coffee warms my frozen fingers and fills the newly carved cavity of my chest. Heat spreads inside me as tears pool in my eyes. I'm yet to process everything that's gone wrong. In twenty-four hours, my perfect fairy tale has shattered into a million pieces. I am the eternally hopeful fool that hopes for the best and ends up with poison apples instead of enchanted roses.

My phone rings and jerks me out of my thoughts.

"Are you enjoying your coffee?"

"It's edible."

"Good." Hunter sounds genuinely relieved, "I've booked a flight for you, it leaves in five hours. Drink your coffee, stand up and go straight to the airport."

"Yes, dad."

"I'm not fucking around here Red." He growls, "No more fuck ups. This is the last time I'm bailing you out."

My head falls back, and I stare at the hanging yellow lampshade, "Yeah. Okay, I get it."

"Make sure you do. I'll text you the flight details and email your ticket."

"Thanks, Hunter."

"Thank me later, when you're home." He hangs up leaving that word hanging between us,

Home.

We haven't had a home in so many years, it feels like an empty joke.

I take another sip as the sky darkens and the rain starts lashing against the windows. Typical. Voices around me get louder as the rain taps outside and everyone competes with one another to be heard above their collective din.

The rain clears the street and forces people under roofs and into the café. The door swings open, heralded by a gust of cold wind. The warmth returns as soon as the door shuts and a shadow looms over my table.

"There you are."

I look up to see Dave slipping into the seat opposite me.

"You should go." My voice is as brittle and sharp as icicles.

"No, we should talk."

"We have nothing to talk about."

"Don't be like that Shortcake."

"Don't call me that."

"You had no problems me calling you that two nights ago." He smirks and I feel the heat rush to my face and somewhere down below.

"Two nights ago, I still thought you were a good guy."

His face twists for a second and he reaches out for me. I yank my hand away and his brow furrows.

"Hey, don't be like that. I'm still the same guy."

"No, you're not," I bite out.

He reaches for me a second time and I pull away again. A flash of anger crosses his face, but he quickly schools his features and pulls his chair closer.

"Don't do this Shortcake, you owe me."

"I *owe* you?" My brow quirks as his jaw clenches.

"I paid for your ticket over, I put you up in a nice apartment, I made you feel *good*." His voice dips with the last word and his expression darkens, like he's imagining himself inside me.

I shiver, "I didn't ask for any of those things—you offered, I accepted. Had I known the truth, I would have never agreed."

His hand slips over my thigh and creeps up. "Don't lie to yourself Shortcake, you had nothing back in London, besides, I know you like me."

"I *did*." His hand creeps up with renewed confidence.

"So, nothing's changed."

"Everything's changed," I growl at him and grip his wrist, yanking it off my body. "You are bloody *married* Dave," I shout loud enough for every eye in the place to stare right at us.

"Keep your fucking voice down, slut." He squeezes my thigh and his nails dig into my flesh.

I bolt up, my chair scrapes the floor and falls with a loud

clang, "Keep your fucking hands off me!" I grab my cup and fling my hot coffee at his face.

He screams, either in surprise or in pain. I don't stay long enough to find out which. I snatch my phone off the table and grab my suitcase then weave my way through the tables.

Eyes follow me as Dave screams my name.

I bolt through the front door and into the pounding rain, and just like I've done all my life, I look straight ahead and don't turn back.

4

Red

I t's not till the plane starts to move that my heart rate finally settles, and I shuffle lower into my seat. Somewhere in the back of my mind, I think I was expecting some kind of chase. Policemen tackling to me to the ground and hauling me away to face Dave and whatever damage my coffee inflicted on him.

Fuck it, he deserved it. Let him explain his burns to his wife, plus a few receipts and pictures I may have left for her.

She deserves better.

I let my head fall back and roll along my shoulders letting the stress slip away as we lazily manoeuvre along the tarmac. I ignore the air hostesses showing off the emergency procedures and check my phone one last time. I have just under twelve hours to get cosy and enjoy this ride.

The crew does their final preparation and soon enough the engine whines and I get sucked into my seat, my stomach flutters with a second of weightlessness.

As soon as the seatbelt lights are off, I press the *'call'* button and a petite redhead—without a hair out of place and enough makeup to cover three dead bodies—smiles down at me.

"How can I help you miss?"

"Can I have a wine please?"

She presses her lips together all judgy and juts out her hip, "The dinner cart will be over shortly, and we will be serving drinks then."

"I know, but I need my wine now."

She gives me a death glare about to explain why she would not be bringing my wine, when my neighbour—which I've been happily ignoring till just that second—pipes up.

"Better make that a double love. It helps with my arthritis, and my granddaughter here is just trying to be polite, pretending it's for her instead of a silly old lady."

At her words, the air hostess' demeanour changes. Her face parts into a wide, lovely smile that seems rather genuine and she grips the older lady's hand, "My grandmother has whiskey," She winks at her, and lowers her voice, "white or red?"

"Whatever's going, sweetheart." The older lady squeezed her hand, then without giving me a second look, she walks down the aisle, presumably to bring me my wine.

I turn to look at the woman sitting in the seat next to mine. "Thank you," I say and watch as her crinkled face stretches in a kind smile and her glacier blue eyes crinkle behind her round spectacles.

"You're welcome," she says, her voice suddenly far less frail and far sharper than it was a second ago, "I usually don't start this early into a flight, but you obviously have something going on."

I sigh, deflating into my seat, "You can say that."

We're interrupted by the air hostess who brings two glasses of wine served in translucent, plastic cups. It's all class.

"Thank you. And keep them coming," I say as I grab my glass from her.

She quirks an eye toward the old lady who just nods then walks away. I know she won't keep them coming, but it felt good to say anyway.

I sip the wine remembering how much I hate the stuff. It always tastes the same, no matter if it's cheap or expensive. An initial crisp bite that turns sour after the second sip. I force myself to drink it anyway. The only real benefit is how quickly the heat spreads through my body and makes me feel lightheaded.

"Well?"

"Well, what?"

"Spill." The old lady's sharp eyes and focused tone unnerve me.

"It's not that exciting, just boy problems."

She nods like she knows what I'm talking about, and I try for a second to imagine what she might have looked like in her youth. I decide that she would have been drop-dead gorgeous.

She stares at me in silence, unrelenting. I sigh and start talking.

"I travelled halfway across the world for the wrong one." I cringe. I can't get over what a mistake it was. But he just felt so *right*.

"Two months ago, I was sitting in a Costa, minding my own business wondering how I would break the news to Hunter that I was just laid off – again. I was having the worst day ever, which was about to turn into the best day ever— which in retrospect, was still in fact the worst cherry on any cake, ever.

I ordered a strawberry frostino with the last of my cash. I wanted to give myself something nice before I couldn't afford anything again. Knowing I would have to beg Hunter for everything and justify all my spending. Ugh, he was such a parent whenever I got into trouble. The barista was cute and winked when I grabbed the drink from him. Our fingers touched as he handed it to me, and two dimples appeared on his cheeks when he smiled. God, he was cute, and I was distracted—which is why, when I turned around, I didn't notice the man standing directly behind me.

Crashing into him propelled my life in an entirely new trajectory. My takeaway cup crushed between us and splashed up like a pink volcano.

'Shit! Sorry.' I cried as a pair of crystalline blue eyes collided with mine while the milkshake soaked through my shirt. The plastic cup a crumpled mess between us, pink milk coating his angular jaw and sliding down his buttoned-up work shirt.

'Sorry,' I mumbled again and took a step back, letting the rest of the drink and the humiliation soak into me.

His jaw ticked for a minute, 'Fuck.' He threw me a look then muscled a path to the men's toilet.

'Sorry,' I ran after him and barged through the door, not paying too much attention.

He came to a dead stop when he saw me in the mirror. He turned slowly and studied my face, then his gaze dipped and tore a path up my strawberry pink body.

'This is the men's,' he said with an amused voice, his lips tugging at the edges as he tore away at his black tie.

'I know, I'm just sorry. I thought maybe you needed help.'

'In the men's room?'

I stilled and shut up, suddenly realising what I was imply-ing. 'Oh shit no, not like that. But your shirt and your suit …'

'Are drenched, probably ruined.'

'Exactly.'

'And you were going to?'

I fumble on my words my hands gesturing aimlessly at all the empty ideas I try to grab from the sour air.

'I don't know, offer to clean your shirt?'

'Now? In here?' Battling a smile, the corners of his eyes crinkled with amusement.

'I guess I didn't think it through.'

He chuckled nodded, then tore away his tie and tucked it into his back pocket. 'Unless you have a spare shirt on you, I can't see you being much help.'

I chewed on my lower lip, 'I could dry clean it for you. Drop it at your office?'

He took a minute to think about it before he shrugged off his jacket and discarded it next to the sink, then unbuttoned his shirt. Slowly, meticulously, watching my gaze follow his fingers as they moved down, till he peeled the shirt from his body.

I stood there and watched, riveted to the spot like someone poured quick-drying cement around my feet. He spun around to the sink and I stared at his strong back. My eyes drifted along his torso till I caught his reflection in the mirror. His smirk vanished when our eyes met and he started washing his shirt under the tap.

'This might take a while,' he said as he scrubbed. I nodded while staring at his chest like a teenager in heat.

'Yeah, right. okay, I'll just wait outside.'

'Sure.' I noticed how hard he worked at keeping his face straight, so I left him to his hand washing and walked out of the men's bathroom and back into the main room where the cute barista gave me a hostile look while he wiped the floor with a grotty mop.

I sighed and leaned against the wall, wondering what other shit this day will throw at me. The pink milk started to solidify in my bra, and everything felt sticky. I wanted to go wash, but I didn't want to miss the man I just splashed after I told him I'd clean his clothes.

I felt ridiculous. I had no money for rent let alone dry cleaning. Guess Hunter will be footing another bill.

I seriously needed a better life plan.

When the man walked out, he seemed surprised to find me. His eyes landed on the giant pink strip across my once white shirt, 'You didn't clean up?'

'I didn't want you to think I left. I promised to …' I wring my hands together and notice he's wearing his shirt again. It's not clean and not soaked but it passed for wearable. I hoped he had another in his office. I felt even more ridiculous as he folded his destroyed jacket over his arm.

His lips curled into a smile and he handed me his jacket and phone, 'Put your phone number in here, I'll call you later with directions of where to drop it off.'

'Oh. Okay.' I put my number in his phone and wondered where the hell I might find a dry cleaner and how I was going to explain this to Hunter.

I handed the man his phone back and he looked at the number. 'Red?'

'That's what people call me.'

His face split into a charming smile and he turned and walked out, leaving me with his jacket and a sticky stupid feeling.

I watched him leave and made my way to the bathroom. My shirt ruined, the rest of my outfit saturated in souring milk. I didn't particularly want to take my bra off in a public bathroom and wash, so I wrapped myself in the jacket and walked out. It smelled like old spice and felt expensive. I promised to wear it just till I get to my apartment, it wasn't too far.

I took two steps out of Costa when my phone rang. A number I didn't recognise, I ignored it. When it rang for a third time I gave in and answered.

'Hi, Red.'

'Hello?'

'This is Dave.'

'I don't know anyone by that name.'

'You just spilt your drink all over me.'

'Oh,' I cringed, 'sorry,' I mumbled again.

He laughed, 'I was beginning to think you gave me a wrong number.'

'No, I just …' I let the words drop off and wondered why I never had the presence of mind to do that.

'I know where I want you to drop off my jacket.'

'Oh?'

'Shishahary, at 7 p.m.'

'I can't afford that place.'

'I'm not asking you to pay for dinner, just to join me for one.'

'But I just spilt my drink all over you.'

'And you offered to help.'

'Which I can do by cleaning your jacket.'

'I'd rather have some company.'

My ears burned. 'Okay, I guess.'

'And Red?'

'Yeah?'

'Don't forget my jacket.' He hung up and I floated the rest of the way home.

I went to that dinner and Dave was charming and smart. He told me he was a stockbroker working on some big project. He was enchanting and charismatic, and somehow after a few too many wines and a lot of laughs, I ended up in his hotel room and later in his bed. I spent two weeks with Dave. He was my prince charming, and I fell under a stupid, delusional spell where I thought this knight in shining armour just solved all my problems.

I knew I was lying to myself and it was only a band-aid solution, but it worked. He let me stay in his hotel room. We dinned and wined and laughed and fucked, and he was pretty good at that too—till his contract ran out and he had to go home.

'Come with me, back to California.'

'I can't, my whole life is here.'

'What life?' He didn't mean it as a harsh reality call, but a cold, sobering truth. 'You have no job and you've been evicted from your apartment. If you've got friends, you refuse to introduce me to any of them, and the only person you vaguely mentioned was your brother—who you don't seem that keen on seeing anyway.'

'It's not like that …'

'Okay.'

'He thinks you're an asshole.'

He·startled, 'We've never even met.'

'He's overprotective.'

'Sure, I get it.' He closed the space between us and drew me into him. His lips tugged at mine till I opened for him and he kissed me long and deep, 'Come with me, I'll take care of you.'

I didn't overthink it. If I did, I'd have found a million reasons why I should have stayed and none of them would have been valid. He was right, I had no life. Maybe this was the opportunity I've been waiting for, something to turn everything around, a fresh start somewhere new. Grabbing the bull by the horns I gave him my answer. 'Okay.'

'Really?'

'Really.' I chuckled and he captured me into a long kiss that ended up with us very naked and very sweaty.

We got on a plane. Hunter hated the idea and drove to the airport to try and talk me out of it. But it was too late, I cleared customs and there was no way I was going back."

The old lady listens in silence, and we eat our plastic meals—which arrived sometime during my pathetic monologue.

"And now you're on your way back?"

I nod with a mouth full of what they classify as food on this airline, in another lifetime it could have been some kind of pasta.

"And do you have somewhere to go?"

"Hunter and his roommate have a spare room for me."

"And you get on with them?"

I grind my teeth, grab my wine, and slug the rest of it into my throat. It curdles in my stomach, but that could just be the thought of seeing *him* again.

"I guess so."

"I see," she says, and pats my arm as if she gets it and realises that I am, in fact, a hopeless case, "better have another wine then."

5

Red

My body protests my movements as I lumber off the plane. The stale air and lukewarm wine making my head throb and my eyes blur.

Exhaustion feels like a word reserved for tired people; I passed it three hundred miles back over the Atlantic, and now I'm well into weariness. It's not just my limbs that hurt, it's everything—my body, my mind, my heart.

I step off the plane and suck a well-ventilated breath of air-conditioned air and my stomach coils. Hunter is angry but he's still my big brother, and if I'm honest, I can't wait to see him. Throw myself into his big arms, wait for him to berate me for the allocated five to ten minutes, and then let him take me somewhere safe.

I find my bag amongst all the others on the carousel, then make my way out towards the arrivals hall. Anticipation bites at my insides and my heart smashes in my chest, reverberating through my entire body. I squeeze my fists a few times in an effort to relax but it makes no difference at all. I'm a knotted ball of anxiety and eagerness, and all I want is to unravel. I suck in one last breath and the doors to the arrivals hall swing open.

I scan the faces looking for Hunter, but I see *him* instead. Shaw Bennett or, as he's otherwise known to everyone else, Wolf. Self-proclaimed lone wolf of Oakridge—no pack, predatory by nature, totally fierce, loyal to a fault, and the last person I wanted to see.

My heart ceases, and for a short eternity stays dead in my chest. His eyes are cast down to his phone, but then he lifts his head and our gazes collide.

A charge of anger, disappointment, and dread strikes me like a bolt of lightning, and my heart restarts just as his face stretches into a beautiful, annoying smirk.

I narrow my eyes at him, and his stupid smile gets bigger. He stands about three heads taller than anyone else in the room. With his wide shoulders and dark hooded eyes, he looks dangerous, just like I know he is.

No, no, no, no, no, this cannot be happening.

As I march over, I study his face. He's not changed at all, just filled out and acquired more angles and sharper features. He remains leaning against the wall, causal as ever, just watching me come to him. As if things were still the same as they were before when I still wanted to go to him.

"Where's Hunter?" I don't bother with pleasantries; I reserve those for people I want to be pleasant with.

"Nice to see you too Red," he scoffs as his eyes zero on my face. "Good flight?"

"I asked you where Hunter was." I fold my arms across my chest and glare at him. I have to glare, otherwise I would be staring at the man that I used to know as a boy. The boy who grew up alongside my brother and has become a beast of a man.

"He had a late night and asked me to come get you."

"That's too bad."

"Come on, car is this way." He grabs my suitcase and

starts walking away. I reach for the handle and jerk it towards me. He freezes, looks down at me and sniggers, "really?"

"I'm not going anywhere with you Shaw!" His eyes widen for a second as I use his real name. I yank on the handle and he just smirks, like the mere gesture is completely ridiculous. Of course it is. He's a goliath at almost seven feet, and I'm barely a full-grown adult at five feet one.

"Don't be ridiculous Red. Come on, I've had a long night too."

"You shouldn't have come."

"Well, Hunter asked me to, so I did."

"And you only ever do what Hunter says?" I stab at him.

He shrugs, turns around, and walks off, pulling me along with my suitcase. I sigh, release the handle, and follow him out of the terminal.

The chilly London air bites at my skin. I draw in a long breath; it feels like it's been too long since I've been back.

"This way," he ushers me towards a fancy looking black car that screams 'I have a shit ton of money and really small dick'. He pops open the trunk and throws my suitcase inside.

Wolf rounds the car pretending to be a gentleman and holds the door open for me. "Get in."

"I already told you, I'm not going anywhere with you."

He scrubs a hand over his face and his jaw ticks, "Red."

"No." I stand my ground.

His knuckles blanch as his grip tightens on the door, "Final warning."

"No."

He glares at me for another beat. "If my presence offends so much, there's plenty of room in the boot."

I gulp at the threat but don't back down, "Get stuffed."

"Suit yourself," The passenger door slams shut, and in two steps he rounds the car, slides into the driver's seat, and speeds off like a demon, tyres screeching in his wake.

It all happens so quickly, it takes me a full minute to realise he's ditched me at the airport, and he's taken my stuff with him.

My pulse hammers and I grind my teeth, considering my options. I could call Hunter but then I'd wake him, and he'd be pissed that I didn't get in the car with Wolf. On the other hand, it would be so much sweeter to let Wolf deal with the brunt of his anger when he gets to the flat without me.

The thoughts make me smile, but only for a second when I realise I'll miss that shit show if I'm still hanging around here.

Hunter should have never sent Wolf. He should know better. Then again, he probably doesn't, and that's how it should stay.

Shit, I should have gotten in the car.

I check my bank balance, brother dearest put just enough funds in there to get a coffee and an airport meal.

Fuck it.

I wave down a taxi and give him Hunter's address.

I flop onto the back seat; the decadent heat engulfs me, and it takes every ounce of strength I have left not to be lulled to sleep by the smooth rocking of the cab.

6

FOURTEEN YEARS AGO

Wolf 14, Red 12

Red

Oakridge was the kind of place where the streets stank of vanity and overindulgence. The kind of place where the rich showed off their wealth and opulence, the kind of place Hunter and I didn't belong.

Although we've lived here our whole lives, we were the outcasts—the ugly dirt the rest of the neighbourhood tried to sweep under the carpet.

I don't exactly know how we ended up in our run-down house. The ugliest house on the prettiest street. But it's been the only home I ever had. Hunter once mentioned living somewhere else, but his memories from our childhood are like fog, blurry and untouchable.

I never knew my dad and I thought I knew my mum, until one day she left to go buy a loaf of bread and never came back. Hunter called the police on the second day, when we were both scared and hungry. After a few scary nights at a stranger's home, they called our only known relative. Our Grandma Julie.

She didn't hesitate when child services called, and she came to look after us. Initially she talked about moving away, about fresh starts and new beginnings, but I screamed and cried and begged her to stay. I didn't want my mum to come back just to find us gone. I always believed she would be back. Then again, back then I was still naïve, and I thought the world was good and that good things happen to good people. Like me. I was only five and I still thought hope was a real thing.

So, we stayed, and Grandma Julie made that house our home and filled it with a love so rich it belittled the piles of gold our neighbours slept on. We didn't know it just then, but she was already sick. Sometimes I wonder if she needed us to take care of her just as much as we needed her. She hid it well, for two years we didn't connect the dots until her 'mistakes' became too regular and much too obvious to be swept away as simple oversights. When the doctors spoon fed us her diagnosis, I watched my brother harden, turn into a provider, a caretaker, and an adult. One that would go on to shoulder all our burdens and responsibilities.

It wasn't fair. But Hunter never—not once—made me feel guilty about it. Between Grandma and Hunter, I always believed I had everything I needed. Until the first time I saw the new boy at Oakridge High.

I sat at the top of the stands as I always did, sketching the tree that hung slightly too far to the left and looked cursed. Gnarled, odd branches that somehow clung on despite the tree clearly being dead. My teeth sank into the softening end of my wooden pencil and the metallic lead flavour coated my tongue when I looked up and saw a boy advance on my brother.

He was taller than Hunter and broader, maybe the mark of a rich boy being fed properly. Fear zinged through me like an electrical current that stopped everything—my muscles, my nerves, my heart.

He crossed the oval and stormed right at him. I thought Hunter was going to die that day. The boy was twice his size and even at fourteen years old, he carried himself like a rugby player out to break everyone and everything in his path.

Sadness flowed through me as I watched him close the distance to my brother. He must have heard about us, the poor kids who didn't wear designer clothes and had an empty lunch box most days. It was like the rest of those rich kids thought poverty was a disease and if they didn't remind us of our place every day, they would somehow catch it.

I guess he had to cement his position in the school somehow, and my brother's face was going to be the way he made his mark. My body seized with fear and knotted with anxiety while Hunter watched him coming.

He didn't move. Hunter never moved, he never ran, and he never stayed down. That's how we survived; Hunter never gave up on us, even when everyone else did.

Fear crawled inside me as the bigger boy advanced, he was running now, his gaze locked on my older brother.

I shuddered.

If he punched him, he could break him.

I stood on weak, wobbly legs that felt more like fragile twigs than solid bones. My heart chugged in my chest as the bigger boy closed the distance, he was only a few steps away. I slammed my eyes shut. I wanted to scream, but my voice died in my throat.

When I opened my eyes again, the boy had stopped.

He looked my brother up and down and they exchanged a few words. The bigger boy smiled, and in the next moment, Hunter let his ball slip to the ground, and they started kicking it around. I fell back into the stands, my fear fizzing in my veins like bubbles in a Coke bottle.

I watched in fascination. This new kid didn't seem to care about Hunter's faded clothes or ruffled hair. He didn't see him as lesser, he saw him as a boy with a ball. They played, kicking it back and forth, running around the oval like they owned it, till the boy kicked the ball at Hunter and he in return, kicked back wildly, the ball sent reeling and landed by the stands.

I studied the new boy as he ran over, and at that instant, I knew that everything in my life was about to change. Like the world whispered something in my ear and it echoed inside me silently, waiting for the day I would hear it scream as it reverberated for eternity.

His dark hair flew about him in a wild frenzy while he chased the ball, long athletic legs and a beautiful smile. He looked up for a second but didn't see me, but I got a look at his striking brown eyes.

"Come on Shaw, we don't have all day," my brother called to him.

Shaw.

Shaw smiled and dribbled the ball then kicked it over to my brother.

Two things happened that day: Hunter found a friend and I found the first boy that would break my heart.

7

PRESENT DAY

Wolf

The door barges open and Red stumbles in. "There's a taxi downstairs that needs his fair paid."

I look at her like she's fallen and hit her head and somehow convinced herself that her problems are now mine, "And?"

"And you need to go downstairs and pay him."

"Why would I do that?"

"Cause otherwise I'd have to wake Hunter up and tell him he has to, and that will entail an entire explanation of his asshole roommate ditching me at the airport."

"Shit," I grumble under my breath as she shots me a triumphant smile and watches me walk out the door.

The taxi driver takes three steps back as he sees me walking downstairs towards him. He puts his hands up and the colour drains from his face. It's a natural reaction from people who see a man my size walking towards them, especially when they're being hostile, and I'm calm as fuck.

He's already apologising like he's done something wrong, "How much does she owe you?"

"£75." He stammers and I pull out my credit card. He seems to sag a bit against his car then grabs his card machine.

"Make it a hundred, for your troubles."

His eyes grow big and he looks at me like I might have made a mistake. I just dip my head once and he doesn't wait for any more reassurances. He hands me back my card and I turn my back on him, even as he mumbles something about taking his card and being available day and night. I don't have need for a driver. I need very few things, the most important one is currently getting Red out of my house and putting distance between us as soon as fucking possible.

My hands still hurt from gripping the steering wheel so tightly. Even though I knew she was about to step out of those double doors she still managed to disarm me completely. I forgot how striking she was with her arresting green eyes and long locks of purple hair. Except now she wasn't a sixteen-year-old girl anymore, she's shed her childhood skin like a cocoon and stepped out every inch a woman.

When I get back upstairs, she's sitting on the arm of the couch and her bloodshot emerald green eyes are drooping.

"Where's my suitcase?"

"You mean, thank you."

"No, I mean where's my stuff?" She leaps off the couch and takes a step closer, a finger stabbing the air, "I've just had a shit day, a long flight and some asshole ditched me at the airport. I'm too tired to do anything other than shower and sleep, so where the hell is my case?"

I study her face. I haven't seen her in almost ten years and seeing her now makes everything I put to sleep in my body come alive. She looks exhausted, but even with her tired face and frazzled hair, she's stunning. "In your room."

She glares at me.

I scowl at her, like it's her fault she has no idea where anything is, "Third room on the left. Bathroom is next door."

She just nods like all the energy has been sapped out of her, and she shuffles out of the lounge and disappears into the corridor.

"Fuck." I grumble to myself as I realise there's no fucking way I'm getting any sleep. I grab my phone and my keys and get the hell out of my house.

8

———

Wolf 17, Red 15

Wolf

I knock on the door and don't bother waiting for an answer before I push it open and walk inside this house which feels much like my own. I've been here so many times and spent endless nights here, it belongs to me just as much as it belongs to the Evans'.

Hunter has been my best friend since that first day I met him on the oval. He didn't even flinch as I sprinted at him, but his eyes did grow ten times bigger when he figured out I wanted to play with him and not beat the shit out of him.

He's become more than just a friend, he's like my brother. He's stood up for me and covered up my messes more times than I deserve, and I've put down anyone that treated him as anything other than equal.

Unlike me, Hunter is a good guy. He's always been a good guy because he's had to be, even at the ripe age of seventeen he already has way too many responsibilities. Responsibilities he took on when he was only seven.

He never really had a choice.

It's made us polar opposites and it's why we get along so well. He's the conscious I never had, and he gets to live vicariously through my sexcapades and other stupid shit he doesn't manage to talk me out of. Of course, he gets laid too. The guy's testosterone on legs but there's one girl that always comes first for him no matter what, his sister Red.

I walk into the house and catch the familiar musty fragrance of old carpets and tired beams. I step further past the tiny foyer and toward the kitchen to deliver 'leftovers' again.

I started bringing food over after knowing Hunter for just three months. He was the only friend that never came over to my house—not ever—and I was upset thinking he was a shit friend. So, at the end of a game one day after school I tackled him to the ground and called him names. He didn't respond, he just got up and walked away. I shoved him again and his eyes flickered to the stands. It was the first time I noticed anyone sitting there. A skinny little thing just like her brother. She chewed on a pencil and had a notepad open across her lap, her face scrunched up.

"Who's is that"

"My sister." He said quietly.

"Is she slow or something?" I leered at him and saw the flame as it sparked behind his eyes, like my words set his insides on fire. He was on me in a second, leaping on my back with his skinny hands wrapped around my neck, and his legs locked around my waist like a steel belt. He was scrawny but he was strong, and darkness crept along the edges of my vision as my throat closed up. I fell to my knees fighting for air, and he increased the pressure. I must have tapped him a hundred times before he finally released me.

I rolled onto my back and sucked in air. That was the only other time I ever let him touch me like that.

He stood above me, "Don't talk about my sister like that. Ever." His eyes narrowed, his voice menacing.

"I'm sorry, I'm just upset that you never come over for a play. Even my mum said it was weird, and you know, she barely says anything at all."

He chewed on his lower lip, and I could see him mulling over my words. His head fell back, and he looked up to the heavens when he spoke, and even now I don't know if it was because he was talking to me or praying.

"When my mum left my grandmother moved in with us. She did her best for a very long time, till she got sick. Sometimes she forgets to make dinner and that Red needs help with her homework, so…"

"So, you help." I took the words out of his mouth as we locked eyes, and I noticed how his glistened with tears.

"Why haven't you said anything till now?"

He just shrugged and stood there clenching his teeth, staying strong.

That day, I learned a few vital things about my best friend.

He's intelligent, resourceful, and kind.

He was what one would call underprivileged.

And he would put his sister first and protect her fiercely no matter the cost.

Hunter offered me his hand, when I accepted, he pulled me up. I stood up and shook the grass form my clothes.

I never asked Hunter to come over again.

In truth, despite his financial situation, I envied Hunter. He had something that I craved dearly—a family that loved him, a grandmother who cared, a sister to comfort; while I had nannies and cooks and parents that forgot about my existence while they holidayed in their summer villas. I guess it's why I cherished my friendship with Hunter so much, and why I would never jeopardise it. He made me part of his family, and when I was at his house, I felt seen and wanted, almost enough to patch up the gaping holes my parents' constant absence left inside me.

After that day, I had the cook make extra dinner portions and I told Hunter it was leftovers. He didn't want charity, he was too proud.

The first time I showed up with food, Hunter frowned for about three seconds before Red grabbed the containers, shovelled them onto three plates and started eating. It was soundless as Hunter and I stared at his tiny little sister do something so mundane, but it also felt powerful. There was no pride, no envy, or anger, just a hungry kid accepting a hearty meal.

When she was done, she grabbed the extra plate and snuck it upstairs. I bet her grandmother was grateful. That was three years ago.

When I walk into the tiny foyer and catch Red sitting on the couch, I'm totally unprepared for what I see. She's clearly not wearing a bra under the white T-shirt that rides up her tummy, revealing a sliver of skin above her black underwear. Her long legs are stretched in front of her and her lips are curled around a pencil, as always.

I take two steps back. *Fuck no.*

In the last year, she has become more than just Hunter's little sister. The skinny girl we use to wrestle in the mud in the back yard and kick a ball around with. She's become a woman, or at least a very attractive teenager. Her perky little tits poke from beneath her shirt and she's gotten a bunch of curves that weren't there before.

The way she rolls the pencil in her mouth makes my blood heat and my cock jerk in my pants.

Shit, I can't look at her like that way.

"What are you staring at?" Hunter's voice slices through my stare and I wrench my eyes away from Red.

"Thought I saw a cockroach," I sling at him.

Red shrieks and scampers onto the couch with a leap,

giving me a glimpse of her tight ass. I swallow the rock in my throat and remind myself she's fifteen and I'm seventeen, and she's just as much my sister as Hunter's, and not a delectable pastry on a dessert platter for me to lick up and devour.

"He's talking shit, there's no cockroach. Go get some fucking clothes on, fuck."

She mumbles something, climbs off the couch, and runs upstairs.

"What the fuck man?" Hunter punches my arm.

"What? I think what you mean to say is 'thank you for dinner, yes I'm ready to get laid at Angela's party tonight', and 'thank you for inviting me'."

"Yeah, yeah," he waves, and I follow him into the kitchen. I place the bag of food on the worn-out counter that sags in the middle as if it too has given up.

"You ready for tonight?" I shove a container of food into his hands, suddenly eager to get out of here as quickly as possible.

"Yup," he smiles at me with a mouthful of food.

"You're going out again?" Red stands at the kitchen door, her voice quivers a little as she asks. She's put on super short jean shorts, which cover nothing and show the underside of her ass.

"I won't be late." His face twists with guilt. I know he wants to do the right thing, but I also know he wants to get laid.

"I'll have him home early."

She crosses her arms around her chest, and I can't help but feel a pang of disappointment as they cover her hard nipples beneath. "As if."

"Scouts honour." I smile and give her a two-finger salute as I drag Hunter out of the kitchen and toward the front door.

"You have no honour," she calls after us.

Of course, she's right.

9

PRESENT DAY

Red

I wake up to an eerie silence, sit up in the unfamiliar bed and take a second to let my eyes focus on the room. Light drips in from the street below and colours the walls a tarnished gold. I suck in a series of quick breaths as my heart settles then scour the room. I find my suitcase laying by the door, right where he left it.

I must have climbed on the bed and fallen asleep.

Big mistake.

My old friend jet lag is about to creep in and bite me in arse.

I check the time. 2.37 a.m. I've been asleep for fourteen hours, and now I'm wide awake and wired. I sigh and smell myself. That was my second mistake. I cringe, slide off the bed, and reach for my bag.

It bursts open the minute I release the zip. All my worldly possessions fly out in a flurry of fabric. A lacy, black number lands by my knees, I grab it fingering the delicate lace. Dave bought that for me, that and a string of other sexy lingerie I displayed for him. Looking back, I really should have seen all the signs, but maybe for just a little bit—and just for once—I wanted to feel like someone might have really wanted *me*. Like my luck had really changed, like I hit the jackpot. Like in that hooker movie with the rich guy and the necklace. I wanted it all to be real. My mouth twitches and I remember that I haven't dealt with any of these feelings yet and that now was probably not the time. I push them back down where they continue to simmer on a low to medium heat, grab my toiletries, and open the door.

The house is silent—and not in the kind of way when the occupants are asleep, but in the way that it's deserted.

I flick on a few extra lights to make the monsters in the shadows disappear, then tiptoe down the hall. I don't know why I do this when I know I'm alone; maybe because it feels a little like being in a museum, all white tiles and white walls. I'm afraid to taint this place with my shit.

All the doors are closed. I take a stab and open the first door to my left and intuitively know it's not where I need to be.

The smell of pheromones and earthy masculinity floods my senses. His bed is made without an edge out of place, like it belongs in a military school. I take a step forward knowing I'm going in the wrong direction. Everything inside me screams to get out—red flashing lights and blaring sirens—and yet I'm acting like the girl who runs upstairs while being chased by the killer when the front door stands perfectly open a foot away.

All his drawers are shut, and closet doors closed. Wolf hides himself even in his own space. There's a bedside lamp and a book on a bedside table. It's too dark to see the title and I find myself taking another irritating step forward.

"Like what you see?" The light flicks on.

I swivel unsteadily to find Wolf leaning against the door frame filling it with his enormous build.

"I was just heading for the shower." I take a step towards the blocked door.

"Well it's not here." His voice drips with distain as if my very existence offends him.

"Obviously."

He doesn't move, instead his gaze rakes up my body.

I study his face and notice the messy hair, the swollen lips tinted with lipstick that's a shade too dark. Something inside me twists.

"Move."

His face hardens with annoyance and he turns just enough for me to slide past him. I feel every single hard, rigid ab muscle on the way out and smell someone else's perfume clinging to his skin.

"Which door?" I ask without turning back.

"The one opposite mine," he growls at me and I turn to it, grab the knob, and slam the door behind me as heat flushes around my body. I lean against the door catching my breath. I've been around Wolf for less than a minute and already I feel strained.

I wash the unease away in the shower, dress and make my way to the main room where gruff male voices drift through the corridor and smash against the cold walls.

They're talking in hushed voices, "Get your shit together man, we've talked about this." Hunter's voice sounds so much more formidable when he's down the hall and not on the other end of a phone.

"Fuck you, you know I'm trying. I didn't ask for this, it could have just as easily been you."

"Fuck you Wolf, no one needs that shit."

"I've already blocked her number and the other's she used."

"Yeah, lets—" Hunter stands up as he spots me walking into the kitchen.

Wolf spins, his gaze lands on me, his eyes narrow and he turns back to Hunter. "Fuck this day, I'm going to bed."

"About that other thing," Hunter catches his arm and they lock eyes in a tense moment, "what I've said before stands —*nothing* has changed."

Wolf yanks his arm out of Hunter's grip and stands to his full height, looming over my brother, "Fuck you Hunter."

"Just remember that it hasn't changed, and it won't, not ever."

"I don't need reminders," he snarls like a rabid dog, turns, and give me a harsh look before storming out of the kitchen and disappearing.

"What's his problem?"

"Don't ask questions none of us can really answer." His stern face breaks into a wide smile, "Red." He steps towards me and wraps me in his big strong arms.

"I've missed you," I whisper into his hard chest and wonder if it's possible that my big brother got even bigger.

"And I've been worried about you." His arms and humour fall away at the same time, and I push away from him.

"Can we not?"

He looks at me as if he's about to drop the lecture of the century, and I hold a hand up.

"Can we just sit and have a coffee and pretend like we're a normal brother and sister for once? And tomorrow you can berate me all day and dissect all my life choices, but not tonight, okay?"

He sighs and eyes me for a second before he turns to the kettle, "How do you take your coffee?"

"Same as always."

He looks at me like I've asked him for the night's winning lottery numbers, "Really?" I shake my head and roll my eyes. Then again, it's been a while since we've seen each other.

He shrugs, throws the sugar and milk on the table, and puts a mug of black coffee in front of me, "You're a big girl."

"Finally, you've worked it out," I say sarcastically as I add a half a teaspoon of sugar and some milk to my mug.

"I didn't say you act like one."

"Didn't say you act like one," I mimic, and he glares at me as if I've proven his point.

Somewhere in the house pipes come alive.

We drink in silence. The coffee is too weak and too watery, but I don't complain.

"So, now that I'm here can you take a few days off and spend some time with me?"

"Sure, I'd love that. I'll just have to clear it with the boss," he scoffs and tilts his head towards the corridor where Wolf is having a very naked shower.

"Boss? What happened to partners?"

"We are, which is why I have to run it by him. We've picked up some new clients last week, and we've just lost a few of the boys to injury and paternity leave. It will take a few weeks for the new recruits to be trained up."

"Yeah, okay, don't stress your pretty little head over it."

"It's not like that,"

I huff, "I know."

The pipes die down and heavy footsteps are followed by a slamming door.

"That's my cue." Hunter grabs his half-drunk coffee and puts the cup in the sink, he looks tired.

"Oh, I thought we would hang out. I have the worst case of jet lag …"

"I would. I'm happy that you're here, but my life doesn't just come to a standstill because you're here. I still have clients and a job to do, and somewhere in and amongst that, I have to sleep."

I nod.

He shifts and sighs, "Look, I'll speak to Wolf in the morning, see if we can shift some things around, and I'll be all yours for a whole day. But after that, we're going to sit down and you're going to work out what you plan on doing with your life."

"Ugh, you were so close."

"Good night Red, I really am glad you're here."

"Yeah, me too."

I watch my brother walk out of the room then force the rest of my coffee down and head for the lounge. Wolf ignores me as he walks in. He's dressed in jeans that mould perfectly to his body and a jacket. His hair is a wet, frenzied mess, and he runs a hand through it before he grabs his keys.

"Where are you going?" I ask when I should be minding my own business.

"Out," he snaps at me, and without a backwards glance, slams the door as he leaves.

As soon as he's gone my body relaxes and I realise that nothing's changed. He still makes me feel like I can't catch my breath.

I snuggle onto the couch and settle for the rest of the morning. All I have to do now, is stay awake till 5 p.m. tonight. With Wolf out of the house —probably with one of his girls— how hard can it be?

Red

The house comes to life at some point. Faint noises, closing doors, and heavy footsteps. I blink open weary eyes. Laughter pours out of the TV as some sitcom plays in the background and it takes me a minute to realise I must have fallen asleep.

Again.

So much for my plan.

The sunrise splashes oranges and yellows across the ceiling, and I stretch my aching limbs. My body is weary—too tired for a twenty-five-year-old to feel—but I know this heavy tiredness that grips me is jet lag. It will pass in a few days. I just have to stay awake long enough to fight it.

I rub the sleep from my eyes as Wolf steps into the room. He's wearing a tight windproof jacket and shorts that show off his tree trunk legs, he's got his air pods in, and he shoots me a sideways glance before stepping out the front door and disappearing.

I check the clock, 6.a.m. and wonder when he got back, and if he ever sleeps.

I shake my head.

Hunter walks into the lounge, still looking half asleep. He gives me a small smile, "Coffee?"

"How about I make it?"

"Sure." He's excited, and honestly, so am I. I don't think I could drink another one of his 'coffees.'

I follow him into the kitchen where he falls into a chair, his head hanging loosely into his palm.

"Why are you up so early?"

"Perks of the job."

"Sleeping four hours is a perk?"

"Sometimes," he scoffs.

I give him a questioning look while I wait for the water to boil.

He falls back into his seat and scrubs his face. My brother looks old and tired. "With the new clients and the boys away, Wolf and I have had to step back into a more active role. I guess it's just been a while since I've done night shifts and day shifts back to back."

"So, business is going well?"

"Really well. You'll be amazed how many people think they need security, when really they're a no one, and they should be saving their money for when everyone realises they have no talent."

"But, you won't tell them that."

"Hey, a man's gotta eat, and anyway, it's been fun doing clubs again."

"I don't want to know."

"I wasn't going to tell." His face lights up in a sly smile, and I shiver with disgust.

I make us coffee then place the mugs on the table. "So, did you manage to shift things around and come hang out with me?"

He shifts in his seat and I already know the answer.

"We're signing a new client this morning, and once that's done…"

"It's okay."

He sighs and runs a hand through his hair, sips on his coffee then stands, "I have to get ready…"

"Go." I give him a tired smile.

It is okay. I don't mind being all alone in a new apartment, that doesn't belong to me, three days after finding out my boyfriend of two months was a lying, cheating dick monkey.

I wrap my hands around my cup and decide that pity parties are for losers, and I'm not going to be one today. I would save that label for another time. I'll grab my sketch pad and go find inspiration and maybe some sunshine. I don't need people to make me feel less alone.

I stare at my cup until it blurs, then finish my coffee. I hear Hunter leaving the shower and suddenly I'm gripped with the need to wash myself.

I head for the shower where I stand under the hot water letting the angry stream wash away the last few days.

I want to stand there forever. I want to let the water erode my humiliation and shame. I can feel it drilling into me, about to crack open the well of emotions I've been keeping shut, when someone pounds on the door.

"Hurry the fuck up." Wolf's angry voice radiates through the door.

"I'm almost done," I call back to him, realising I haven't even started to wash. I grab the soap and start scrubbing.

"Not almost, now! I have to get to work."

"Just hang on," I scream at him as I throw some shampoo into my palms and start scrapping my scalp like a crazy person.

"You have one minute or I'm ripping the door off its hinges and coming inside! I have a meeting to get to."

Heat explodes in my core at the thought of Wolf bursting

into the shower, but I quickly douse the fire with painful memories.

I run conditioner through my hair when he pounds again, "Tick-tock, Red."

I run my hands through my hair in a growing panic, I suddenly feel like a very small pig in a house made of straw and the big bad wolf is about to huff and puff and blow the door down.

I turn off the tap feeling the remains of conditioner in my hair, it will dry later and will either make my hair super soft or ultra-crusty; I guess only time will tell. I grab my towel, wrap it around me and swing the door open just as Wolf starts pounding again.

His sweaty face is set in a scowl and his eyes land on my face, then trail my neck down to where my hand clutches the towel closed.

"Excuse me." I nudge by him, my shoulder sliding against his hard body. I ignore the shiver that runs up my spine and trudge to my room. I close the door behind me and lean against it panting. Fuck. Why does being around him still make me so fucking nervous, like I was that night.

Disappointment eats up my skin as the memories flood back inside me. My heart pinches with pain and I let loose a long breath. If only my body would forget the past, the promise he never kept. Maybe then I could move on and not have to pretend that he doesn't affect me.

Wolf

I'm glued to the floor. I can't shake her. Her smell is everywhere and so is her stuff. I rip my sweaty clothes off my body, step through the steamy veil into the shower and cut the water on.

I smirk when I spot her open shampoo bottle on the floor —discarded in a hurry. When I pick it up to close it, I can't help myself but inhale the fruity smell that I've come to associate with her. It's been so long since I've smelt it in such powerful concentration, my whole body grows rigid like a cold finger just ran a path up my back and left an icy trail.

I step under the hot water letting it pelt my tingling skin. I wait for its magic to work, for the streaming rivulets flowing down my face to help me forget, set my mind into a dreamy fog, and let all my dirty thoughts spill into the drain.

But the memories nick at my heart and won't stay buried in their coffin. Just having her in this city pulls everything back to the surface; all the ways my body wants hers and my heart craves her. But it doesn't matter, Hunter's threats and my guilt gnaw at me. She'll never be mine. I won't let the way I feel about her take away the only family I've ever had.

I grind my teeth and wash my aching body, dreading the day ahead.

Red

The morning passes in cold white walls and tiled floors. My phone slices the silence of the apartment. I've been pacing. Nothing feels like it's mine. I feel like I'm a hostage in a building with too many 'no access' areas.

"Hi."

"Hey, Red." By the tone of Hunter's voice, I know it's not good news.

"What's up? You gonna be home soon?"

He's silent for a beat too long, and I know the answer. I sigh.

"I can't. Actually, have to leave for a few days."

"What?" I shout into the phone.

"The client needs to fly out and I'm head of his security team, it's just what we signed up for Red."

"So, send Wolf."

"Doesn't work like that, he has his own clients. Anyway, I'd feel better about it if there was someone there watching over you."

"I don't need him to watch over me, I don't need anyone—"

"—not really up to you."

"Hunter." I grind my teeth, this conversation feels awfully familiar.

"Shit, I was hoping to do this in person…" He trails off for a second, moving the conversation into a new direction, and I already know what's coming.

"You don't have to say it - again." I stop him before he does.

"Don't I?"

"I know. I owe you. I need to get my shit together blah blah blah."

He doesn't answer, like he's nodding on the other end, forgetting I can't see him.

"How long will you be away?

"About a week."

"A week?"

"It's not that long and you'll have company, you guys used to be good friends."

I scoff, "He was never my friend."

"It will be just like old times." *But I don't want it to be like old times.* I wilt. "Just play nice. I have to go. Try get along and maybe get a job?"

"Ugh. See you when you get back." I hang up, not letting him have the last word, knowing the annoyance will churn in his stomach on whatever flight he's going to endure.

A smile flickers across my face at the thought. It's a small victory, but one I'll happily enjoy.

I look around and sigh. Now that I have nothing to wait around for, I grab my backpack from my room and head out to the tube station.

The station is a teeming mass of humanity, a murky consume of people shouldering past each other, rushing to live their lives in hyper speed. Somehow being on the platform finally cements the fact that I'm back home. It's all so familiar; the noise and smell and leering angry glances of everyone competing for space on the metal worm that will take us to our next destination. Even the crude graffiti made me smile.

The train shakes beneath my feet, and the passengers sway along with the movement like we're a strange living wave. They all have blank empty faces. I study them as they lock eyes with anything but another human and wait till they can get off and on with their day.

The train comes to a stop with a whine and a hiss, I mind the gap and meander my way to the escalators.

I squint when I step out of the station. The sun is beautiful, and the air holds the autumnal bite that stings my cheeks as I make my way to Hyde Park. It's always been one of my favourite places. A green haven teeming with life, I always found inspiration in its ever-changing landscape and colours. Jailed by concrete, this green mass blooms in splendour.

The bench is dwarfed by the giant oak which casts a long shadow across the walking path, allowing the sun to bathe the beautiful sculpture on the other end.

I sit on the bench and pull out my sketch pad and a pencil, and soon I disappear into the page.

My phone rings and I'm dragged away from my pad, the cherub face smiles back at me from my pad.

"Hello?" I don't recognise the number.

"Why aren't you home?" Wolf growls at me.

"Because I don't want to be."

"Hunter told you to wait for me."

"No, he told me he has to leave for a week, and I'll be stuck with you. Not the same."

"Where are you?" He snaps.

"Somewhere you'll never find me." I hang up and tuck the phone back into my backpack pretending I can't hear it ring.

After the fifth try he gives up, and I hear the ping of a message. I ignore that too.

Wolf

I hate how predictable she is. And it's not because she's boring or stupid, it's because she's passionate and that passion takes her to the same place it always has. My heart stings with a stab of memory and I push it away. Like every other feeling I've ever had for her.

I find her curled up on a bench, her shoulders hunched, her eyes squinted as her hands move in a delighted frenzy over her sketch pad.

I step closer. She doesn't notice me. She's so deep in her own world, and for a second, I wish I could see it through her eyes, a beautiful array of colours and shapes and voids to fill with her talent. She rips her gaze from the page and studies the sculpture across the path, Peter Pan—her favourite. My heart constricts as she studies him with intense concentration, her pencil darting in and out of her mouth making my cock twitch as she rolls it around along her lips.

I clear my throat. She startles, looks up, and her eyes land on me, instantly narrowing.

"How did you find me?"

I stare at her like an idiot, completely drawn to her lips. When I don't answer she rolls her eyes, and I wrench my eyes away.

"I told you I don't need a babysitter," she starts.

"It's a free world and I've just come to enjoy a stroll in the park."

She trails an annoyed path along my face and shakes her head, returning her attention to the boy who never grew up.

I stroll over to the bench and sit down right next to her. It's the closest I can allow myself to get.

She turns her back to me, and I can't help but smirk at her irritation—it rises off her like steam.

"What are you doing?"

"Sitting." *Stalking.*

"Can you go away?"

"I can." I shrug and don't move. Instead, I stretch my hands out over the bench, enjoying being close to her, even when I know I shouldn't be.

She bristles and brings her legs up. A smile tugs at my lips and I look ahead as we sit. The pencil hits her pad and she sinks back into a trance as her hand sketches across the paper. She doesn't even notice as she relaxes and leans against me. But I do. My fingers could so easily reach out and stroke her naked shoulder.

My body is way too aware of hers, of how it's changed since the last time I saw her. How all the teenage marks of womanhood have shed away, and what's left is a woman's body, all curves and dips and holes I'd love nothing more than to explore for the rest of eternity. My cock jerks at the thought and a dark ball of sensation builds in my chest.

I clear my throat and shoot up, erasing the thought. Red falls backwards and her hands flail, her pencil marks a long black line across her work. Her eyes latch onto mine and she gives me a death glare.

"Let's go."

"I'm not done."

"You are."

"No, I'm not." She gives me a scathing look and goes back to her pad.

"I'm not fucking around here Red, you've had enough time. Now it's getting late and I have work to do, and I say we need to go." It's not that she needs a babysitter, and it's not that I actually need to be here or watch her, but it's easy to twist Hunter's words and use them for an excuse to be around her. Lying to her is easier than lying to myself.

"So, go."

"If you don't stuff that pad back into your bag and get up, I will pick up you up off this bench and carry you over my shoulder." I don't have to be so cruel and I have nowhere to be, but siting next to her is making me spiral.

"You wouldn't"

"Try me?" I look down at her and wish with every fibre of my being that little Red would decide to fight me like she always did. I want my fingers to slither up her thighs and hold on to her fleshy ass, feel the weight of her above me as her perky tits hit my back. The thought sends my cock reeling.

Red snatches her pad and shoves it into her backpack then makes a show of zipping her bag and standing up. All the while shooting me fierce looks that make my body so hard, I grind my teeth till my jaw hurts.

"Lead the way," she taunted me with a heated stare and a wave of her hand.

I turn to walk away and Red takes the chance to stomp off in the opposite direction. A small smile tugs at my lips then vanishes. Red will always fight.

I follow at a safe distance admiring how her body moves in space, all curves and femininity.

Maybe if I spend enough time with her today, I'll realise

that all this time I've spent trying to avoid and forget her was unnecessary, and that she's just bland and boring and has always been more of an infatuation than anything else. Maybe I only want her because I know I could never have her.

But even as I try to talk myself into disliking her, I'm drawn to the way she moves and the way she looks at things —like she's taking everything in, storing it for later just to bring it back to life on paper.

I hate how she intrigues me and how I crave to know even more about her, everything there is to know. Every speck and crumb of information she would throw my way, I want to devour and keep for myself.

Most of all, I hate that the more I think about it, the more I know how much I still want her, how her smell does things to my body on a molecular level, how her smile makes me fight every impulse to taste her lips, how her skin makes mine simmer with savage desire, and how none of it matters because she is Hunter's little sister and that means she's off limits.

Nothing has changed. His warning echoes inside me.

Besides, she deserves someone better than me.

Red speeds up, exits the park, and takes a sharp right disappearing out of sight. I roll my eyes and start after her.

I don't need to run; I know exactly where she's going.

I get to the tube station and scan the crowd, the advantage of being my height is that I can see over everyone. I spot her backpack; it peaks behind a column and I can't help but be amused by her silly little games. Doesn't she know I will always find her?

We get on the tube and it shakes beneath us as it shoots out of the station. I get the usual suspicious looks, and everyone gives me a wide berth. It's another advantage of being tall and broad, and a little battle weary—people can read that on you, and they stay the fuck away. Red sits on the opposite side of the carriage, pretending I don't exist. The space between us makes it easier to think again.

She walks ahead of me when we head home, giving me her back and her silence. I unlock the door for her and she barrels inside, side steps me, and goes straight to her room.

I close the door and clench my fists. I wish I was anywhere else than here with her.

13

Red

I've locked myself up in the room like a child, and I'm furious at myself. Why should I be punished because he's here?

I draw in a breath and reach for my door. All I have to do is forget our history, forget our pain, forget how he used to make me feel every time he walked into a room.

I stroll out and find him in the kitchen, he's pacing with a phone glued to his ear and a laptop open on the table. Words like 'shifts' and 'per hour' drift into the lounge room and blend with the voices that spill from the TV.

I'm not really listening. My heart pounds so hard, it drowns everything out anyway. He's not even in the same space and I'm falling apart.

When he walks into the lounge he sighs and falls into the couch. He looks too big to be sitting in it, all tangled, long limbs. It's almost comical. I stand up to leave and a strange look crosses his face.

He stands up and blocks my way.

"You can't keep avoiding me if we're going to be living together."

"Don't worry, I won't encroach on your space too much." I try to move around him but he's too quick for me.

"That's not what I meant," he says and runs a hand over his face.

"It's fine, get out of my way please."

"Not till we talk this over."

"Nothing to talk about."

"Red," he warns me.

"I have nothing to say to you *Wolf*." I watch how it stings when I throw his nickname at him. "You made your feelings about me perfectly clear." I try to storm past him, and he snatches my arm, his fingers biting into my flesh as he spins me to face him.

"Red…"

"No."

"Stop fighting me."

"Never!"

He growls deep in his throat and his face twists into something menacing, "This doesn't have to be so difficult."

I try to tug away from him but he's too strong, and his fingers dig deeper. "Let. Me. Go."

"Fine," he growls and releases me; I stumble backwards and my back hits the kitchen counter. He scowls when I wince, "Keep carrying your stupid grudge. It was one little betrayal, years go."

I freeze at the harsh cadence of his words and my insides shrivel. My gaze finds his angry eyes, "It was more than that, I trusted you," I whisper and swallow all the hurt that tries to scramble into my throat.

He says nothing, like everything I say bounces right off him.

"You. You knew how lonely I was, how abandoned I felt,

especially after my grandma…" I suck in a ragged breath, "You were the first person to look at me like I was more."

I swallow all the pain as he looks at me like it's the first time he's ever seen me.

"You made me feel… *More.* You gave me hope and you snatched it away in the cruellest possible way."

Our eyes collide and a single tear slices my cheeks, "It wasn't a *little* betrayal. It was the biggest, and it broke everything. You were meant to be my everything and instead, you destroyed me."

With that I turn away from him and return to my room.

This isn't going to work.

14

Wolf

I watch her walk away and my heart crumples at the pain on her face. Pain I caused. Pain she's been carrying with her all these years.

Fuck.

A heavy groan rips from my mouth and remorse pinches at my gut as I glare at the deserted corridor. The house feels empty, even with two heartbeats.

I need to make peace with Red. I have to make this work, just till she gets herself back on her feet and leaves. Then things can get back to how they were. She can be happy and I can go back to fucking randoms—to help me forget about her. Again.

My stomach growls and I'm guessing she'd be hungry too.

In the kitchen, I scour around the cupboards and open and close the fridge aimlessly. When I slap the last cupboards closed, I grab my phone and dial the Chinese shop. I order the Peking duck for myself and a chicken chow mein with two extra portions of spring rolls. Her favourite.

I nod to myself, happy with the effort, then sit and watch the clock like I have nothing better to do. But, food means an excuse to go knock on Red's door and coax her out, and maybe even have a conversation while I get to look at her face, the delicate contours of her lips, and the deep soulful emerald of her eyes.

The doorbell finally rings, and I grab the plastic bags, pay the delivery guy and set the containers on the table.

I edge to her room and stare at the door like an idiot for a second before I pound on it, "Red."

It swings open and my body stalls for a second when she stands on the other side, her eyes burning with unshed tears. She sniffs in a tattered breath and her fingers lace together then pick at her shirt.

I clear my throat and take a step back, "I got us some food."

"I'm not a hungry little girl anymore Wolf, you don't need to feed me."

"Don't be like that. I got your favourite, chow mein with extra spring rolls." Her eyes grow wide for a second.

"Yeah, I'm good thanks." She goes to close the door, but I shove my foot in the gap and force it open. She stumbles backwards, and I reach for her. My hands land on her delicate waist and I draw her to me. My body instantly hardens, and I get a whiff of her strawberry shampoo.

She claws at my hand, "Let me go!"

"Come eat with me!" I growl drawing her closer, trying to quell the anger in my voice, but I can't. It floods through me with crushing force and I know it's not anger I'm feeling but bitter disappointment—at myself. I'm trying to be the good guy, trying to pretend that everything I ever felt for her stopped that night, but she's fighting me, goading me, making it fucking impossible. I have a gnawing need to take care of her. I need her to forgive me.

"Get one of your whiney girls to eat with you," she sneers and shoves away from my touch. "You can screw her afterwards too."

"I don't screw whiney girls."

"Pffft, that's all you screw."

"What the fuck are you on about?"

"All those chicks you fuck, just to ghost them the next day… You're the same asshole you've always been."

I snort and wonder how the hell the conversation derailed this far off its tracks. "Whatever."

"The only reason they sleep with you is cause little girls sleep with little boys." She digs, trying to hurt me.

"Watch yourself Red."

"Or what? The big bad wolf is going to run away and come back in the morning?" She taunts and fury flares inside me.

In a swift, savage move, I grab her shoulder and throw her against the wall where my hand curls around her neck. I lean down so I can look into her infuriating eyes, and we glare at one another, frozen in a silent, angry battle.

"What are you going to do?" She smirks and swallows hard against my palm, her heartbeat thrashing beneath my fingers. My body tenses and my hand closes just another inch around her while the other rises to her shoulder, and my knuckles glide along her perfect hot skin. I relish the way she feels, though I'm bitterly aware that I'm perilously close to her. It's too dangerous, her very presence makes me want to rip into her, to annihilate her senses and make her mine— like she's always been.

Red doesn't back down, her eyes burn into mine.

"Fuck," I growl and release her. She has no idea what she's doing to me. I storm out of her room and into the lounge. The food forgotten on the dining room table. I grab my keys and head for the door letting it slam behind me.

My heart threatens to shatter my ribs and my nails dig

into the flesh of my palms as my fists clench tighter. I suck in breath trying to calm the raging tempest of emotions that grows inside me. I step away from the house, needing to put distance between us, uncertain why I feel so rattled by her. I take off sprinting. My feet pound the ground as I dart along the darkening streets. I don't want to think about anything— not how she felt or smelt or how her burning eyes looked at me with so much pain. I push myself, straining my body till my throat rasps and feet are too heavy, and then I push even harder till my heart screams and my lungs burn, and all I need is air.

I jog back home and stare at the building while catching my breath. Yellow light from the lounge room spills onto the roadside. I suck in a galvanising breath then crack the door open.

She's on the couch, sketching again, lost in a world known only to her. Her earphones are pushed into her ears and she doesn't notice me.

My parched throat aches with thirst, I go to the kitchen and grab a drink. On the table, the plastic bags have been disassembled. A single spring roll lays abandoned on a plate and one of the containers is gone.

I find it in the fridge.

I gulp the rest of my water and swipe my t-shirt over my face, it comes away with a wet sweat stain. I walk back into the lounge and fall on the couch across from Red. For the first time, she sees me. She startles but doesn't move as I shuffle closer to her. I reach for one of her earphones, pull it from her ear and push it into mine. Strange ambient music filters through the earpiece and I lean back into the couch, tension leaking from me and into the pillows.

"What are you doing?" Red is still looking at me her big eyes suspicious and wary. She looks like prey that's just been found by a very hungry predator.

"I need to stop thinking," I shrug and let my eyes close.

"About what?"

"About you."

Her sharp intake of breath makes my heart pinch. I ignore the sensation and sink into the music.

15

TEN YEARS AGO

Wolf 18, Red 15

Wolf

I stroll into the house and spot Red sitting on the couch. As always, one leg crossed over the other, her sketch pad on her lap, her pencil rolling between her glistening red lips. I stare at them for a minute then shake myself awake as I find her looking at my face, a ghost of a smile tugs on her lips.

"Brought dinner," I hold up the containers. "Where's Hunter?"

"Thought he was with you?" She shrugs and her eyes dart back to her sketch.

"Must be out with someone else."

"Must be," her pencil brushes the page.

"I brought dinner."

"You said that already." She doesn't look up.

"Well, do you want to come and eat with me before it gets cold?"

"In a minute," she says absentmindedly, "I just want to finish this."

She doesn't look up as I walk to the kitchen and dump the food on the counter then plummet next to her on the couch. "What are you drawing?"

Her head snaps up and her big green eyes land on my face, "Nothing." She grabs the sketch pad and holds it close to her chest.

"Don't be like that, show me."

"No," she whines and curls further away. It's such a sweet sound it makes my body tighten, and I have to remind myself it's not allowed to feel that way.

"Come on, I won't bite." I lunge for her and she squeals rolling onto her stomach and into a small ball. I smother her with my bigger body and reach for the pad. And suddenly, I am way too aware of the way her body curves against mine and how soft her skin feels when I graze it and how she shudders when I touch her.

"Let me see," I growl in her ear.

Her muffled 'no' amuses me.

"Final warning, Red."

"Get off me," she wriggles beneath me. "It's not finished yet."

The way she says it piques my curiosity, and instead of letting her go like I should, my fingers find the delicate soft flesh over her hips and dig in. She shrieks in surprise and her body arches with the pain. I seize the moment, flip her over, pin her legs down with my body, then dig into her flesh again.

She giggles and screams, and the sound sends a thousand electric volts into my cock—which is already hard.

"Get off me," she squirms beneath me trying to slither free, but I have her locked down.

"Show me." I dig my fingers in again and she shrieks with insane, beautiful laughter followed by irritated embarrassment.

"Stop it, Wolf."

"Show me!"

"Get off!" She struggles and tries to pry herself loose. This time I let myself lie on top of her, my larger body pinning her down into the couch.

Her ragged breath is inches from my face, and I drop my forehead onto hers—all too aware of how she feels against me, all too aware of the way her mouth is inches away, and my cock is only a few cotton fibres away from being inside her. All too aware of how wrong this should feel, except that it feels a little too right.

She gasps as she feels me, and I smirk covering up my sudden desperate need for my best friend's little sister. "You can't win, Red."

"It doesn't mean I'm going to stop fighting."

"Why fight when you can just give in?" I whisper against her cheek and I wonder which one of us I'm actually asking. "Just give me what I want, and I'll let you go."

"And what about what I want?" Her hips rise just a touch and she grind against my hard cock.

My breath catches in my throat with her sudden move and my body stiffens. I shuffle slightly down, breaking the contact, needing to get away from how good she feels; except that she slides down after me and brushes against me, taunting, again and then a third time.

Our hot breaths mingle as my cock swells and sensible thought is about to disappear. She smirks and I realise she's playing a game. Anger flares and floods my veins, it's an easier feeling to latch onto then disappointment. For a second, I thought she wanted me as much as I want her.

In a swift movement I push up and rip her wrists from her body, the sketch pad falls to the floor and I roll off her, snatch it and stand.

She's on me a second later, clawing at my chest and neck as I hold the pad above my head knowing she'll never reach it.

"Give up Red."

"Give it to me."

"You want me to give it to you?" With one hand still above my head, I grab her and smash her into the wall. My body pins hers with cruel intention. She gasps and her mouth falls slightly open in a delectable pout and I can't help myself, my lips graze hers, "I'll give you everything Red," I whisper.

Her wide eyes lock with mine for a beat, and my heart ricochets in my chest before she pushes me away with all her strength. I take a small step back. Red slides beneath my hands and rushes upstairs. I hear her door slam behind her, my forehead kisses the wall while I catch my breath.

What the fuck was that?

I roll onto the wall and lean against it then look at her precious sketch pad. I was anticipating doodles, so what I saw took my breath away.

An intricate and delicate pencil drawing of *me*.

The boy on the paper looks directly at me, like he's somehow looking right into my soul. Her haunting realism stings. Linear grey-black strokes that smash into powerful, blunt lines, tipped with darker, sharper, wirelike delineations that create a dramatic composition and stunning tonal shadings. The picture glares at me and a shaky breath rattles out of me as I find air in the suddenly oppressive room.

I flip through her pad, searching through a few of the pages. Half-done drawings of fruit and other still lives, but none as delicate or intricate or loved or worked on as the one which held my image.

For a second, I allow myself to wonder if Red did want the same things I did; maybe the girl who was growing up into a beautiful woman wanted to be mine as just much as I wanted to make her mine. Maybe she saw me as more than the guy who brings her food and hangs out with her brother.

I take a steeling breath and take the stairs two at a time,

stopping at her door. I knock and wait in the silence that followed.

"Red?"

"Go away."

"I'm coming in," I say and push the door open.

She's sitting on the edge of her bed, staring out into the evening, the colours ink into murky shades of purple and dark blue. She doesn't turn around.

"Your artwork is amazing."

"It wasn't for you to look at it, it was personal."

"But it's stunning."

She turns to face me and her face burns with anger, "You shouldn't have…"

"You're incredibly talented Red, why do you want to hide it away."

"I wasn't hiding my *talent*…" she bites out the words. She says nothing more. Her burning wanting eyes lock with mine, like she can really see me behind all the masks I wear—all my desires I thought I've hidden so well.

I clench my fists around the pad as I fill in the rest of her words. I want to reach for her, desperately, but I don't because I crave her too much. She fills me with more. More emotion, more want, more desire, she's not like the other empty girls.

I step closer to the bed knowing I shouldn't, "It's beautiful."

She chews on her lower lip and her cheeks colour with crimson.

"You could have just asked, I would have sat for you."

The crimson turns a shade darker and she shakes her head, "I don't need you to sit for me, I know what you look like."

I nearly cave then, nearly wrap myself around her, make her mine, take away the burning ache in her voice. But I don't. Instead, I break the cord that tethers us together in the moment, cause if I don't … I throw away the thought.

"Not in the nude," I deadpan and the red in her cheeks burns hotter spreading down her neck.

"No thanks, I'm creating art not horror movies."

I chuckle at her insult while my insides burn.

"Can I have it back now?" Her voice breaks a little.

I hold it out to her, and she snatches it away and clutches it to her chest.

"You really are amazing."

She nods, "I'm going to apply to UADL."

"The arts university?"

"It's the best one in London, plus if I get a job and Hunter picks up some extra shifts." she shrugs.

Shit he hasn't told her.

"That's great Red." I grip the back of my neck to stop myself from reaching for her.

"It will be." She's beaming at me.

I'm about to tell her not to get her hopes up when the front door opens.

"Red?" Hunter's voice echoes through the house. "Wolf?"

He must have discovered the food I left in the kitchen.

"Up here," she calls, then by passes by me, our shoulders touch and I thrill at the feel of her skin.

She runs downstairs and their muffled voices travel up to her room where I sit for a moment and stare at myself through her eyes.

A shiver wracks up my body as I realise I'm done for.

16

PRESENT DAY

Wolf

When I wake up Red is gone. I stand up and the blanket that she threw over me pools at my feet. I glare at the fabric and my traitor heart wants to expand, like it thinks she might care about me. I snuff out the feeling, pick up the blanket and march to her room.

She's not there.

"Fuck." I mumble to myself and wonder how I managed to sleep twelve uninterrupted hours.

I check my phone. Fourteen voicemails and a few emails. They'll have to wait.

I call Red.

"Hello?" she puts on an innocent voice, like she doesn't know who it is and the urge to strangle her returns.

"Where the fuck are you?"

"Someone woke up on the wrong side of the couch?"

"Where?'

"You didn't get my note?"

I hesitate and brush my hands over my face, "No."

"Awe, must be cause I didn't leave one."

"Red," I warn her, "where the hell are you?"

"None of your business,"

"Red—"

"Find me if you can," she taunts me before the line goes dead.

"Fuck!" I growl into the empty corridor.

I grab my phone and grind my teeth as I flick it open. I shut my eyes for a second then open up the tracking app Hunter installed on her phone the first night she arrived. It's not like she needs a babysitter or that she can't take care of herself, it's just that I know she'll be safer if I was around. At least that's what I can keep telling myself.

It's all about her.

She's in the city again, near a gallery. I head for a quick shower and spend the next thirty minutes apologising to people for missing their calls and answering all the emails that can't wait, all the while keeping an eye on the app. Red doesn't stray from the gallery.

I shut down my laptop and head out.

1 7

Red

For a second, I forget about all the problems that wait for me outside, and I smirk as I picture Wolf's face when I hung up on him. He'll never find me here. I almost feel guilty about putting his phone on silent and letting him sleep. But he looked so peaceful, so beautiful like an ornate sculpture.

I step into the gallery and my Doc Martens stick to the tiled floor, they rip away in silence, and I don't feel like too much of an intruder.

There's a beautiful silent hum that hangs in the air, like it's holding its breath at the artwork that lines the walls. I fear my thundering heart will disrupt the silence.

"Can I help you?" the voice drawls and rips me from my thoughts as a young man dressed in a black suit and styled hair steps from behind an oversized desk.

"I hope so," I give him my best smile as he gives me a disapproving once over. "I'm here about the traineeship." My breath stutters on the intake and nerves crawl up my skin.

He purses his lips like he's totally unimpressed with

everything I've said so far then turns around towards his monstrous desk, "Follow me."

His dress shoes echo on the tiles, and he rounds his table making me wait on the other end while he picks up the phone and dials a few numbers, "Hi sweety, your next victim is here." He smirks at me as he speaks, and I try for a smile. It seems to be the wrong response as his smile dies like a dark planet.

He puts the handle back in the cradle and turns his attention to his computer screen.

"Ignore Caleb, he's just being a bitch cause he was dumped last night," a honied voice startles me.

I turn to find Becca Oakford floating towards me. Caleb glares at her and she raises an eyebrow. He folds his hands across his chest and pouts. I watch the silent exchange with awe then turn my attention back to Becca, who is now directly in front of me.

My words lodge in my throat as too many of them want to escape all at once. "I work you," I spit out and wait in vain for lightning to strike me down.

She grins and Caleb snorts, "Let's get to know each other first," she winks at me and heat rushes to my ears.

"I meant to say I love your work."

"Good, then we'll get along just fine." Her smile is so sincere I relax instantly. "Caleb baby, be a dear and get us a couple of coffees, I have a feeling about this one."

She winks at me a second time and ushers me to her office.

Today is going to be the best day ever.

1 8

Red

Today is the worst day ever.

I step out of her office and fight the urge to run away screaming and crying like a toddler mid tantrum. I feel like a fool and wish I would have never made this stupid appointment. How could I ever think that Becca Oakford will hire me.

Me.

Uneducated, unqualified, pathetic little me.

"Thank you for this opportunity," I mumble feeling like I'm just wasting more of her time.

"Can I help you sir?" Caleb's voice sounds enthusiastic as his shoes tap along the floor.

"No thanks, I'm just here for her."

All the hair on my neck stiffens and I swivel to find an agitated Wolf; he ensnares me with a fierce look.

"Oh," Caleb sulks again and shuffles back to his desk. "Lucky bitch," he mutters as he passes by me.

"He's… we're… it's no…" I pinch my eyes closed and turn back to Becca. "Thanks again." She nods.

I sidestep Wolf and walk outside, wanting to find a dark corner to collapse into and partake in a pity party. *What the hell is he doing here anyway?*

"Stop running away from me." He's suddenly by my side.

"How did you even—" I clench my jaw and pinch my eyes closed for a second, then sigh, "you know what I don't even want to know." I keep walking and he stalks me like a shadow. "Go away!"

"No."

"Go away, please?" I try again.

"No."

"What are you even doing here, Wolf?"

"Making sure you don't get yourself into any sticky situations while Hunter is away."

I huff and trudge off. He catches me easily which only infuriates me more.

"How about you tell me what that was all about?"

"How about you die in a blazing hellfire."

He grabs my elbow and my pulse kicks up at the touch. My free hand flies to my neck, remembering his grip, the way he squeezed just enough to make my body shiver with terrible, treacherous thoughts. I bat the feelings away as I tug my hand and he releases me.

"Red," He calls me, "Red!"

I stop and turn to him, "What?"

"I'll make you a deal."

I wait in silence for his terms.

"Walk with me once around the block and tell me what happened, after that you won't see me for the rest of the day."

"For the *rest* of the day?"

"I promise."

I scoff, "Your promises mean shit."

He purses his lips and runs a hand through his hair, "It's all I have for now, you'll just have to trust me."

"Trust you?" The idea is laughable.

"Just… try." He almost looks desperate, and I hate how that makes something inside me twinge.

I sag with my sigh, "fine."

His wolfish smile takes me by surprise and my heart staggers at the sight. I feel the ivy around my heart rip away and tear me with reminders.

When I look away, he starts walking.

I fall into step with him, he's silent as he waits for me to start spilling. But every time I want to, embarrassment coats my throat, burns my ears and coils my stomach till all that comes out are feeble ragged breaths.

"Do you remember that day when we cut school and the three of us sneaked to Hyde Park? It was so hot and everywhere was packed with stupid tourists."

A happy memory begins to float inside me as he speaks.

"And then we got those ice creams."

I nod and a smile ghosts my lips, strawberry vanilla with a flake. I lick my lower lip.

A dark look crosses Wolf's eyes then he blinks it away. "Then later, when we walked by the lake, I pushed Hunter into the water." He starts laughing, a low rumble that thunders inside me.

"You were always such an asshole."

"A charmer you mean." He winks at me.

I arch a brow as the rest of the day plays out in my head, "and then you two idiots threw me in too."

"You wanted to swim."

"It was my only set of school uniform, and I was in a white shirt."

"Hey, I gave you the option to take it off," he smirks and I glare at him, just for his smile to broaden. I can't help the stupid grin that creeps onto my face as he keeps talking.

"Then we chilled on those deckchairs till the cops chased us off. We ran all the way to the tube station."

"You mean, you two ran and I was dragged."

"Not our fault you have short legs."

"It was your fault the cops were after us in the first place."

"Neither of us knew those chairs were occupied, or that the money in the purse belonged to someone else."

He chuckles and I can't help but do the same. I hate when he can make me feel so at ease, like being around him is so easy.

He stops and turns to me, "Remember we were friends once?" He cradles my face in his big hands and traces his thumb over my cheek before he releases me, "Do you think we can get back there?"

"I don't know if I could ever be your friend, Wolf." He nods, but he doesn't understand.

I can't be his friend because when I'm around him, every part of me screams for more of him. I want him so badly it hurts, and my heart rips a little more each time I smell another girl on him. I can't be his friend because I want to be his everything.

Silence follows us through narrow streets and busy alleys and still he doesn't push or ask. He lets me explore shopfronts and dwell on my feelings of sour failure before I finally start spilling.

Wolf

I watch her with a fascination I don't want to feel. Red should be mundane, a dime a dozen kind of girl. She should be totally forgettable—except that she isn't, and everything about her interests me, makes me want to know more, dig deeper. Just like before. I find that I enjoy spending time with her, looking at her. Any part of her, and that when I do, it's easy to forget that Hunter is my best friend and Red is his little sister.

I follow her in silence knowing there's no need to push her. She'll spill when she's ready, not because she's a talker, but because she wants to get as far away from me as possible. The thought stings and I swipe it away.

"That was a job interview for an internship," she starts but doesn't look at me, her attention is focused on a near naked mannequin holding a book. Her eyes flash as she reads the title.

The Count of Monte Cristo. Another classic. Like her.

She moves on and I follow like the stalker I am.

"Becca Oakford is a legend, at fifteen she was already

exhibiting her work in some of the world's most prestigious galleries," her hands fly to her chest like she's breathless, "since then she's been a household name around the world."

I nod pretending I know what she's talking about, but we both know I don't. I've never heard of this Becca woman. Or if I did once, I'd forgotten about her just like I've forgotten about a long line of other women.

We keep walking and she stops at another shop front, I get the feeling she's avoiding looking at me, because it's vacant. A 'to let' sign hangs limply on the glass door and the floor is littered with unopened mail.

"I wanted that internship so badly." She shakes her head, covering her mouth with a hand. "When I saw she was hiring, I didn't even think about it, I just called and made an appointment."

Her hand slips away from her mouth and she sucks in her bottom lip. My eyes zero on her glistening lips while I keep my mouth shut, my jaw relaxed, so that she can't see what I'm really thinking. How that one singular action affected me. How I crave to tear her clothes off, push up her up against that storefront, thread my hand through her long, purple hair and fuck her until she cries for me. I want to hear her moan; I want to make her whimper, and then I want to make her beg for more of me.

My body riots and I wrench my eyes away.

I wait.

She turns to look at me and her face is a crumpled mess, she wears her sadness like a red cloak that wraps around her entire body. "Anyway, it was a total disaster. I'm such a fucking mess Shaw, I didn't know anything." My heart rate kicks up at the mention of my name, and I feel compelled to hold her, comfort her, take away the tortured blanket of pain that follows her everywhere she goes.

"I was totally unprepared and made a complete fucking fool of myself. I—"

I step in, reaching out for her, when her phone rings. She swings her backpack into me as she tosses it from her shoulder into the cradle of her hands, then pulls out the phone.

I freeze, feeling like an idiot and watch as she takes a few steps away.

"Hello?" Her voice wavers. She clears her throat and her face twists with annoyance, "Just call me Red."

I battle my smile, I'd also be annoyed if my mother gave me her ridiculous name, Ruby Esmeralda Diamante Evans.

My heart twists with the memory of the day I pried that piece of information out of her.

Her name is a collection of precious stones, and she guards its secret like it's a chest full of treasure. I know she hates it, but I think even when she was born, her mother knew how precious and special she was going to be, so she couldn't name her just one beautiful thing—she wanted her to be all of them. And of course, she is a combination of all those precious stones.

Her red ruby lips and smart mouth, her emerald green, piercing eyes that floor you when they really focus on you, and her hard, sharp and beautiful exterior like the diamond she is. She's been put through so much shit, pounded down by life, but all the pressure just made her shine even brighter.

I watch as her face changes. Her eyes lift to mine and with each passing second, they grow bigger, her mouth falls open and her sharp features soften.

Impatience skitters along my skin as she bites down a creeping smile, and my cock is all too aware of her glistening lips.

"Okay. Yes. Thank you." She says and hangs up.

Before I can ask, she shrieks, "I got the job."

And before I know what she's doing, she wraps herself around me. Her sudden heat sends my body into a frenzy, and I can't help but draw her in and inhale her. Her strawberry shampoo saturates my senses, and familiar feelings that should not resurface try and push themselves up. I hold her, pulling her ever closer and she looks up at me, her mouth split into a beautiful delicious smile, and without thinking, I dip my head and brush her lips with my own. Wanting so much more than a whisper of a taste.

She stiffens in my arms. And the moment shatters around us.

"Shit," I growl and release her.

She stares at me for a long moment, her face a myriad of emotions all crashing against one another. She looks rattled and sad.

"I'm going to go now." Her voice quivers and she steps away from me, her eyes boomeranging from me to the narrow alleyway, her smile all but vanished. I've robbed her of another beautiful memory and tainted it with my own flavour.

She takes another step away and I go to follow when she puts a hand up, "You promised."

I take a long breath, retreat, nod, and open my hands in a 'you're free to go' gesture.

She hesitates before finally turning around and walking away.

I watch her leave. She turns around twice to see me still rooted to my spot. When she turns again, I retreat behind a wall.

I wait two full minutes before I start to follow her. I don't need to hurry, and I can't lose her.

Red is easy to track and easier to follow. She lives in her own bubble where the rest of us don't exist.

She spends the next few hours in futile wanderings around the city, taking notes and randomly sketching. I spend the time answering the rest of my emails and snatching glances at anyone who moves too close to her. A would-be pickpocket catches a glimpse of me glaring at him as he approaches her and quickly walks away, like he knows he's about to lose a vital organ. Even at a distance, I can protect her. I find that suddenly being close to Red and knowing where she is and what she does has become vital for me.

When she returns to the apartment, I wait for her to close the door behind her and watch for the lights to come on, then turn around and go to the store.

2 0

Red

The delicate brush of his lips still lingers on mine all these hours later, and each time I think about it, my entire belly explodes with a violent eruption of butterflies; but his lips are like poison and as soon as the butterflies reach my throat they sink to their agonising death.

I sigh hating the way he makes my body feel, hating the way my anger towards him saturates everything.

An hour later and he walks into the house with bags under his arms. He sets them on the dining room table then packs the food away.

I pretend he doesn't exist by looking down at my phone.

"Are you hungry? Thought we could celebrate your new job."

"We?"

He shrugs, "If Hunter was here, you'd be celebrating."

"So, what are you, my new big brother?" The thought sits like a rock in my stomach.

"No, but I'm his best friend and I'd like to try be your friend again."

My heart clinches in my chest at the word again—
'Friends'. I give him a lopsided smile with a side of shrug.

"So, dinner?"

"Are you cooking?"

His face scrunches and his head tilts a little, "You can call
it cooking."

"What do you call it?"

"Not burning."

I hate that I snicker. "So, what will you not be burning for
us this evening?"

"French toast? With a side of Champagne?"

"It's all very continental…"

"I was trying to be classy."

"Must be hard for you. Did you hurt yourself?"

"Only a little." He winks at me and tangles his hands in his
hair.

My body hums with sudden electricity, "Did you mention
Champagne?"

"We are celebrating."

I nod and my pinched smile is back. Maybe I can throw
this wolf a bone. "Sure, sounds great."

He flashes me his teeth and disappears into the kitchen.
Moments later the clang of pans and pots fill the air followed
by sizzling and the smell of melted butter.

"Dinner is served," he calls out a while later and I go sit at
the table where he'd set two plates.

I sit down and he places a plater piled with toast in the
centre of the table then goes to a cupboard and grabs two
whiskey glasses. He fills them with Champagne and places
one in front of me.

"Cheers," he says, raising his glass.

I eye the tumbler and raise an eyebrow.

He shrugs, "We don't entertain much, or drink much
Champagne."

I kiss his tumbler with my own and it clinks softly. I take

a small sip and the bubbles rush down my throat in a churning waterfall.

"Why don't you entertain much?" I ask as I grab two toasts and start eating.

"We prefer the quiet."

"That doesn't sound like Hunter."

He chuckles and nods, "I didn't say we don't party, I just said we don't entertain much."

"So, what you're saying is you don't bring people back to the house?"

"I'm saying we prefer our privacy, and in our line of work, it's safer. The less people know about you, the better."

"Is that why you always act like such an ass?"

"Excuse me?"

"Push people away, keep yourself closed off."

"It's not all as simple as that?"

"Isn't it?"

"Nope."

"Enlighten me."

"Red, you know I can't talk about my job."

"Why not, you're basically a glorified babysitter."

His lips purse for a second and his brow furrows, "It's a little more than that."

"Is it?"

"Yes." He tucks into his food and gives me a stone wall.

"The way I see it, your job is to sit around all night then go home and sleep."

He glares at me and his mouth thins into a long line, "If it was that basic, I'd have a lot less paperwork at the end of every night." He bristles and swipes his palms over his thighs. "There's lots of red tape and procedures. Our job is to make sure everyone has a good time and doesn't see the ugly side."

"The ugly side?"

"The weapons, the drugs, the fighting…" he tampers off, "we make sure our guys are highly trained."

"Are you 'highly trained'?" I mock him and he shots me an annoyed glance.

"Yeah, I have a brown belt in Jiu-Jitsu."

"So, your speciality is hugging?" I drive the poker deeper.

"What can I say, I'm a lover not a fighter."

I scoff, "Think you're in the wrong line of work then."

"Well." He smirks, shrugs and attacks another piece of toast.

I ignore the flutter in my chest as I watch him. The way he tears at the toast, and the way his hands move and how his throat bobs as he swallows with his wolfish expression locked on me. I pretend not to notice how his full lips glisten with a buttery shine till he licks it away.

I have to talk just to clear the constriction in my throat, "Do you ever get scared?"

He rolls his eyes as a smile creeps on my face, getting under his skin is going to be my new favourite hobby. "Nothing scares me."

"Liar." Something passes across his face, and he stuffs more food into his mouth.

He takes another sip of his drink, "I don't want to talk about my work. Tell me about this internship,'

"Nothing to tell, I don't start till next Monday."

"But this Becca Oakwood, she was the one that painted 'Roses in the Fields'?"

I give him a sideway glance and my brow furrows, "Yeah?"

"It's really dark isn't it?"

"Only in its story. The colours are actually incredibly vibrant, it's what makes it so powerful."

He nods like he agrees, "It was a bold statement at such a young age."

I bite the inside of my cheek, holding back a snicker. He sounds so well versed, like he practiced. There's something incredibly sweet in his manner. But I have no intention in putting him out of his misery.

For the rest of dinner, I talk to him about mood, colour and composition in Becca's work then spill over to other influential artists. By the time I'm done his eyes are rolling to the back of his head, and I can see he's suffered enough.

Almost.

Sometime between Becca and Monet we have nearly finished the bottle of Champagne and I'm on the right side of buzzed. A lovely warm hum that sings under my skin and makes me forget that I should not be enjoying myself as much as I am.

"Thanks for dinner," I say as he piles up our empty plates and clears the table.

"Want to watch a movie?" he calls from the sink, and my eyes jerk to his face. He looks like the Wolf I used to know, his shoulders hang with confidence and his mouth quirks up in a half smile. His searching look makes something drag down in my lower belly, and I ignore the tugging inside me, ripping my eyes from his as I stand up.

"Sure," I say it even as every fibre in my body screams for me to call it a night.

His smile spreads and he lazily pushes away from the counter and heads to the lounge, where he drops into the couch and grabs the remote.

He flicks the TV on, and I take a hesitant step into the lounge and sit on the other side of the couch.

Where it's safe.

"What do you want to watch?"

"How about *Ghost*?" I clench my teeth to keep a straight face. Nothing tortures Wolf more than emotional chick flicks.

"Fine." The muscles of his jaw twitch for a second before he puts it on.

There is a trench between us; it's deep and wide, and I

don't know how to cross it as he shuffles closer to me, his eyes darting over every now and again.

He's like a lazy current, languidly closing the distance between us, till I can feel the heat of his shoulder against mine, and his fingers twitch alongside my own. They stroke a long, slow trail that sends shivers down my spine and spread like ink inside me, blotting out all the empty spaces, sketching images into my head, threatening to awaken dead things.

I want to touch him so badly, I want to feel so much more of him, but I can't.

I jerk away from him and feel him turn to ice beside me. His eyes shoot to mine, and for a second, I think he's going to say something, but his phone rings and he pulls further away as he shifts and yanks it from his pocket.

He eyes the number before swiping, "Hello?"

A muffled female voice on the other end. He grinds his jaw and anger flashes in his eyes, then he abruptly stands up.

He storms out of the room, "Je—."

He's gone for another few minutes and when he comes back, he's a different man. Tension leaks from him and his neck is taut with agitation. He paces and rips a hand through his hair like he's forgotten I'm here.

"Are you okay?"

He stalls and his eyes snap to mine, "Oh shit, I'm sorry about the movie. I just have to take care of something."

"Of course." My heart pinches in my chest.

His gaze lands on my face and in two steps he's in front of me, and his hands come up as if to cradle my face, then freeze in mid-air. They drop to his sides, "I'm sorry Red, I know we're celebrating, but I *have to* take care of this."

I nod and stand up, moving out of his reach, feeling the anguish claw my insides, "Thanks for dinner."

I shut the door to my room and climb into my cold bed, it feels like every chamber of my empty heart.

Wolf

Her sunken face spikes the rhythm of my heart but I wait for her to close her door then shake it off and call Hunter.

"What's up?"

"She's gotten through again."

Hunter sighs, "Again?"

I shrug even though he can't see me, "I've already blocked her a hundred different times, but I'll need to have a chat with boys about giving out my phone number without my consent." I growl.

"Did she confirm it was one of them?"

"How else?"

"We own a business Wolf…"

"My number isn't listed." I remind him.

"Fine, but *I'll* talk to them."

I bristle, "Fine. But they better get the fucking message."

"They will. How's Red?" He changes the subject and electricity tingles along my skin.

"Fine, she got herself a job."

"Really?" He sounds too surprised.

"At some gallery."

"And you?"

"Just keeping an eye on her."

"Just an eye?"

"We've had this conversation." My stomach rolls.

"I just like to know you're keeping your end of things."

"You know she hates me."

His silent reply is confirmation.

"Just talk to the boys and get this sorted." I hang up before he can say anything more.

22

<hr>

Red

The rest of the week passes as if I'm nothing but a mosquito in Wolf's life soup. He snaps and growls at me, giving me precious little time and endless icy looks that I pretend don't stab my insides. He follows me around in silences that see him stuck with his nose to his phone. He doesn't mention our celebration and I use the quiet to prepare for my internship. The echoes return to my empty heart chambers, and the world feels normal again.

My first week at Becca's gallery is a black and white blur, smeared with too many colours. I'm given endless dates and a virtual calendar that's going to be my new best friend, along with Caleb, who despite being a 'bitch,' as Becca called him on our first meeting, is really gentle and kind. He's also been shagged in a back alley at least twice that I know of during work hours, and I think that helps his mood. He's only asked about Wolf one other time, but I shut it down.

Becca isn't around as often as I'd hoped, and Caleb placates me with reassurances that once we start doing exhibitions, I'll be sick of her. I can't wait to be sick of her. He tells me about an upcoming charity fundraiser in a country estate.

Becca has agreed to contribute a percentage of her sales, and we will have to oversee the installation. A buzz of excitement thrills through me. I spend the rest of that week learning about Becca's social media accounts, yearly planners, and art installations.

When the weekend finally arrives, I'm exhausted and thrilled and, most importantly, alone. Hunter is back, but with three guys still down, him and Wolf have been covering shifts at clubs. They leave one celebrity client and go straight to work standing outside a door somewhere. Sometimes I hear them slipping in in the early hours of the morning.

When I get up, they're still down or have already left. It feels almost like I'm living alone. And it feels safe, because I don't have to see Wolf at all, and my heart can stay intact just a little bit longer.

I spend my day off sketching in the rare sunlight, autumn is creeping in and with it, cooler days and darker nights. I shower and pull on some comfy tracksuit pants and a white singlet.

I make some popcorn and snuggle on the couch ready for a thrilling Saturday night with the cast of *Dirty Dancing*.

I'm mid chew and Johnny just threw Baby into the water when the doorknob rattles and opens. I swing around to see Wolf coming through the door, he turns his face away as he notices me, and I check the time on my phone.

"You're home early." Suspicion leaks from my voice.

He mumbles something under his breath and disappears into the corridor. A litany of noises tells me he's gone from his room to the bathroom and is now showering.

I keep watching the movie till I see movement in the corner of my eye. Wolf slinks back into the room. I can smell him before he arrives, spice and the things gods are made of, enticing delicious smells that make clever girls like me do stupid things. I pretend not to notice him. Given his entrance, he obviously doesn't want to talk.

He slides onto the couch and we sit in silence watching the movie.

"Can I get some of that?"

I turn to look at him and gasp. He points to my popcorn as if everything is fine.

His eye is a dull red, swollen almost shut and his lip is split. "Shit, what happened?"

He shrugs, "It's the job."

In a second, I'm out of the couch and in the kitchen throwing ice cubes into a towel. I bunch up the fabric and bring it over to him.

"Here."

"Don't need it."

"You do."

"I'm okay."

"Take the fucking ice Wolf."

"Just drop it."

"Please? Shaw?" His mouth twitches and I know I've hit a nerve.

I pass the towel over, and he winces as it lands on his face.

"What happened?"

"Not important."

"Was Hunter involved?" My heart spikes with worry.

"Oh, he was involved all right." He grumbles then hisses.

"Is he okay?"

"He won't be when I get my hands on him."

"Don't say that!" I jab his ribs and he sucks in a pained breath, his head falls back, and I realise I'd hurt him.

"I'm sorry." I don't know how to help.

His eyes peak open. "It's fine." But I can see that it's not, in the way his face is grim, and his shoulders are bunched up, and the way that he breaths—slowly, like it hurts.

"Is he?"

"He looks better than me," he grizzles and winces, and I wince along with him, my hands feeling helpless and useless at my sides.

"Where is he?"

"I'm sure he's got someone looking after him." He smirks then groans as his eyes pinch shut.

"I guess that sounds about right." I don't spend too much time thinking about it.

He chuckles, and sucks in a sharp breath, "Yeah .It's his fault this whole thing started in the first place."

"What do you mean?"

He shakes his head and I know I won't get anything else out of him. He pulls the ice away from his face and grimaces. My heart cracks a little at the sight of him.

"I think you need to get to a hospital."

"No, it's fine."

"Wolf."

"Just a few bruises and a probably a bruised rib. I've had worse." He's tight jawed, his eyes find mine.

"Probably?" I draw in a shaky breath, my eyes sting with unshed tears.

"Hey," his voice softens, but I can hear his pain underneath, "I'm fine, so is Hunter. Everything is okay."

Anxiety swims inside me on a loop. Worry and fear I never imagined I'd have to feel for these two big men who seem so invincible. My stomach locks up and I find myself sucking air into my lungs through choppy breaths. I push down the worry.

"Let me get you into bed." I offer him my hand as if I'd be able to pull him out of the couch. Instead, he snatches my wrist and rips me to him. I land in his lap and he hisses behind me sucking in a long, agonised breath. His entire body stiffens for almost a full minute before I can feel it relax again.

"Shaw." I make to get up, but his strong arms close

around me.

"Stay," his guttural, breathy voice whispers over my neck and goose bumps erupt along my skin.

I nod and he releases me, but only enough to slide in beside him, then his hand tightens around my shoulder, and his eyes lock firmly onto the TV. His long fingers trace a line from my neck, along my shoulder, slipping off the thin shoulder strap of my singlet. My heart thrums in a frenzy while he trails slow circles on my shoulder.

"Relax Red," he whispers above me, "everything's fine."

But it's not fine; I'm in Wolf's arms, and I can feel his warmth around me and hear the pounding of his heart as it smashes through me calling to my own heart, asking it to wake.

I watch the movie, totally aware of all of him. I want to relax, it should be easy and feel more natural, but with every stroke of his fingers and every sharp breath, I feel the tension build inside me. He unnerves me, he makes me feel totally vulnerable, and it scares the shit out of me.

Every time I move, he winces, and each time I try to pull away, his grip around me tightens. His presence tears at my defences and threatens to unleash my longing. My heart suffocates as he claws at the scars, and I clutch to his lies as a last ditch effort to save myself. *Everything's fine.*

We sit there till Johnny dances with Baby and announces that no one will put her a corner, and we watch the credits reel up the screen. I try to get up but he holds me. His hands wrap around me and he pulls me to him, and just as quickly, he lets me go and I'm on my feet at a safe distance. Except that I know there's no such thing. Not anymore.

"Let me get you to bed." I take a small step towards him.

"I'm going to sleep here, it's easier," he speaks through gritted teeth, and I wonder how much pain he's hiding from me.

"Are you sure?"

"Yeah." His eyes shut and his head falls to the back of the couch.

I retreat.

I go to his room and tear his blanket from his bed and return to the couch where he leans back. His body tense.

I throw the blanket over him. He doesn't move.

I turn away.

"Red?" I falter and turn back towards him. "Thanks." His hoarse voice screams of agony.

I nod, because I can no longer speak or stand here with him in the same room.

The desire to hold him and take away his pain consumes me, seeing him like this shatters me into a thousand pieces. I know if I go back in that room, I will be signing my fate to him again. I can't risk a second fall, yet it's all my body wants to do. Instead, I close my door and pull the blanket over my head and pretend I'm far far away.

The next morning, when I check the lounge, Wolf is gone. I don't see him again for the rest of the week.

23

———

TEN YEARS AGO

Wolf 18, Red 15

Wolf

The muffled sniffs and slight moans travel through the silent house and smash against my chest as I close the door behind me. I round the foyer wall to find Red curled up on the couch, her notepad and pencil deserted, her face twisted with grief, her green eyes swimming in red pools.

Her eyes shoot up and when they land on me, her hands fly to her face and wipe away the tears. She looks so broken and frightened sitting there; I want to pick up all her pieces and put her back together.

I'm by her side in two strides, and she doesn't pull away as I wing my arms around her and draw her into me. She's been avoiding me since I've discovered her secret. One she's not voiced, and I haven't been brave enough to ask about.

"What's happened?"

She sniffles and draws in a few sharp breaths steadying her voice, "Grandma Julie."

"Is she?"

"No," she wipes a hand over her tear streaked face, "they just took her away to the nursing home."

My hand tightens around her. Grandma Julie's been sick for so long, we all knew it was coming. She needed real help. I never understood why Hunter insisted she stay as long as she has.

Red pushes away from me, but I keep my hands on her.

"They said less than a year." She falls into a muted cry and I let her shiver against me.

"I can talk to my parents, maybe they can help."

She shakes her head, her hair tickles my chin, "Yeah? Where are they, Shaw?"

Her words stab with their truth, and I discard the idea.

"What if they take us away? I'm still underaged." her voice quivers with uncertainty.

"I won't let that happen."

She scoffs.

"Hunter will be an adult next month and your sixteenth birthday is not long after."

"I'm not sure if we can hang on that long."

"Hey," my knuckle finds her chin and I lift it, so that her burning eyes can look into mine, "I won't let anything happen to you."

"You can't make a promise like that."

"I just did." I whisper against her hair and pull her to my chest. Protecting Red has suddenly become the single most important thing in my world.

The door bangs open and Hunter appears in the doorway.

His brow furrows as it lands on us. "What's going on?"

"Red is upset, about your grandmother being taken away today."

He nods once and his jaw tightens, "I have some good news."

Her head jerks up and her eyes grow wide with desperate hope, my heart forgets to beat.

"I got another job."

"Oh, that's great Hunter," she leaps from my arms and into his, leaving a hollow cold cavity where she was a second ago.

"It is, and good money too." He looks down at her, "But it's after hours, which means you might be alone a few nights a week."

"I can stay with her," I pipe up before I can think about what I'm saying.

Hunter raises an eyebrow, and Red jabs me with a long look.

"I don't need a babysitter." She pushes away from Hunter.

"That's not a bad idea," he says, ignoring her.

"You know I'd be here anyway." we talk over her like she's not even there.

"I said I don't need a babysitter."

"Well I say different, at least until you're sixteen."

"That's only three months away Hunter, it will make no difference."

"It's settled then."

"What?" She huffs and her eyes narrow, bounding from his face to mine, "I'm not a little kid anymore."

"No, but you are my little sister and I'll feel better if I know there's someone here with you," he says it with so much sincerity, the fight falls from her like an avalanche.

"Fine, but I don't have to listen to anything he says."

Hunter laughs, "Fine."

"We'll just see about that," I play along, folding my arms across my chest, my mind flooded with a thousand images of Red doing *exactly* what I tell her to do. My cock jolts in my pants, and I swivel away walking towards the kitchen.

When Hunter follows, I grab two beers and put one in front of him.

"Hey, thanks man," he says and grabs the can, "I'll feel better knowing someone I can trust is looking after her."

"Don't mention it." I tip my beer towards his and take a long sip hoping the cold contents will cool my suddenly boiling insides.

"I mean it."

"Yeah I know." I shrug. "Have you told her yet?" He shakes his head slowly and I nod. I don't agree with his plan to keep delaying it, but I can't interfere. "When are you planning on doing that?"

"Soon," is all he says and drags another long sip of his beer.

24

PRESENT DAY

Red

Caleb grabs my wrist as I make to stand up and bolts out of the chair himself, a smile slicing his face as he takes in the tall, blond man that's just walked in. He strolls in like he doesn't have a care in the world and takes time to examine the first painting hanging on the wall. A striking art nouveau piece inspired by the great impressionists of our time, colourful with bold, confident strokes. Becca tells the story of the sea and his mistress; the white cliffs, as they chase each other through time, cursed to forever remain apart. The piece stirs something inside me, and I let my eyes fall away.

Caleb's shoes echo on the tiled floor as he goes to help the man who's moved on to the next piece. He introduces himself and his smile loses some of its shine when the man shakes his hand. He must be straight. Caleb's shoulders drop a little—yup, definitely straight. I cover my smirk as they walk over to the desk and Caleb rounds it, moving towards his seat.

"This is Red, she can answer any of your other questions."
He's stiff as he sits down and turns to his computer.

"Hi." I stand up and the man flashes me a sweet smile.

"Ethan," he gives me his hand and we shake, perhaps a little too long before I snatch my hand away.

"How can I help you?"

"I'm looking for a piece for my new office."

I give him a side glance, "You got a promotion?"

He chuckles, "No." He doesn't elaborate, and I feel ridiculous for asking.

"Did you have any particular piece in mind?"

He looks around the gallery, "Not really, thought maybe you could take me through some of the pieces."

"Of course."

We spend the next hour talking brush strokes and composition. I'm surprised by his knowledge of painting and the way he chooses to interpret the images that scream at us from the canvases.

"Are you an artist yourself?" I ask as we stand in front of the final canvass.

"I used to dabble," he sighs, like he's letting go of a dream, "but I was always better at arguing than creating, so I studied law instead."

I nod wondering what it's like to finally let the flame burn out on your dreams. I shift my focus back on the canvass. "How about this one?"

"It's nice," he says.

"*Nice?*" I bite my tongue too late, but his face breaks into a smile.

"What's wrong with nice?"

I shake my head, keeping my mouth shut.

"What's wrong with nice?" He prods again.

"It's just such a lazy word, too simple. It doesn't describe anything. It has no real substance." I cringe internally at my honesty, wondering how hard Caleb will be on me once I tell him I lost him a client.

"A lazy word?" he smirks, "it's a painting of a vase."

"It's a painting about standing out. Being unique."

He studies the painting and his brow furrows, "Explain."

I look at the painting, stepping inside of it as I start speaking, "At first glance, it looks like an ordinary scene, a dark table with a vase of flowers. But when you look at it, you'll notice that your eyes keep getting drawn to the singular red rose in the vase. The only real burst of colour in an otherwise dull background."

He nods.

"The rose draws your eye because it's unique, she stands out and shines brighter than the rest of the flowers because she has no equal. She is totally incomparable to anything else in the painting."

When I finish talking, Ethan is looking at me instead of the canvass, and I squirm a little under his scrutinising gaze.

He doesn't say anything for a beat, then his eyes finally swing back to the artwork. "Unique," he says it so softly, I'm not sure if that's what he actually said.

I wait for another few seconds before I open my mouth again, "So, what do you think? See anything you like?"

A small smile crosses his face as he turns back to me, "I think so."

"Great," I say possibly a little too enthusiastically, "which one?"

He shoves his hands into the pockets of his pants and looks at me, "This one."

"The *nice* one?" I let too much sarcasm drip out and kick myself instantly.

He chuckles and his gaze bores into mine, "I've since learned to look at it again and found that it is rather *unique*."

I feel heat rise to my face and ears, though I'm not sure

why. "Fantastic. Should we go back to the front desk and start the paperwork?"

"Sure." He gestures for me to lead, and I step ahead of him feeling sheepish.

At the desk I turn to Caleb, "Caleb can help you with the paperwo—"

"No," Ethan cuts through my words. He's not aggressive but calm as his eyes lock with mine, "I'll deal only with you or not at all."

Caleb's eyes dart from his face to mine and shrugs, "Just fill everything in and let me have a look before final delivery." He turns back to his computer as Ethan winks at me.

We spend the time going over the paperwork, payment, and delivery options. He's nonchalant and seems to agree with everything I say. I wonder if all clients are as easy to deal with as he is.

"Before I sign this, I want to add a condition."

I feel myself about to get lawyered and regret not forcing the issue of Caleb taking charge. "What is it?"

"I want you to be there when it gets delivered, to make sure it's installed properly."

"That's not really something I do."

"Well, do it anyway."

"It's not up to me."

"Well, who is it up to?"

"Becca."

"What's her number?"

I look at him like he's one sandwich short of a picnic, "I can't give you her number."

He puts his phone away and looks at me, "Fair enough. Go call her."

"Now?"

"Do you want me to sign?"

I stare at him for three seconds before standing up, "No."

His confidence shatters and his brow furrows like I have completely taken him aback. "No?"

I inhale deeply, calming my pounding heart. I'm about to let a £3000 deal walk out the door. "No," I repeat and cross my hands over my chest, "If you want the artwork, you should buy it because you love it. But you can't blackmail me into jeopardising my job because you're an arrogant ass who thinks he can walk in here and intimidate me."

"My intention wasn't to intimidate you, I just enjoyed spending the last hour with you."

Heat slithers up my neck.

"You were so passionate about the piece, I wanted to make sure it was installed correctly."

"Oh."

His eyes gleam with amusement and irritation prickles my skin. He calmly moves to the stack of papers on the table, takes the pen and signs the paperwork without further argument.

He drops the pen on the table and pulls out a card, "If you won't come to install my artwork, would you at least consider having a coffee with me?"

"Coffee?"

"Yeah coffee, it's a dark drink you have during the day between meals."

"I know what coffee is," I say stupidly, and he sniggers, battling full-on laughter.

"Think about it, Red." He places his cards on top of the contract, slides it across the desk towards me, and steps out of the office. His voice echoes through the gallery as he farewells Caleb, and then there's silence.

Caleb bursts through the door, his face all smiles. "You sold 'The Rose?'"

"I think so." I reach for the card and pocket it.

Caleb runs to me, shrieking and next thing I know, we're jumping up and down giggling.

2 5

Red

In the autumn air, the breeze bites at my cheeks while the sun kisses it. It's a lovely feeling, a contradiction, like everything else that has been going on in the last few months.

Hunter walks towards me, a large grin across his face, "Hey." He takes me into his arms.

"Hi," I smile back.

"Sorry we're late. I got… delayed."

"I don't want to know."

He shrugs and another of his too telling smirks flashes across his face.

"We're?" His words suddenly register.

"Oh yeah. Wolf is coming too, with someone."

"Someone?"

Hunter grins and my stomach does a long, aching roll that slings a knot into my throat. I hear the shrieking giggle and his low, gruff laughter, and I hold my breath behind pursed lips.

Wolf walks towards us with a girl draped around him.

She's clingy like Glad Wrap and just as transparent. He's still dressed in last night's uniform, his white shirt wrinkled, and the top two buttons missing. His hair is ruffled and unkempt, and I hate how his hand is hooked around her slim shoulder. He whispers something in her ear, and she bursts into another shriek of over the top laughter.

They make their way to our table and he stalls for a second as he sees me.

His date slips into the bench across from mine and smiles at me, then claws at Wolf who's still staring at me. He falls stiffly into the bench, his gaze still locked with mine, "What are you doing here?" He barks out, his face pinching with irritation.

"Hunter invited *me* to breakfast."

"Oh, we were carpooling."

I wave my hand, "Whatever, I don't want to know."

I grab my menu and stare at the words, instead of at the over made up doll sitting across from me, gripping Wolf's arm like it keeps her from drowning in her own stupidity.

I grind my teeth and try to soothe the angry green flames that lick at my skin. Jealousy is not a good colour for me. But then again, why should I be jealous? There's nothing romantic between us. In fact, there's nothing at all between us, and there never will be.

I order a full breakfast, so do Hunter and Wolf. *She* orders a fruit salad, and I'm glad my sunglasses are dark enough to hide my eye roll.

"How was last night?" I turn to Hunter.

"Fun." He winks at Wolf, who looks suddenly very uncomfortable. His relaxed demeanour when he walked in, all but vanished.

"Yeah it was a great night," blondie's syrupy voice drips, and her hands slide under the table onto Wolf's thigh. His jaw tightens.

The waitress brings a round of coffees and I sip on mine.

I can't help but examine this specimen hanging off Wolf. Maybe if I had endless legs and bottle blonde hair, he'd let me touch him the way her hands roam around him.

I try and shake the thought away, but jealousy has taken hold of me. I can't shake it, like an insipid river, it's filtered inside me and the water drips into the hollow cavity of my chest, creating sharp angry stalactites that slice me each time I breathe.

I guess I'd never been good enough for him. Not my taste in my music or the way I dance; like I actually feel the music, rather than to a hungry audience putting myself on display. And when he tells jokes I laugh—real and loud—till my belly hurts and not just turn on fake laughter to stroke his ego. The stalactites slice my insides, I never could compete with girls who starve themselves so they could look like they just stepped out of a fashion magazine. Maybe I'd always wished he would see me, the real me, and that somehow, I could touch him in all the places hands can never reach. I guess I was wrong

"I'm Tracey." She looks at me as she leans into Wolf. He hasn't touched her since he came in.

"Red." I say over the lip of my coffee cup.

"That's such a unique name, I wish my mum gave me such a fantastic name. I've thought of changing mine. Tracey is just so bland."

I nod, unsure what she wants me to say.

"What do you do Red?" Her hand moves under the table and Wolf jerks up. I arch an eyebrow at her, and she wiggles her eyebrows. My hands tighten around my cup.

"I work in an art gallery."

"Oh, you're an arty-farty type? That explains a lot."

"Oh?" I put my cup down and tilt my head a little.

"Explains what exactly?" Hunter bites out beside me and warmth floods my insides. He's always so protective of me.

Tracey shifts in her seat and her eyes dart from my face to Hunter, "Oh, no, it's just how she looks… and… erm…"

Hunter leans forward steepling his fingers in front of his face and glaring at her, while I sit in silence waiting for her to keep digging her own grave.

"You must be super smart." She tries to correct, and I wonder what about my wild hair, unmatched clothes and boots gave her that idea.

"And you must not be." The words slip out before I could bite them down. A ghost of a smile touches Wolf's lips and vanishes while Hunter bursts into laughter beside me.

"Excuse me? Did you just call me stupid?" Tracey looks indignant as she leans forwards.

"Me? I'd never say anything like that." I deadpan.

Her face colours a shiny pink and she looks at Wolf, "Are you just going to let her talk to me this way?"

"Which way is that?" His face is taut, but I know that expression, he's holding back laughter.

"She just insulted me."

"You were the one that started talking to her."

"You're defending her?"

"No," he shrugs, "just pointing out the sequence of events."

She huffs and stands up, "Come on, we're leaving."

He looks at her and remains seated, then pulls out a wedge of notes from his pocket and fishes out a £20. He holds it out to her, her pink face turns a dark red.

"What's this?" She hisses.

"I'm hungry and that should cover your Uber."

Her eyes narrow and she gives him a scathing look, I bite down hard on my lip keeping my face schooled. "You're un-fucking-believable."

"That's what you've been saying all night," he says it loud enough to earn a few chuckles from the table near us.

She snatches the note from his hand and stomps off towards the front door.

As soon as she is gone, Wolf and Hunter fall into a fit of laughter. I can't help the grin that erupts across my face, even as I shake my head. I know I should be mortified for all women kind, but right now, I'm just glad she's gone.

Wolf turns his attention to me, "Thanks Red, she just wasn't getting the message."

I look away, "Yeah no problem. Maybe you should have ditched her last night, like all your other girls."

"I would have, but your brother here wasn't done till this morning."

My hands shot to my ears, "La la la la." He laughs and gestures to me that he's done talking. I let my hands fall away. "You guys are all class."

They nod and smirk in unison.

"At least now I know how to ditch them if they get too clingy."

"How?" Hunter asks.

"Let them talk to your sister."

They burst into laughter again and my stomach churns. The idea of meeting a string of Wolf's conquests makes me physically ill. I clear my throat and am about to excuse myself when our food arrives. The waitress can't keep her eyes off Wolf as she puts our plates down and doesn't leave till he notices her flirty grin and winks.

My appetite vanishes. I pick at my plate as Hunter and Wolf talk shop.

Hunter pays the bill and I turn to him, "Thanks for breakfast."

"I needed it," he yawns, and I grimace.

"You should get some rest."

He nods and stands, "What are your plans for the rest of the day?"

I shrug a single shoulder, "Don't know. Walk around, get lost a little bit."

"Want some company?" Wolf's voice has me whiplashing to meet his gaze.

"You must be tired." I try the easy way out.

"I'm fine."

I let out a long breath, "So am I."

"Great, then it's settled."

"How do you—" I clench my fists and bite the inside of my cheek, "I don't need a babysitter."

"How about a friend then?"

The word stabs me in the gut and twists. A small cry claws its way up my throat, and I swallow it down. The fight leaves my body.

"Fine." I'm resigned.

Hunter eyes us then pulls me in for a hug. "Enjoy your afternoon Red, see you later."

I watch him leave, then make my way out the door. Wolf shadows me outside and waits till I pick a direction.

I walk, letting my legs do their thing without thinking too much about it. London on a Sunday morning is much like any other day but times a hundred. The streets are packed with families, tourists and locals all making their way somewhere. While the hundred-year-old buildings stand like silent witnesses, watching the world go by them.

We stumble into Soho. The crowded alleys full of shoppers and curious tourists wanting a peek at the famous underbelly of this area. I love it for the atmosphere. A concoction of light, colour and history that's soaked into the stones and clings to the air. I come here sometimes just to breathe inspiration into my veins, and right now, I need to clear my head and pretend that all the tingling in my skin is not the remnants of burning jealousy lingering from breakfast.

We walk idly, silently. Wolf keeps in step as I wander

around the streets, soaking up images, shapes, and textures to record later on paper. We walk till we stumble into Soho square, the little, green grass peppered with people soaking up the last of the sun before winter sets in.

I find an unoccupied square of grass where sunlight beams through the gaps between the building and few trees scattered around the place. They are mostly barren, shedding leaves in the light breeze, getting ready for their naked winter slumber. Wolf falls beside me, all tangled limbs and discomfort. I bite down my smile as he stretches his long legs in front of him and leans back on a hand. His shirt pulls open at the chest, and I see a few black lines peak out. He has a tattoo. My curiosity piques but I tear my gaze away, sweeping over the missing buttons. I ignore the harsh pang in my stomach then pull out my sketchpad and observe.

He scans the park, "This place looks very different at night time." His voice cuts through the hum of the park.

I nod as I look at my surroundings taking it all in. "Different how?"

"It's full of undesirables."

"Like you?"

"Ouch," he smirks at me, and I can't help but smile. "It's guys like me that keep undesirables like them from hurting people like you."

"I can take care of myself." I straighten my shoulders and stare at him.

"Is that why you ended up living with us?"

"Fuck you, Wolf."

"I would, but I'm too tired from last night." He winks at me.

Heated anger and jealousy smashes inside me, and goosebumps erupt all over my skin. "I don't want to know," I bite out and his smirk evaporates.

"Sure?" His voice is suddenly dark and husky.

"Never been surer of anything in my life. You're probably a petri dish of STIs."

"I get checked regularly," he says it like it's the most natural thing in the world and falls back onto an elbow, letting the sun kiss his beautiful face.

"Delightful."

"They always come back negative."

"I'm sure that's great for the female population of London."

The cocky grin is back on his face, and I hate it for all the wrong reasons.

"You're the worst."

"Actually, I've never had a complaint," he winks at me and my stomach knits and roils with all the wrong emotions.

"Like I said, I don't want to know." My hands tighten around my sketch pad, and I look away scanning the park, looking anywhere other than at Wolf—because I'm a big fat liar.

"What are you looking at?"

"I'm not looking at any one thing really."

"So, what are you doing?"

"Looking to capture something."

He looks around us then returns his attention back to me, "What do you mean?"

"I mean I want to capture a moment in time, but not the thing, the emotion of the thing."

His brow furrows like he's trying to understand me.

"Look at that tree." I point to a tree. His gaze swings in the direction I point, and he studies it for a few seconds.

"It's a tree."

"No, it's a story."

"I don't understand," he says with a sigh.

"Look at her."

"Her?"

"The way she's been stripped naked and put out on

display, the way she's rooted to place, unable to run or hide, the way she's been exposed just after being draped in the most glamorous coat of leaves. She's in pain, she's alone, but she'll stay and suffer and grow and will emerge stronger and bigger, and her next dress will be even thicker, more lush, and more exquisite."

He scrubs a hand over his face and looks at the tree, his face twisted as he tries to see the story. "I still see a tree."

I shrug, "Maybe once I draw her, you'll see what I see."

"You'll show me when you're done?" His eyebrow arches, "You never used to show me your work."

"I never wanted you to see the subject matter," I let slip and my heart stops beating for a short eternity.

I stare at my pad and grip my pencil too tightly.

"How do you know where to start?" he asks, pretending neither of us heard what I said, and my heart resumes its pathetic rhythm.

"Just a naked sketch at first and then the real art is in the shading."

"You've always—" his words fizzle out as his phone rings.

He gives me an apologetic look as he studies the number. "Hello?"

A female voice answers on the other end and my insides burn. Wolf bolts up and walks away, his face contorting in anger as he whispers harshly into the phone. He hangs up and slides it into his pocket before returning and squatting in front of me.

"Who keeps calling you?"

"It's no one."

"Doesn't feel like no one, Shaw. Whenever they call, you get off all flustered and angry."

"Trust me, nothing about those phone calls gets me off," he tries to break the tension, but his face is still set in a frown.

"So, who is it?"

He gives me a long, thoughtful look as if he's considering his answer.

"Please don't lie to me."

"I wasn't going to." He holds his hands up. "It's just work stuff. I don't want to talk about it."

I draw in an irritated breath and let it out slowly, diffusing my irritation. "Fine."

"Look, I have to go take care of something."

"Something or someone?" I can't help the bitterness that creeps into my voice.

"Sorry Red, will you be alright to get home on your own?"

"I swear if you pull out a £20 for an Uber, I'm going to stab you with my 5H."

He does something between a laugh and a snort, opens his mouth to say something then smirks instead, "See you later Red."

I watch him go, my body humming with mixed emotion as he leaves the park. I feel like the naked sketch of the tree is looking back at me from my notepad, and I realise at last, that when Wolf looks at me, he will never see anything other than a girl lost in a long line of other women who were able to give him what he wanted.

I clutch the notepad to my heart, feeling the ivy rip through the seeds of hope I keep trying to plant. I reach for my bag, pull out the card, and twist it around in my hand before I draw in a long breath and dial Ethan's number.

Wolf

I'm pacing again, my body chemistry is all over the place—a concoction of mixed emotions which consists mostly of irritation, irrational anger, and pathetic jealousy.

I was pissed when I got home early just to find it empty. It's nearing midnight and Red still isn't home. I rip a hand through my hair again and fall to the couch. I snap the remote, turn on the TV then flip channels not really paying any attention to what's on. I turn it off and bolt out of the couch circling it like a caged animal.

My whole body shakes and burns. I should have gone out for a run, let this flood of emotion seep out of me. Instead, I'm here watching the door, waiting for her to step inside.

I feel eighteen again and Red is out on one of her stupid dates, and I can't help but want to murder everyone. My loose shirt starts to cling to my back in places, and I'm about to punch the wall when a key jangles in the lock. I throw myself on the couch, grab the remote and turn the TV on, then swipe my phone and lock my eyes on the screen. Their voices drift inside from the other side of the door before it swings open.

She's giggling and the sound is accompanied by a low husky laughter that has my blood heat in my veins. I look up to see a man pinning her against the door. His mouth is so close to hers, too close to hers. I have to fight every urge in my body not to rip him away and hurl him down the stairs. Instead, I clear my throat and two sets of startled eyes fall on me.

"Wolf? You're home?" All the happiness drains away from Red's face, and she puts a hand on the man's chest and pushes him away gently. He takes a small step back and the constriction in my chest loosens.

"I took the night off."

"Oh." She looks lost and I stand to my full height, making sure fuck face at the door knows exactly who he's dealing with.

"Ethan, this is my *friend* Wolf. He's my brother's housemate. And mine, I guess, till I move out."

Friend. The word feels like a fist in my guts that grips my insides and pulls viciously.

"Nice to meet you," Fuck face mumbles and offers me a hand. I make sure to squeeze a little extra hard before retracting my hand. He pulls away and rubs his palm with his other. Pathetic satisfaction slithers through me.

"So, we thought we might have a nightcap." Red looks at me and her face tells me she wants me to make myself scarce.

"Oh, well, sorry. I'm in the middle of watching something," I say, and all our gazes swing to the TV. It's news in some foreign language.

She glares at me with an annoyed questioning look.

"One of the boys is over there with a client," I lie smoothly not even knowing where *'there'* is.

Red's eyes grow wide and she tilts her head meaningfully.

I pretend not to notice as I turn back to her date, "Nice meeting you Emmett."

"It's Ethan," he corrects, but I'm already halfway to the couch settling in to watch subtitled news.

I sink into the couch, my gaze secured on the TV as they stand silently and awkwardly at the door. When they realise I won't leave, I hear him say he had a good time, she agrees and promises him a raincheck for the nightcap. He says he can't wait, and I hear the desire in his voice. I want to strangle him till the only noise he makes is a pained gurgling sound. My jaw is so tight, it aches, and my head feels like it might explode when she finally gets rid of him and the door closes.

A second later Red's gorgeous body is blocking my view, and I can't help but rake my eyes over her before I meet her dangerous glare. That seems to make the situation worse, but I can't help myself. Her short, short skirt drives high enough up her thighs to show off her shapely legs, and her tight as fuck singlet pushes her up her perfect tits, clinging to all the stunning curves of her body that make mine hard.

"Watching the news?"

"Well, I was till you blocked the TV," I huff at her.

"Fuck you Wolf."

"Looks like that's what you were about to do with Evan over there."

"It's Ethan," she corrects on an exasperated sigh, "and what's it to you what I do?"

"I don't like him," I say plainly, biting back the irritation that creeps up my spine.

"You're not the one that's meant to like him, I am. And I do, and seeing as me and you are just *friends*, be a fucking friend and leave the lounge next time."

I brush my hands through my hair and swallow down my agitation, "It's my fucking house."

"Well, you'll have it back soon enough."

"What the fuck does that mean?"

She glares at me for another second then turns away and goes to the kitchen. I scramble from the couch and follow, watching her as she flicks her violet hair to the side revealing the length of her neck. I want to sink my teeth into it. I feel her eyes on me and I realize I've held my gaze too long. *Fuck.*

"You're moving out?" I keep all the emotion out of my voice.

"Maybe." She throws it out like it's nothing and my fists clench into tight balls.

"What does that mean?"

She shrugs with one shoulder, and I can't help but trace the lines of her neck with my gaze. "It means maybe I'll move in with Ethan."

"That little prick? You've known him for all of ten minutes." Anger flares inside of me and I'm picturing my hands closing around that man's throat.

"He's not a prick, he's a lawyer. Successful, intelligent, kind."

It's like she's trying to throw it in my face, all the things she thinks I'm not.

"We've been dating a while."

"Three dates, is not a while."

Her eyes grow in surprise, "Keeping tabs on me?"

Fuck. I glare at her deciding silence is better than a confession.

"You're pathetic."

"I'm pathetic?" I take a step closer to her, "That man is just another version of your last string of boyfriends, you'll be back and crying to Hunter in a month."

Her hand moves in a swirl and she slaps me hard across the cheek. It's barely a sting. I scoff, "That's all you got?"

She swings a second time—harder—but I stand there and smirk. When she tries for a third, I grab her wrist and hold it easily between us. She yanks it out of my grasp, and I let her. Red glares at me, her eyes drenched in disdain.

"Screw you Wolf," she says as she steps around me.

Without thinking, I swivel and grab her nape, jarring her and turning her towards me. I pull her close—so close that our breaths mingle—and her lips feather my own and there is nothing between us but a few angry particles of air. My heart rips through my ears and screams, as heat floods me all over. I could take her, I could sink myself into her, bruise her lips with mine and claim her. Her eyes burn into mine, and I want to believe I see the same desire inside them. Her hands slide up to my chest slowly, gliding along all my tight muscles, her touch burns. Her hands rest on my chest for a beat and she heaves.

I release her and she smirks before turning and leaving the kitchen.

She fucking smirks, and I have to grip the cabinet to stop myself from running after her and wiping it off her face with my cock.

I draw in a frayed breath as my heart thrashes in my chest, and her door slams shut.

TEN YEARS AGO

Wolf 18, Red 15

Wolf

Hunter shoots a couple of zombies on the screen and I keep looking at the clock. It's like time has decided to stand still. I declare it my enemy as another thirty seconds go by. Agonisingly slow.

My skin prickles with irritation and I pace around the small lounge. I've been looking forward to spending some time with Hunter on a rare evening off. But when he causally informs me that Red is out on a date, the news tip my nerves.

"You got anything to drink?"

Hunter pauses the game and looks at me with a quirked eyebrow, "What's up with you tonight, you're all twitchy."

"My mum is being all up my grill about uni."

"Since when does she give a shit?"

I give him a half shrug, "Plus, fucking Angela won't get off my case."

Hunter bites down the edge of a smile, a futile attempt to

keep his creeping grin at bay. "Fuck, she's got it bad. Just put her out of her misery."

"I would, except I'm worried it's not the only thing she's got."

Hunter falls back laughing, "Oh come on *Wolfy*," he mocks me, "Just give it to her, stick her with your big, fat–"

"Fuck off," I snap at him.

Hunter doubles over, his laughter ripples through the house and I resist the urge to punch him. I can't stand Angela. I wish she'd just get the hint and leave me alone, but she hasn't and she won't.

"So, do you have anything to drink or what?"

His breath comes in quick gasps, "You know where everything is." Hunter's laughter settles down, and he returns his attention back to his game. I don't mind, it gives me something to do and get out from under Hunter's watch. I know he notices more than he says, I keep telling him he should be a detective. But he has a thing for justice, and that doesn't always happen when you do the right thing and follow the rules.

I open the cupboard where Hunter used to hide bottles from his grandmother in case she confuses them for something else. Nothing there. The fridge is empty too.

I slam it shut and swear at the white door, wondering who the fuck Red is out with, and where she might be, and why Hunter would even allow it. My stomach knots at the thought of another guy's lips on her, any guy's anything on her.

I bristle and go back to the lounge where blood splatters across the TV screen as Hunter takes out another troupe of zombies.

"You're out of everything."

Hunter pauses the game again and sighs. "So, go get some."

"Why don't you go?"

"Cause I'm busy." He signals toward the paused game.

"With a game I brought over."

He shoots me a look and I know it was a low blow. I don't care. I pull out my car keys and suddenly he's far more interested.

"You can stop by at Lacey's." I wink at him and notice how his body shifts at the mention of her name. He's definitely been enjoying quality time with her on her knees, and I know she's asked him to wait till they get to know each other before they go all the way. He's hanging on by a very loose thread, and I just threw him a lifeline.

He grips the back of his neck and sighs, "I need to wait for Red."

"I'll wait." I pretend like I don't give a shit.

"I don't know how long she'll be."

"Where the fuck did she go? Oxfordshire?"

"Don't be an idiot, she's just gone to the movies down the road."

"And you didn't give her a curfew?"

"First of all, she's fifteen, and anyway, you know Red, she'll be home before ten."

I peek at my clock, half an hour to go. I shrug, "She'll be here soon. You come back with beer, a smile, and all the details."

A salacious grin crosses his face. "You sure?"

"How many of these opportunities do you think you'll get out of me?"

He grabs the dangling keys from my hand and runs upstairs. He's down two minutes later with a washed face, a fresh shirt and enough cologne to drown six virgins.

"If I swing by Lacey's, I don't know how long I'll be."

I smirk, "Three extra minutes?"

"Fuck you!"

"No, go fuck Lacey, and bring me back some fucking beer."

He scoffs then bolts out the door like he's been bitten by lightning.

With Hunter gone, the house feels abandoned. When his grandmother was moved to the hospice two months ago the house lost some of its light.

Red used to go visit almost every day, till her grandmother forgot her face and her name, and it cut her too deeply. I hated to see her cry. Her beautiful green eyes bloodshot and swollen, and her small body tense with anxiety.

She's accepted that she's gone, but I still catch her looking out the window any time a car lingers for too long outside.

The sound of a rumbling engine pulls me from my reverie, and I look out the window to see a beat-up Nissan. There is only one fucker I know that drives that car. Oliver Brown. That slick fucker. I can't believe Hunter let Red go out with *him*.

The car remains idle and I see two figures sitting in the front seats. The movement is bleary and it's too dark to make anything out. My body twitches and knots, and my fists clench and tighten by my side.

They don't move, the sound of the engine drilling a hole into my brain. Images play in my mind, and I suddenly regret sending Hunter away with my car. I should be rinsing them away with alcohol and pretending all these feelings I have don't exist.

I tear my eyes away and I'm about to retreat from the window when I think I hear a faint scream. The truth is, it didn't matter whether I did or not, I wasn't going to wait for a second one—and maybe I was just looking for an excuse to get out there.

I run outside and rush to the car where I rip the door open and grip Oliver by the shoulder. He's on the ground before he has time to blink and my fist connects with his face. His nose exploded in a spewing fountain of blood. He shrieks like a stuck pig.

It all happens so fast, and yet I'm moving in slow motion; sounds have fallen away, and my fists feel slow and heavy instead of lightning fast.

"Wolf!" Red leaps at me, "Wolf!' My name is like an insect flying around me, I'm just aware of its being there, but I flick it away.

"Shaw!" My heart squeezes and her shrill cries stills my fists, "What the hell are you doing?"

I look at her horrified face and follow her gaze, Olive's pulverised face looks back at me, he's whimpering as blood leaks from everywhere, his complexion ashen.

"I heard you cry for help."

"I didn't, I…" she looks at me—a strange, wonderous look —then shakes her head, "help me."

We reach for Oliver. He snatches his hand out of mine and tumbles upwards, swaying slightly off balance.

"What the fuck is wrong with you, Wolf?" Oliver spits a mouth full of blood and staggers to his car, wiping a hand across his mouth, it comes back stained a dark red.

Red follows him tentatively, "I'm so sorry Oli—"

He shots Red a scathing look, "Yeah, whatever."

"Oli—"

"Just stay away from me," his eyes shoot to me before they flick back to Red, whose hands are folded like a protective barrier across herself. "Not like you were gonna let me do anything anyway."

My fists tighten and I suck in an agitated breath.

He climbs into the car and throws her a final look, "Virgin." He grates it out like it's a swear word, and Red's face twitches.

He drives off with screeching tyres, and I make a mental note to pay him another visit later.

When I turn around, Red is already halfway to the house.

"Red," I call after her, but she doubles her speed and

ignores me. I catch up easily as we reach the front door, and I block her way, "Red?"

"What the hell Wolf? You totally ruined my date."

"I thought you were in trouble," I say again as her gaze drops to my hand where blood drips from my fingers and splashes silently on the floor.

"You're hurt." It's a mixture of anger and compassion.

"It's probably all his."

"Just… come on." She takes my hand in hers, the touch is so gentle it sparks electricity under my skin. Sensations I have no right to feel.

She leads me silently to the kitchen and holds my hand under the tap. Blood drips into the basin and disappears along with her touch. I turn the water off and swivel around to find her sitting at the table with a bag of frozen peas.

She gestures for me to sit down, and I do. She takes my hand in hers; it's cold from the peas but oh so soft as she examines my hand. It's swollen and sore, but the skin is intact.

She takes the peas and places them over my knuckles.

Our eyes collide. The brown flecks that swim inside her mesmerising green swirl around like my emotions.

"Why did you do that?" Her voice is as soft as her touch and sends a shiver down my spine.

"Like I said—"

"—tell me the truth," she doesn't shout or scream, but her demand is silent and loud enough to rattle my insides.

I tear a hand through my hair and exhale a long, anguished breath, "Because," I shift on my chair, "the thought of someone else touching you makes me go a little insane."

She sucks in a sharp gasp and her eyes narrow, "It does?"

"You have no idea what it does to me." I let the peas drop from my hand and reach for hers. My frozen fingers seek her warmth.

"You can't say things like that if you don't mean them," she says in a shaky voice, her gaze drops to the ground.

My fingers travel up along her arm, rounding her delicate shoulder and my knuckles lift her chin. She's too fucking beautiful and innocent and young, but I can't help it. "But I do."

"Shaw?"

My heart squeezes as she uses my name, it drips with raw emotion and twists inside me. No one else uses my name. I don't know if anyone ever remembers it.

"I want you so badly it's eating at me, but—"

"—please don't let there be a but, not yet."

My mouth falls open and her hand delicately, tentatively pushes my mussy locks out of my face, it lands on my neck and her cheeks flush with pink, and I'm done.

I rip away from the chair, which smashes into the ground with a loud bang as my lips fuse around hers. She's so fucking sweet and her lips are so fucking soft, and everything I'm doing is so fucking wrong, but I can't help myself.

My tongue sweeps by her lips and clashes with hers. Everything about her is so delicate and fragile, and I'm reminded that she's still fifteen.

I pull away from her, breathless and trail kisses down the length of her neck. I want her so badly it hurts.

"Shaw," the name falls from her lips on a shaky breath, "I've wanted this for so long,"

"Me too." I find her lips, take her sweet words and make them mine.

I want to kiss her forever, to take her upstairs and make her mine in all the ways that I know I can. But she's still too young, and I'm eighteen and I can't. I wrench myself from her and look at her face. Flushed pink cheeks and eyes dilated by desire.

"We need to stop."

She nods and her face drops. I lift her chin and graze my

lips with hers, "I don't want to Red, but we *have* to because if we don't, I'll take you upstairs and…"

"I want you too," she whispers and my breath falters as the words tumble from her mouth, and every nerve in my body comes alive. "I want you to be my first."

I swallow the lump in my throat, "You're fifteen."

"My birthday is next month." The heat of her breath whispers across my skin, and I feel it *everywhere.*

"Then we'll wait until your birthday and then…" It's a choked response as my dick jerks against my pants, straining with the images that flood my mind.

The sound of an engine ripples through the house, it idles outside for a few seconds before turning off. A car door slams outside. Our eyes lock for a split second, then Red slips from my touch and runs upstairs just as Hunter walks inside.

"You got hungry?" he eyes the pea packet on the table, and his gaze flickers over me.

I shrug and go over to the counter where he's unloaded a six pack.

"Lacey didn't want you?"

"Her parents were home."

"That's never stopped you before." I chuckle as I grab a beer and hide my massive erection behind the table. I gulp on the beer and try to fill my mind with anything other than how Red felt against me.

"She was good for a quick blowie," he chuckles and swipes his palms over his jeans, "Want to tell me what's going on with you?"

"What do you mean?"

"I mean you're home alone with my sister and have a raging fucking hard on."

I grimace and try to cover up.

"Don't bother, if you want to cover that shit up wear looser jeans."

I jut out my chin and take another swig off my beer. He

grabs his own, twists the cap off, chucks it into the sink then takes a long sip.

"Look Wolf, you know you're like a brother to me, and you know I appreciate everything you've ever done for us," he gives me a long-pointed look, and I wait for the 'but'.

"I didn't think the day would ever come when I had to tell you that Red is off limits."

"Hunter–"

"Don't bullshit me. I see the way the two of you look at each other, how every time she walks into a room you stop breathing, and any time in the last year that the two of you are together, you're suddenly awkward and weird. Whatever you think you feel for her, don't. She's off the menu —permanently."

"We're not awkward." My hand tightens around the cold bottle in my hand.

"If you can't see how much she wants you, you're as stupid as you are blind. But it doesn't matter, because you will never touch a hair on my sister's body. You will never kiss her or touch her or think about her in any way, shape, or form."

"Or else?"

"Or else I will end you." He says it with such finality that it's hard not to laugh at his face.

I know I could take him in a fight—I could break anyone —but Hunter has never threatened me before and has never really asked me for anything at all. I know deep down it's not about violence for either of us. It will be the end of our friendship, and it will cut me in ways that would be hard to recover from. Having Hunter as my family has been the only thing that's gotten me through the last few years. Every downward spiral, every painful moment, every time my parents never showed. Hunter was there.

"What about what she wants?"

"She's fifteen, what the fuck does she know about what

she wants? She only thinks she likes you cause you hang around here all the time and give her some attention."

"And yet she went out with Oliver fucking Brown tonight."

"And she'll keep going out with other guys until you're nothing but the man standing next to her brother on her wedding day."

He swings the beer back and sips again. Our eyes lock and his burn into mine till I nod once and he does the same —as if it's settled, as if everything I feel for her, think about her, need from her can get erased with a few sentences and a pathetic threat.

"Have you told her yet? About our plans?" I redirect the conversation and he knows he's made himself clear.

He shakes his head, "I figured I'll tell her after her birthday."

Her birthday, fuck.

"She needs to know."

"I said I'll tell her."

"My mum is still happy to let her stay at the house."

"She'll make up her own mind."

I nod, knowing neither of us knows what Red will do once she finds out. I sip my beer hoping the cold will freeze her taste on my lips forever.

PRESENT DAY

Wolf

The night already feels too long, and it's only just begun. I sit on the chair like a rookie wondering why I agreed to fill in on this gig when I should be at home, pretending I'm not watching Red. I bat the thought away. knowing it was a bad idea to keep scratching that same raw wound that won't let go, and look at the growing line of desperados wanting to get in.

On the upside, I'd only have to be at the door for another couple hours. Once Hunter and Rob get here with the client, Rob can take over and I can sit inside and watch the rich prick drinking and treating everyone else like trash.

If I'm being honest, I didn't want to take this guy on. We have a long list of good clients that have been loyal and satisfied, and have made us more than comfortable with our retainers.

This one just smelled off, like he was broken on the inside but tried to patch it up with too much silicone and makeup so no one would notice. But I deal with evil on a daily basis, I could smell it on him, so I don't know why Hunter insisted we take this fucker on.

I only agreed because I couldn't spend another minute arguing with him, when all I wanted to do was think about Red and how being close to her makes me unnerved, excited, aggravated. How feeling her soft skin under my touch makes me want to run my lips over every inch of her body, to feel that smooth skin glide beneath my lips and tongue.

Knowing she's dating some other guy has me frazzled. I scan the crowd for a potential code twenty-two that could help ease some of my tension later on.

I grind my teeth again as Dylan lets a few girls inside. They shriek and squeal like teenagers, but if you scrap their makeup off, they'll probably age ten years in front of your eyes.

They're all the same; bottle blondes with tight dresses that should be at least one size bigger, stupid uncomfortable shoes that make their legs look longer in their too short skirts, and inflated, plastic lips covered with fuck me red lipstick that stains everything.

The place starts filling up and music blares from inside. My gut churns with unease. Like I know a storm is coming but the sky is perfectly clear. I wipe my palms over my thighs and tap Dylan, we've filled out the quota of randoms and hopefuls, the only ones that will be allowed in from now on will be on the list.

I hate that fucking list—like we've put a price tag on having fun and being human.

They give me their names, and Dylan lets them in if I nod.

It's a perfect system, just not for anyone who gets left standing out in the cold.

The girls in the line start hustling us—as they always do. They huff and puff and threaten to give me the best blow job in town if I let the red rope down and let them in. But I'm no fucking piggy, I'm the fucking Wolf and I'm already inside.

They croon and bend over thinking they are the sexiest ass I've ever seen. Five years ago, they might have been; these days, I've seen so much ass I'm just not that easily impressed.

I wink at one anyway, just for shits and giggles. Her gaggle of friends all shriek and they fall into a huddle. *That was too easy.* I could take my pick of any of them, or if I really wanted to, fuck them all one at a time tonight. I shoot one of the other girls a little smile, she pushes her tits up and licks her lips. All too easy.

A skinny man pushes his way to the front of the line. He's draped in ridiculous gold chains and his jeans hang dangerously low—his shoes are too white, like they just came out of a box, and I'm pretty sure he's got a diamond stuck on a tooth. *Idiot.*

He comes forward with a crew of eight or so friends who all surround him. They stand with their chests puffed out all geared up in suits that look expensive but smell cheap. The entourage. They look as ridiculous as he does.

"Corbin Smith Junior." He looks at me like I'm snot on his shoes and crosses his arms.

I arch an eyebrow and remain seated.

"I'm on the list."

I glare at the guy letting my eyes track him from top to bottom then shake my head. He squares his shoulders like he's a big man. I grab the list and check the names.

"You're not on the list." I put the clipboard aside and remain seated.

"Check again."

"No." I say calm and casual and watch his nostrils flare.

His crew of friends step a little closer and I inhale, already exhausted from this show.

"I said check again. The name's Corbin Smith Junior." His friends cheer him and hoot like he's some kind of tough guy, and I already know whoever he thinks he is, he will never amount to anything.

"Even if you were on the list, which you are not, you can't come in dressed like that."

"What's wrong with the way I dress," he seems visibly offended.

"You can't wear a hat inside, and your pants have to cover your entire buttock area. We can't let in any sexual predators that might assault the guests."

"Seriously man?" His mouth falls open and he recovers. "Do you know who I am? I don't need to assault anyone. These girls..." he waves at the long line, "they assault me, and I let 'em—if you know what I'm sayin'?" He gets a few high fives and leery looks and nods from his friends.

"If you say so."

"I do. Now put down the rope old man, and let me in." The humour is gone from his face.

"You're not on the list." I make a mental note to fuck around with Henri a little on his next shift, to make him pay for this.

"Check again, you lazy piece of shit. I'm a celebrity around here, I shouldn't even have to ask."

I squeeze my eyes shut for a moment then stand to my full height, the group takes a collective step back as I take a step forward, while a few of the spectating ladies throw their own remarks about my size and my shoes. I ignore them.

"Sir, I'm not aware of your celebrity status, nor do I care. Your name is not on the list, so I suggest you clear a path for the guests that are, or we will be forced to remove you."

He looks me up and down with cold, angry eyes, humiliation soaking through his big boy underwear.

He takes a small step towards me and signals with his hand that I come closer and bend towards him. I don't move, so he closes the gap as much as I let him, and he pushes up on his tiptoes, "Come on man, how much is it going to take?" He flashes me a bunch of fifties, I eye them for a second then stare ahead.

"Not interested."

His face drops and his face furrows, "Come on man, you're embarrassing me in front of my girl."

I wish I gave a fuck about his problems, but I don't. Not when I have enough of my own.

"Can't help you, you're not on the list." I step back from him and turn away; this conversation was boring when it started.

"Fine, fuck you. This place is lame anyway, so old news, we'll take our business and our money elsewhere."

Like I give a shit. I plaster on my best fakest grin and wave at him, "Have a good night sir."

He stares daggers at me before he turns to leave.

I remain standing till they put enough distance between them and the club. I'm about to sit down when a wave of purple hair catches my attention.

No.

She's standing with that guy from the gallery, Caleb, and I can't tear my fucking eyes off her. She can't fit in even when she tries, which is why she's so fucking unique—because she never really tries. Her long, purple hair cascades over her shoulders, and she's wearing a very tight, very short black skirt and a black shiny singlet that rises just above her midriff every time she moves her hand even a centimetre. Those straps are so thin, I know I could rip them with my teeth.

I shake my head batting the thought away. She finished the look with her black Doc Martens boots. They are worn and loved, but they're a part of her.

Fuck.

They step forward, and when Dylan reaches for the clip board, I snatch it from his hands. He knows better than to argue with his boss, so he sits down and shuts the fuck up.

I will wipe the smirk on his face later when he's trying to

pick up, and I'll throw out a loud comment about his STI test results.

"Hi," she smiles at me and my entire body catches fire. She's fucking gorgeous with the simple, natural make up she has on and fuck me red lips that I want wrapped around my cock.

"What are you doing here?" I grind my teeth trying to stay in my own skin.

"Celebrating."

"Celebrating what?"

"That she's amazing," her friend chirps in, and I pay him no attention.

"Celebrating what?'

"Today marks four months since I started working, and I just sold my second biggest commission." The two of them squeal like it means something.

"Go celebrate somewhere else."

She cocks her head at me and grins, "We're on the list."

Her friend wraps his hand around her arm and squeezes. Red remains cool as fuck as she stared into my face.

"Doubt it." I shrug not even checking.

Red's face twists with annoyance and she juts out her hip in that way she does. Her singlet pulls up revealing nuances of her hip bones that curve beautifully from her smooth belly.

The moisture from my mouth vanishes and I try to swallow to no avail.

"Check your precious list. Hunter put my name down."

I grab the list and flap through the pages. I scan the names and clench my fists around the fucking board when I find hers and two others. The board snaps under the force of my hand.

I can't believe Hunter. I'm going to kill him and bury him in a grave so deep they will never find his body.

She must see something in my eyes because her face relaxes and breaks into an exquisite smile. "See?"

I don't even argue, there's no point

"Where's the third?" I don't even try to hide the hostility in my voice.

Her mouth twists a little, "Ethan had to cancel."

A combination of hot sticky joy and irritation spreads through my body, and I nod to Dylan who's been watching with his mouth shut the entire time. He drops the rope letting them in.

"Thanks," Red says as she sashays inside.

Dylan's gaze remains dangerously on Red's ass as she walks away. I step into his field of vision and he straightens up, "Fuck me, did you see the a—"

"—she's off limits."

"Oh, I didn't know you guys—'

"—we're not, that's Hunter's little sister."

His face visibly falls, and I know the kind of blow he's just experienced, I've felt it too, "Got it boss."

I run a hand through my hair, my entire body feels restless, there's no fucking way I can keep sitting on this fucking stool out here while she's inside. Every muscle in my body is suddenly tense.

"You got it here for a sec? I'm going to see how far away Hunter is."

"Sure."

I throw the clipboard at him; he eyes the cracked wood but says nothing.

I'm breaking protocol here. This is not the way we do things. I'm being stupid and emotional when I should be practical, but Red is inside and I'm not—and that just doesn't work for me.

Hunter picks up on the second ring, "Everything alright?"

"What's your ETA?"

"Twenty minutes at most, I'll text you like I always do. You good?"

"Yeah, yeah, just forgot how much I hate the stool."

He chuckles into the phone, "I won't be long.'

"Right."

I hang up and return to my place by the door where Dylan does his best to look at anyone but me.

Time stretches like an elastic and winds me up so tight, that by the time twenty minutes have passed, I'm about ready to break everything in my path. Hunter said twenty minutes, and even though I'm pretending not to look at my watch every thirty seconds, I'm painfully aware that it's been over forty and that Red has been inside—unprotected.

I can't find an excuse to change position with any of the boys, and I don't want to be a dick and abuse my position as their boss. We're still a team, so I suffer.

When my phone finally rings, I'm a jittery fucking mess and I'm pissed off at myself, at my inability to get my shit together.

I text Frank who will greet Hunter and Rob at the back entrance. When Rob comes to take my place, I push right past him without a word. I'm sure Dylan will have his own version of what he thinks is happening. I don't give a fuck, I just want eyes on Red.

My eyes.

Only.

Wolf

I walk inside trying not to run. A big guy like me scares people when I head in their direction at a speed other than a snail's pace.

I meet Hunter, who's led the client to the VIP area and introduced me. Again. The fucker doesn't even remember my name, and I'm not a forgettable kind of guy. Our celebrity offers us a drink which we both decline. He proceeds to ignore us and talk to his guests.

Hunter runs me down on the schedule, then goes and checks in with all the guys before he takes his position on the other end of the VIP room.

I scan the dim club and find her almost immediately. She's leaning against the bar talking to Caleb, they're giggling as they look around and sip their drinks. I wonder how many she's had. A new song starts and Caleb shrieks while Red smiles. She's radiating energy and happiness; in fact, I don't think I'd ever seen her so happy, so relaxed. Maybe it's because she thinks I'm still outside. I ignore the thought even as it makes my stomach coil.

They weave their way through the throng of people toward the dance floor.

Music blares everywhere and the dance floor is full, bodies moving like a singular wave, clashing against one another in churning swells. Limbs and torsos twisting and flailing.

Caleb points to the middle of the floor but Red seems content to stay on the fringes, the edges, like she always does —and then she starts dancing. She's a mesmerising fucking distraction. She shuts her eyes and lets her body move, her hips roll with the music as she moves around, a total oddity in a sea of sameness, and I notice and then I notice everyone else notice. And they are all fascinated, like me, by this new, rare thing that doesn't fit in. She's still a cog, and without her, the machine would fail. But somehow, she doesn't fit anywhere.

I don't like the other eyes on her and grind my teeth, my jaw already aching. I swivel around when a hand tries to reach up to my shoulder, and I find my new client leering at Red.

"She's something, isn't she big guy?"

I fucking hate it when people call me that. "Sure thing, sir."

"Go get her for me."

"Excuse me, sir?"

"Just march yourself up to her and ask her to come join me here."

"Sorry sir, that's not part of my job description."

He glares at me like I'm stupid, and I don't know who pays for my next meal, "It is tonight."

"Sorry sir, I can't leave you unguarded."

He pouts and taps my hand like it's okay.

Of course, it's fucking okay. It takes all my energy not to punch him in his smirky little face.

"Right, well good job...?"

"Wolf, sir."

"You howl at the moon, Wolf?"

I don't reply and a minute later he's back with one of his guests, "Can he go and get her?"

"If you want him to, sir."

"I do." He gives me a sly grin, and I want to break every last one of his perfect white teeth.

The friend leaves and stops Red mid dance. It pisses me off that he interrupts her, but I have to stand like a moron and watch as he shouts in her ear and points to the VIP room. Her eyes land on me first and her smile falters for a second, before they swing over to the rest of the VIP area. Her face lights up, and she nods.

The guy puts his hand on her shoulder, and I make a mental note to break it later. It slides down her back and he guides her towards me and the roped VIP area. I'll break every one of his little fingers, making it slow and painful. The thought brings me an ounce of relief. As they approach, Red turns to the man again, he nods and disappears into the dance floor. I'm guessing she doesn't leave her friends behind and sent a search party.

"I've been invited into this area," she smirks at me.

"So I've been told," I say dryly, irritation saturating my body.

"So, let me in."

"I can't let you in without searching you first." I bite the inside of my cheek to stop from grinning.

"Fuck off, Wolf.'

"It's protocol."

"I don't give a shit."

"What seems to be the problem?" His smarmy voice pierces my nerves, and I inhale through clenched teeth.

"Your lady friend needs to be searched if she wants to join your party."

"Look at her, unless she has something stuffed in a hole somewhere, there's no way she's carrying anything."

"It's my job sir."

Red's eyes narrow as she pierces me with a death glare.

"It's ok," he pats my arm again and my fists clench, "I'll pat her down myself."

"Sir—"

"—let her in. Now."

My jaw is iron clad as I reach for the velvet rope releasing it. Red walks by me and I grab her upper arm, "Are you sure you want to be in there?" My stomach twists with uneasiness.

"Let go of her, dog," the client calls behind me, and I let my hand drop. He'll pay for that later.

"His name is Wolf." Red corrects him taking me by surprise. She glares at me like she has more to say, but instead of speaking, she snatches her arm away and walks by me. Her mouth splits into a gorgeous fucking smile as the celebrity douche draws her in for a hug and kisses her cheeks. Hers flush pink and his hand lands on the exposed low of her back as he guides her towards his table surrounded by friends, a second later she has a drink in her hand.

I almost find myself wishing fuck face would have shown up, that way she'd be away from this prick. He's a predator. I can tell cause he wears the same scent as me. Except that his intentions reek.

I know Red isn't stupid, maybe a touch innocent. She's celebrating, indulging. It's not every day a movie star invites you to his shiny side of the rope. I know how bright lights can look when you've been on the dim side of the tracks your whole life. They are enticing.

I want to believe that I know Red. She's not there for his charm, she wants to make connections, hoping that his status will afford her a step into some gallery, or push start her career; but what she doesn't realise is that all that glitz and glamour are a thousand bright lights all blinding her to the ugly truth.

Every time I look up, her drink is topped up. She's sitting next to him, her eyes all lit up as he tells her about his movies no doubt. He's shuffled way too close to her. One of his friends is keeping Caleb occupied with his tongue while another keeps topping up Red's glass.

I grind my molars. I can see what they're doing and there's fucking nothing I can do about it.

She giggles and the sound carries over the music and straight to my cock, I can't stand it. I finally understand the meaning of torture, draining away your sanity one second at a time. Under the table I can see his dirty little fingers draw circles on her thigh, and I imagine him screaming in pain as I break each of them in turn. My lips twitch at the prospect.

The music grows louder and the crowd rowdier. It's the way most nights go. The ebb and flow. It's when the drugs and the alcohol reach their peak, and the testosterone and pheromones in the air start to mingle when trouble will start —sex always leads to fucking trouble.

I grunt pulling my thoughts away from my issues, and watch the stupid rich fucker as he strokes Red's cheek. She flicks me a look and licks her lower lip, and I have to fight every fibre and savage need in my body not to rip the fucking rope in half and wrap it around his neck. A low growl vibrates from somewhere inside me and I breathe, sucking in alcohol doused air and dry, cherry flavour smoke. *What is she playing at? She's not being herself, she's been fed too much alcohol. Where the fuck is Hunter?*

They laugh and he swipes his thumb over the soft pads of her lips, and all I can hear is buzzing. He leans towards her and their foreheads touch, her lips are curled into a shy smile and her cheeks are flushed by alcohol. My chest tightens as a hot flicker of hatred pumps through my veins. I glare at them, their lips an impulse away. Breathing is almost impossible. I don't want to look but I can't tear my eyes away.

Maybe this torment is what I need to finally crush this desperate desire for her e—to cleanse myself of my need for her, to be force fed my own medicine of bitter disappointment and a savage knife to the heart. And maybe at last, I can stop pinning for something that never happened.

Their lips

Almost

Touch.

I suck in a sharp breath.

One,

More,

Inch.

A bottle explodes at my feet and screams slice through the music. Lover boy bolts up at the sound the vice around my heart eases a fraction. A group of men to my right are throwing punches, while a girl cries on the floor. I don't know if she's been hurt or if she's the cause of the punching. I suspect it's a bit of both.

Red is more slumped then seated on her chair and the fucker is touching her legs sliding his fingers too high. She doesn't protest, her head lulls back and forth.

Fuck.

I knew I hated this guy. I've seen this shit happen more than once, and right now, I hate that my fucking job is to stand still, shut the fuck up and turn a blind eye till I can fire his ass in the morning. Till then, I'm bound by our contract and an NDA.

My fingers curl into a tight fist till the nails bite into my skin, I imagine driving it through his nose. I suck in a long breath knowing I'm about to lose my futile effort to calm down, to push some of the tension out of my body and rid myself of the raging fury building inside me.

The fight on the dance floor spreads like an infectious

disease. It's not so much that people get involved but sucked in; they all want to help it or stop it, and soon there's a mass of bodies that tumble through the club.

My boys jump in. They are bigger, stronger and highly trained, and they rip through the amassed crowd as it starts to surge towards me. Someone throws a glass at my head and it bounces off and into the VIP area. It explodes on the floor where the guests all screech like headless birds. I don't wait for another excuse, instead I tear through the rope and within two steps I grab the client, rip him from his chair and pull him behind me.

He tries to protest for a second but he's more of a waif that a man. Pulling him towards the exit is easy and satisfying. I snatch my radio and call for Hunter.

The line remains static.

Fuck.

I turn back to Red. She's sitting on the chair unperturbed by the commotion around her.

"Sit here and don't move."

She looks at me through glazed drunk eyes and smiles. "Hi Shaw." She traces a hand over mine.

Fuck.

I try Hunter again just to get more static from him. I call down to Rob and tell him to get the car to the back exit.

The crowd grows rowdier and busier and tension slithers up my spine when I finally spot Hunter. He rushes out of the bathroom brushing his blonde hair out of his flushed face and tugging on his pants. A petit little thing follows him out, her googly eyes ogle him, and she wipes at her mouth.

Me and him will have words about that later.

I'm dragging the hot shot by the wrist, and though I know I can't break it cause he's in the middle of shooting a film, a harsh bruise can be covered up by makeup. I tighten my grip round him and yank. He whimpers a little but keeps up as we catch up to Hunter.

"Nice of you to join us," I growl at him.

"I was held up."

"More like she was being held down." I nod towards the girl dreamily gazing at Hunter.

He shrugs and a stupid grin crosses his face, "What can I say?"

"Nothing. We'll sort it out later. That and the fact you forgot to tell me Red would be here tonight."

The afterglow falls from his face in a second and he starts scanning the dance floor where the mob is starting to settle and the boys push the rowdy ones toward the door. "Where is she?"

"I've got eyes on her. I'll make sure she gets home safe if you deal with him."

I shove the client into Hunter's hard body, and he doesn't argue. Instead he takes the lead and they disappear towards the back exit.

Once they're gone, I turn back to Red. She's exactly where I left her, glazed eyes, and silly expression. She has a drunk smile plastered on her face and it cracks wider when she sees me.

"Hi."

"Yeah, hi, where's your friend?" I scan the deserted VIP area and the dance floor that's once more throbbing with dancing bodies.

"I don't know, he went off with a new friend. He was cute." She waves and giggles.

"Right." I run a hand through my hair, this night is not going how I thought it would. I grab my radio and call Dean to find out if they have things under control. When he assures me the offending parties have been dealt with, I stare at Red. She's barely conscious and I need to get her home.

I grab the radio again and growl, "I need to get out of here and Hunter and Rob just left with the client, do we have anyone around that can cover?"

Dean's voice crackles into my ear, "Let me call around."

I grab a waiter while I wait and ask him for some water. He comes back with a bottle. I put it on the table for Red. She glares at it like she's unsure what it does. It's part adorable and part frustrating. Mostly frustrating, because of how cute she looks.

Dean calls me back and tells me that one of our guys is a few minutes away.

"Good, let me know when he arrives, I need to get out of here."

"Everything okay there, boss?"

"Dean?"

"Yeah?"

"Do you like your job?"

The static grows silent on the radio, all the guys are holding their breaths and shutting their fucking mouths.

"I do."

"Then shut the fuck up and mind your own business."

"Copy that."

The radio silence screams in my ear and I wipe my forehead. The back of my hand comes back wet with sweat and I swipe it on my dress pants.

Fuck.

Dean calls back a few minutes later letting me know Sean just arrived. "Get him set up, I'm leaving out the back. If there are any issues, call Hunter."

"Yes boss."

I pull out my earpiece and thread my hands beneath Red's knees and hands. She giggles and tucks her head into my chest and everything inside me comes alive like it's been consumed by a wild, hungry hive. I'm a buzzing thing—I know I have eyes on me and that this will get back to Hunter, but fuck it. I told him I would get Red out and I'm going to tell him to fire that fucker for what he did, and everything else he was about to do. My body clenches at the thought and my skin feels too small for my own body.

I push through the back door where Sam pretends he doesn't see me, and I make a beeline for my Jaguar.

I slide Red into the passenger seat. "Buckle up," I growl at her and slam the door, then round the car.

When I get in, she's looking at me all doe eyed and fucking stunning, with pink flushed cheeks and a sweet little pout.

"Why are you angry at me?" She's more slurring than speaking, and I'm regretting putting her in my car without some kind of vomit bag.

"I'm not."

"But you're shouting."

I clutch the back of my neck and let out a heavy sigh, "Just buckle up."

She fumbles with the belt a few times till it finally clicks in place and I put the car into gear, I drive faster than I should.

The road blurs as I swerve around corners and break a few speed limits getting us home. Her head lolls with the car and her eyes grow heavy. I put on the radio and she shrieks with glee, coming alive. She starts singing and moving to the beat, and I hate her so much because I'm fucking mesmerised by how beautiful her voice is and how lovely and ridiculous she looks as she moves around obstructed by the seat belt. But she doesn't care; the alcohol has lowered all her inhibitions, made her open and vulnerable and totally fucking desirable for all the wrong reasons.

I park. She lets herself out and stumbles into me as I round the car to get her.

"Can you walk?"

"I think so," she giggles and stumbles around then falls against me. Her silky, frozen hands land on my chest and she giggles even more, totally unaware of how her touch affects me, of how much I want her to touch me everywhere, of all the things her touch makes me want to do to her.

"Come on," I lead her to the front door and then the couch, "Sit down."

She falls backward into the couch and slithers up the cushions, the movement forcing the strap of her singlet down and the skirt up. I am being punished for something, and at this point, I'm almost prepared to fall down on my knees and repent for all my sins if I could just bury myself between her legs and taste her.

I wrench my eyes away from her and go to the kitchen. I adjust my cock that's been pushing against my dress pants all night. My balls haven't ached this much since I've been sixteen. I grab a glass of water and take it to her. "Drink."

Her red lips split into a sloppy smile, "Thanks Shaw."

Fuck.

No one ever calls me by my name, and suddenly, the moment has become more than what it should be. My heart kicks in my chest and I want to make time stand still, I want to rip it from the thread of the universe and push it back. Back to before I fucked everything up, back before I let her go, back to when she was mine.

She gulps down the water totally oblivious to what she'd done.

She hands me back the empty glass and her head tips to the side. Her brow furrows for a second and her eyes almost focus before she nods, and that drunk smile plasters itself across her face again.

"What?" I growl at her.

"You're like a marshmallow."

"Excuse me?" I tense up, my muscles growing rigid as if offended.

"A camp fired one—you're all dark and hard on the outside, but inside you're all gooey." She curls up on the couch as she talks.

"Gooey?" I rip my hands through my hair. "Un-fucking-believable," I mumble, "Gooey?"

"And soft," she purrs.

Every fibre in my body stands on edge, I love that Red thinks about me, but I hate that she thinks of *any* part of me as gooey. I need to make her think of other adjectives.

"There's nothing about me that's soft or gooey." I hate that word. It's my new favourite word to hate in the English language, fucking *gooey*.

"And delicious." Her eyes close and I stare at her. *Is she talking about me or marshmallow? Fuck.*

"Red?"

"Mm mm." She nods slightly but her eyes remain closed, and I know that she's gone.

I stand over her and watch her sleep. The flush of her cheeks begins to drain slowly away as her breathing becomes even. The strap of her singlet falls to the side again and reveals her delicate fucking shoulder and long neck. I want to run my tongue all over her skin and taste every fucking inch of her.

I rumble in frustration, go to her room, and pull away the blanket, ignoring the pile of clothes on the floor and stuff everywhere—the room is a window into her life, frenzied and in a total fucking mess.

I go back to the couch and wrap my arms around her, picking her up. She purrs against me, wraps her thin arms around my neck and nestles her head into my chest. Her warmth radiates through me, and I'm loath to release her. I hover over her bed and hold her, keeping her there, close. Feeling her chest move against mine, feeling her breath as it filters through the fabric of my shirt and teases me with its warmth. I've never found it this hard to release someone.

I set her down on the bed where she curls up like a cat. She would make the perfect little spoon. I shake my head wondering where the thought came from. Maybe she was right, maybe I am going soft.

I throw the cover over her and march out of the room.

Fuck.

I pace the hallway, stopping just short of her doorway each time. Undesirable thoughts slosh inside my brain like a well stirred martini, and I fight them off. When my phone rings in the lounge, I'm finally ripped away from the door.

Hunter's number flashes on my screen, "How's Red?"

"I got her home and put her in bed."

"Wolf." the warning in his voice is clear.

"*Her* fucking bed, you asshole. The client invited her into the VIP area and got her legless, he was pulling all sorts of moves and if that fight hadn't broken up, we would have had another 'Alabama Chichi' incident."

He's silent for a long time. "I owe you man."

I nod into the phone; well aware he can't see me.

"I'll get rid of the fucker first thing tomorrow, but till 6:00 A.M., we're still under contract."

"Do you need back up?"

"No, just watch over her."

"I will."

Wolf

I end the call and stomp to the kitchen where I grab a beer. I fall onto the couch. My brain hurts. My head falls back, and I stare at the ceiling, replaying that night over and over in my head, wishing I would have done everything differently.

Alabama Chichi was just like Red that night. Fiery and feisty and unstoppable. She probably had hopes and dreams too and would have never expected her night to end like it did.

None of us did.

I sip my beer and it sours in my mouth as everything comes flooding back. She was so excited when she was invited to the VIP room, her body was vibrating with it. Her eyes were wide, and star struck. You could tell it was her first time. If I'd known it would be her last...

I slam my eyes shut at the memories, but they won't go away; on nights like these, they always come back.

They started feeding her drink after drink, and I guess at one point someone slipped something in it. None of us saw, which is why we all share the blame equally. We all missed it, and it all happened so fast.

She went from being lively and excitable to almost paralytic. She was sitting down which was why it wasn't so noticeable when he started kissing her. That type of shit, it happened all the time—celebrities and randoms hooking up, people wanting to touch that kind of famous like it might rub off on them.

My stomach curdles with the thoughts and my hands tightens around the beer bottle. On the upside, that celebrity fucker will only ever be famous for his infamy. Turns out, no amount of money could cover that shit show up, and once you're tainted enough, no one wants to work with you.

When they asked to be taken home, he held her up at the waist. She stumbled and giggled, but she wasn't the same girl that stepped across the velvet rope. I suggested we get her a cab home, he suggested I mind my own fucking business.

She looked drunk, but I think somewhere we knew it was all wrong. We made excuses to ourselves that we were just starting out, that we had to keep our reputation in this town or none of us would work again, but what we really did that night was fail. Fail as men and people and protectors. We were protecting the predator when we should have been protecting his prey.

She looked drunk, and drunk girls go home with celebrities every day of the week. Fuck, drunk girls go home with me every day of the week.

We just didn't see it coming.

I take another long sip and the cold beer sears my inside. It took three days for the video to surface, and when it did, it spread like a raging fire consuming everything and everyone in its path.

The thing is, people do that sort of fucked up shit all the time. But when rich people do it and their friends take videos and they don't want to shell out the blackmail funds, that's when they get burned.

And everyone got singed by that fire.

Overnight the name 'Alabama Chichi' became the most spoken about in every household in the UK. Not for anything that she did, but rather for what she endured.

The fucked-up thing about that night is that she probably woke up the next morning feeling sore and foggy but happy. Happy because she thought some celebrity picked her from a line of girls. Picked *her*. She should have felt special and precious. Fuck it, for all I know he could have kissed her good morning and smiled to her face before sending her on her way.

She told the police that she didn't remember anything. I bet in the end she wished everyone else would forget.

It's amazing what the human body can bear when it's debilitated. It's equally amazing what sick fucks would do to it when they can control it. The worst thing was the moaning; when they hurt her and fucked her and shoved shit down every hole, she moaned and it drove them crazy, it drove them to more, to extremes.

I groan wanting to wipe away the sounds.

When she killed herself, I took it personally. I mourned for her. I stood at the funeral and wished I could take it all away, and I swore I would never let that shit happen again. If that fight hadn't broken out tonight, I would have started another. I'd be sitting in jail right now and that celebrity dickhead would be in the morgue, but Red would be safe. I may not have been able to save Alabama, but fuck it if I ever let another woman get hurt under my watch again. Never again.

I down the rest of the beer and my stomach curdles with distain.

I set the empty bottle down and lean back on the couch. Everything still hurts.

Wolf

My phone rings and I groan, reaching for my bedside table to find an empty space instead. I shoot up and my back complains with the movement, realising I'm not in my bed.

"Shit." I mumble and find my phone on the floor. I grab it and fall against the couch, my entire body reminding me why it needs a bed.

"Yeah?" My voice is full of sleep, and I scratch at my burning eyes.

"Wakey, wakey sleeping beauty."

I check the time on my phone, 6.01 A.M, "Fuck you, Hunter."

"My shift is over. Thought you might want to sit in while we break this guy's contract."

I grind my teeth and draw in a long breath, picturing his hands creeping up Red's thigh, his thumb over her lips; and my hand tightens around the phone. "No."

"No?" He doesn't hide his surprise.

"I might kill him if I'm there." I go for honesty. Hunter knows how much Alabama's death affected me.

"Maybe you should be here so that *I* don't kill him," he throws back at me.

"Maybe if you weren't getting your dick sucked and saw what was happening, you would have killed him already."

Hunter grunts over the phone, "How is she?"

"Asleep, like I should be." I growl back.

"Good."

"You know I would have never let it—"

"—I do. See you later."

"Yeah."

He hangs up and I feel a little lighter knowing we're about to be a client short. It also means that my night has just cleared up cause I was scheduled for babysitting duty.

I stand up and my body protests, my muscles ache and scream as I shuffle to my room. My bed looks inviting, but I know I'm done sleeping and I'll just be lying on it, starting at the ceiling.

I take a quick sneak peek into Red's room. She's passed out, her duvet covering all but her face that's a little twisted as it pushes up her pillow.

I get in the shower letting the hot water tumble against my skin and wash away the night.

3 2

Red

My eyes feel glued together; prying them open I regret it instantly and slam them shut. My dry mouth is thick with sticky dribble, and I groan into my pillow before throwing the duvet back over my head.

I roll onto my back and let my body sink into the mattress. The beginnings of a headache knock at my skull, and I know I need to get some water in me. I push the blanket away and find a glass of water and two headache tablets on my bedside table. My eyes dart to the door. It's closed.

I listen to the house and hear only silence.

I down the water and swallow the pills then slither out of my bed like a broken marionette. Waves of nausea flit in and out, threatening but never amounting to anything. All I need is a shower and then food.

I step into the shower and turn the water on, the water trickles down my back bringing with it flashes of the night before. Dancing with Caleb, meeting some celebrity. Wolf. Cradling him, touching him, calling him a marshmallow.

I groan into my hands and shake my head. I called him soft and gooey, I told him he was delicious. My head falls back against the tiles. He is delicious, that much I remember.

I switch the water off, dress and head for the kitchen. I freeze as I enter the lounge. Wolf is sprawled across the couch, his long legs stretched in front of him, head tucked on a palm as he scrolls on his phone.

He lifts his eyes to me, "How's your head?"

"Could be worse," I say with a croak, and a flicker of a smile crosses his beautiful face. "Thanks, for last night."

His eyes fall away, and he nods a little. He looks exhausted.

"Have you slept?"

"A little," he sounds weary.

"Breakfast?"

"Are you cooking?"

"Sure." I shuffle to the kitchen, leaving him on the couch.

My stomach rolls and nausea claws at my throat. I need something greasy to soak up the alcohol still sloshing around my veins. My body feels dull and abused. I find some eggs, bacon and bread and get frying. My stomach growls as the acidic hunger gnaws inside me. I douse it with another glass of water, which still doesn't settle my endless thirst.

Wolf steps into the kitchen, "Smells good, I'll make coffee."

I throw him a sideway glance and put some bread into the toaster. I pretend not to watch as his large, broad body moves, agile and precise. He feels like a contradiction.

The silence is broken by the pop of the toaster. My heart leaps at the sound and I chuck the toast on a plate, blow on my fingers, then add two more pieces.

"About last night..."

He looks up at me. "Don't want to talk about it," he says flatly.

I bite my tongue for a second, "Well, I just wanted to and say—"

"You already did," he ends the conversation, and I watch as he adds a half a teaspoon of sugar and milk into my coffee without asking. Knowing exactly how I like it. I frown as I contemplate this. He places the mugs on the table as the second batch of toast pops up, and I grab the pieces piling them on a plate.

I take the butter from the fridge and turn find Wolf standing next to me.

"Would you like me to butter your toast?"

He shoots me a sly smile and I regret my words instantly, "I bet you'd love to butter my toast wouldn't you, Red?"

"Wolf…"

He takes a careful step towards me, his grin spreading as he speaks, "Maybe once you finish with the bread you can see what you can do about my buns." I roll my eyes as his gaze falls on my lips. "What's wrong Red? Too toasty in here for you?"

"You're an idiot," I say and stab the butter knife into the air in the mock threat. Wolf catches my wrist and pins my body against the counter with his.

His forehead drops to mine and his eyes are full of mischief. "Let me make it all butter for you Red." his hot breath tickles my mouth as it splits into a ridiculous smile.

"Wolf," I groan, "stop it."

"Too cheesy for you?"

I close my eyes and sigh. When I open them again, all the humour has drained from his face. Instead, his chocolate brown eyes bore into mine, staring holes into me. His lips dangerously close to mine. My breath hitches and my heart trips as time stands still, suspended like dew on a blade of grass. Tension ratchets up my spine until it has nowhere to go but up and out. I push up on my tiptoes and my lips crash into his, where they've always belonged.

All my defences crumble before this desperate, hungry mystery that pulls us together. His lips are just as I remember them, soft and full, and his kisses are just as desperate, just as needy as they beg for mine.

For me.

For more.

The knife clatters somewhere on the floor and a hand tangles in my hair. He draws me against his rippling muscles that flex and tense around me. Heat crawls inside me as he deepens the kiss. I claw at his back, at his neck, at his shoulders. My body recognises his, like an addict taking a hit after a long sobriety.

When we hear it, Wolf untangles himself from me and rips away in a single swift movement, while I find air and suck it into my lungs. A second later, the door slams shut and Hunter's key's clatter into the key box by the front door.

Wolf's eyes dart to mine for a single moment, his face pinched with regret as he wipes a hand over his mouth erasing the moment.

Hunter walks into the kitchen, "I'm in time for breakfast? Is there enough for one more?"

"Of course," I say on a shaky breath and turn away from him.

"Red was just buttering up the toast..." Wolf adds, and a flicker of a smile touches my lips.

"Great, thanks Red." Hunter says and falls into a chair.

Wolf doesn't look at me once as he stabs his food with his fork and talks business with Hunter. I tune out, thinking about Wolf's mouth on mine and a warm shiver wracks up my body. I try to douse it with memories, but it's like I've swallowed an ember and it's sparked something inside me that's spreading and catching on everything it touches. It's already out of control, and I don't know if I want to put it out again.

33

TEN YEARS AGO

Wolf 18, Red 15

Wolf

Hunter has been working at his new job for two weeks, three nights a week where I get Red all to myself. Where I don't have to share her with anyone, when we can both be who we are. Where I can put my arm around her when we watch movies, and I can trace the long slender shape of her thigh as she sits and sketches and purrs. Where she can tell me her dreams. Where I can tell her lame jokes and listen to her laughter and then kiss her mouth till her lips are red and swollen and we're breathless. When we have to stop every time it gets too far, and my body wants to take over.

I never let her touch my cock. I'm too afraid, and it scares me that she isn't. But I can be patient, for her. I can wait just one more week.

For her I can wait a lifetime.

I don't know when she became mine. I can't pinpoint the exact moment, all I know is that everything about her fascinates me, and all my thoughts are consumed by her I find myself eager and happy for no reason other than the fact I'd know I'd be seeing her, that she'd be there, that we can steal a piece of time to ourselves each night and no one could touch it. I craved that time with her, like a heroin addict. When I was with her, I felt peace—like all the restlessness of the day was set aside and her presence, her voice, her laughter soothed me from the inside out.

We sat on the couch. Her long legs outstretched before her and her hand moving frantically over the pad.

"What are you drawing?"

"It's not done yet."

I nod and hold back the desire to rip it out of her hand again, "Will you show me?"

"When it's done." Her eyes glint and a smile ghosts her lips. "It's a surprise."

"For me?"

She nods and sucks her lower lip into her mouth, and my body explodes with envy wanting to be that lip. I let my gaze fall away in fear of doing something stupid.

"It's getting late." I look at the clock.

Not that it matters.

She sets her pad down, and her gaze dips to my lips and she licks her own.

"Take me to bed?" It's shy and delicate and totally devastating.

"I shouldn't."

"Just this one time. You can tuck me in." She hops off the couch and waits for me.

I know I shouldn't get off this couch, I know I should sit here and watch her go. Send her away and wait for Hunter to get home before I go back to mine and release all the pain in my groin. But I don't, I get up and follow her.

She takes me by the hand and leads me upstairs to her room. She's a combination of nervous energy and confidence. She bites down her fear, but her eyes can't lie. She pushes her door open and keeps the lights off as she leads me to her bed. We lie down facing one another, her eyes glisten in the darkness and silence that engulfs us. And then her hand is on my face, tracing my jaw with soft delicate fingers and taking away my breath—Which I find on her lips.

I kiss her like she's mine. My hands weave through her hair and explore every part of her I want to claim. My greedy hands touch and feel but don't take.

Not yet.

I push her away, my body aching and needy, and my breath coming in in short sharp pants.

"Not yet, sweet, beautiful Red. You know we can't."

She lets out a frustrated huff, and I feel her head move against my palm in a nod.

"Just one more week till your birthday, and then I can make you mine."

Her hands tighten around me.

"What do you want for your birthday, Red?"

"Just you," she whispers against my neck, and I shiver.

"But you can have anything," I kiss her neck, wanting to sink my teeth into her delicate flesh, wanting to make her moan.

"But I don't need anything else."

"Are you sure?"

"Yes," she whispers, and it sounds like a wish.

"Then that's what you'll get." I nuzzle her neck wanting time to move, to stop, wanting this moment to last an eternity but also end. End and move faster—till Saturday, when there will be no more waiting, no more holding back, no more stopping.

"You promise?"

There's something so needy and desperate in her voice, it cracks at my resolve.

"I promise." I find her mouth and seal my promise with a kiss.

My mouth can't leave hers; I snatch endless kisses and touches, I want her so much I wrench myself away till it hurts.

"I better go, Hunter will be home soon."

"Shaw?"

She grips my hand as I sit up, and I find her silhouette on the bed.

"Yeah?"

"I think I love you." She sounds relieved, like she's been carrying that weight around for so long.

"I think I love you too, Red." And as I say it, my heart soars and I feel light, like maybe I was carrying that weight too and I never even realised.

"Good night."

"Good night, Red."

I reach for the door handle and step out of her room, and what I see makes my heart stop.

3 4

PRESENT DAY

Red

We spend the next two weeks working out the planning and installation for Becca's show. I've become Caleb's favourite friend since I got him into that club, and he's been paying me back by not only doing the bulk of the work, but by teaching me everything he knows —Willingly.

We took a day trip to the estate house to meet with the owner. The place was enchanting and beautiful, and I knew exactly why Becca chose it as the venue.

We drove into the estate over the grandiose driveway that seemed to stretch for miles, lined on each side by thick dark woods which opened up into a sweeping, wide circle drawn in front of the manor with an ornamental fountain in the centre.

The ornate sandstone walls seemed to grow from the manicured lawn, reaching into the heavens. The greyish stone bare of any ivy growth but peppered with too many oversized windows, almost cathedral like.

When we stepped inside, all the rooms were bathed in

natural light that cascaded through the multitude of windows, and when the curtains were drawn and the chandeliers above lit, I could see the enchantment of this place and how Becca's work would truly come to life here as the light bounced from the polished oak floors and danced on the antique furniture still scattered around. We spent that day taking measurement and inspecting walls, spaces, and going over endless procedures and protocols.

By the time I got home each day, I was exhausted and elated and feeling like a contributing, functioning member of society. Wolf's kiss all but a dimming memory. In fact, I haven't seen either Hunter or Wolf since that breakfast.

We're back to being ships in the night.

On the Thursday morning before the show, Becca calls me to her office.

"Hey Red," she doesn't look up from the pile of papers on her desk, "are we all set for Saturday night?"

"Yes." I beam at her, but she doesn't see me. I don't mind, I'm proud. Tomorrow Caleb and I will spend the day at the manor putting the last of the installation together, and I couldn't wait to see all my hard work take shape—at last—into something real and tangible. "It's looking amazing."

She looks up then and gives me a wide genuine smile. "So, you'll pick me up at five?"

"Excuse me?"

"Well you didn't think you're not coming, did you? There's no better learning opportunity than being at the opening night, seeing how everything really works behind the scenes. Plus, schmoozing with all the money people and getting your name out there in the arts world won't hurt either."

"Oh, I didn't realise. I…"

"You've made other plans?" she arches an eyebrow.

Drinks with Ethan. I sigh, "No."

"Great, it's settled." Her smile broadens, "Wear something tasteful."

"Tasteful?"

"Sexy, revealing, saucy. Get those people to notice you. After they notice *you*, they'll notice your art."

"Oh." I grimace and shudder internally at her words and wonder what I have in my closet that could pass for 'saucy.'

"It's how the world works, darling."

I nod, not hiding my unease. "Can I bring a plus one?"

"Of course."

I thank her, glad I don't have to cancel on Ethan, and as I turn to leave she calls me back, "Red?"

"Yes?"

"What's this?"

She hands me a paper with one of my doodles, a half face of a boy. I startle as a shiver slithers up my spine. "Oh, it's nothing."

"He's a very sad nothing."

I shrug. I'm not getting into this now.

"Well, if you ever want to make that nothing into something, I suggest you create a professional portfolio of your work and have it on my desk, by…" she waves her hand in the air like she can magically pull out a number from it, "the end of the month?" She grabs her calendar and squints as she reads the numbers, "That gives you three weeks. Ask Caleb to help."

I stand frozen to the floor, unable to move. Trying to comprehend what she's just said. I stare at her till she looks away and back down to her papers.

"You can go now, I'll see you Saturday."

I mumble something that could have been thank you and open the door. I walk out and into what feels like a brick wall.

When I look up, my eyes narrow at Wolf. "What are you

doing here?" My stomach drags in a long roll as my gaze finds his lips, then his eyes.

"I have a meeting with your boss."

"What? Why?" My voice catches in my throat.

"Come in Mr. Bennett." Becca calls from her office and he sidesteps me, closing the door behind him.

I hurry over to Caleb. "What the hell is he doing here?" I try to cover the quiver in my voice, but seeing Wolf again makes my body remember. I need to remind myself I'm with Ethan.

"Who? Mr. Hot Stuff?" he says dreamily, and I punch him on the shoulder. "Ouch." He gives me a dramatic look and rubs his arm, "Becca needed security for the next two nights —"

"So, you gave her Wolf's number?"

"I thought you'd be happy, he works with your brother. You said they lost a client the other day."

I sigh and mumble an unbelievable thanks.

"Anyway, we're going to be stuck there for hours, I need some eye candy to help pass the time." His eyebrows bounce up and down as he gives me a dirty smile.

I giggle then frown, "Wait, you knew we were going?"

"You didn't?" he chuckles, and I stop myself from punching him again, he bruises like a peach. "It's in your contract."

I purse my lips thinking that maybe I should have read it. "I have nothing to wear."

He takes a step back and clasps his hands to his chest. "I've got you babe." By the way he says it, and the way his eyes roam my body, I'm not so sure.

"Caleb." I cringe.

"Trust me."

And I do.

3 5

Wolf

I've been here for over two hours, watching the rooms fill up with London's rich and infamous. Fortunes built on the misfortune of others stuffed in everyone's faces. Dressed up, pompous peacocks all out to impress with feathers, when the meat underneath is rotten. I see a few familiar clients and we ignore each other. In this space, I don't exist. I scan the room for the hundredth time, pretending I'm not waiting for her while inconsequential polite conversation, canapes, and wine woosh around me.

The ebb of conversation dims for a few seconds, then the room erupts in applause as Becca Oakridge makes an entrance followed by Caleb and Red.

Red.

The air in my lungs squeezes out in a sharp breath, and my heart staggers in my chest.

Her fingers are entwined together in front of her, and I know it's to stop her from pulling at her scant dress. She's all long legs in shiny, red heels and curves in a stunning, off the shoulder tight black number that makes my body crave hers and burn with heat.

I shuffle backwards into the shadows, watching her move and smile, watching the rich pricks roam her body with their eyes and taint her shoulders with lingering, uncomfortable touches. I see the way she steps out of them, keeping the fake smile firmly in place.

Every now and then, she scans the room like she's looking for something, someone. I wonder where fuck face is and why he's not wrapped around her. Truth be told, I don't give a shit. I pull further into the darkness where I can watch her.

Only her.

Resigned to suffer in shadows.

When the auction starts, I swap with Dean. I stand by the glass backdoor- fresh air, sealed exit, and no Red anywhere to be seen. She'll be inside somewhere, wearing that sexy stunning number that makes my indecision about her impossible. I'm so drawn to her that if I don't touch her soon, my atoms will rip me apart from the inside.

I pace along the glass door. Light from inside piercing the lattice windows, throwing strange shapes on the ground, and that's when I see a flicker of movement. A flash of colour catches my eye and when I look up, I see Red. She slips out of her bright red shoes and leaves them by the path, then she steals into the woods where the darkness swallows her whole.

Red

It's hard to breathe in there, and I just need a minute to collect my thoughts. The excitement and pressure overwhelms me. Becca's art all sold in the first forty minutes for ridiculous and exuberant sums. I know it's mostly for charity and the rich out doing their rich friends; but the numbers are large and intimidating, and I'm increasingly aware how far I've fallen and how far I have to climb if I ever want to enjoy as much success as Becca.

After the sale, she flaunts me like I'm an accessory. I get assessed and passed around by all her rich friends and plaster a fake smile on my face as they all prod me with their questions and dirty looks. I'm somewhere between flattered and needing a long shower. Ethan is running late on the one night I really needed him to be around.

I just need to breathe.

There's no sign of Hunter or Wolf or any of their boys, but I know they're around. They must be blending into their environment. Becca will be pleased.

Although I don't see him, I can feel his eyes on me wherever I go. I feel watched. My skin tingles like it's aware of his presence. I can't see him whenever I scan the room, but I can *feel* him. *Everywhere.*

I slip out of the manor and take off the high heels. My feet thank me instantly, and I curse myself for letting Caleb talk me out of my Doc Martens.

I follow the short path through the manicured lawn and steal into the woods. My feet follow the narrow strip of naked earth edged by giant gnarled roots which weave in and out of the ground.

I let my hands touch their husks as I pass, feeling their rough bark beneath my cooling fingers. The cold air bites at my flushed skin, and I fill my lungs with air. The tension leaking out of me.

"Red," I hear Wolf's voice slice the darkness and my heart trips, "you are out of bounds, come back here."

I don't. I press my back against a tree and search the dark —which would have been absolute, save for the yellow flickers cast by the flaming torches in the garden, the flames ripple in the light breeze and shadows dance on the ground.

"Red," he taunts me, "I'm not playing games."

I stay silent, shutting my eyes and resting my head against the tree. The crunch of small rocks beneath his feet tell me he's close.

Too close.

Time to move.

"Red," he calls.

I shoot a glance over my shoulder and smirk before I step away from the path and into the woods. I know it's out of bounds, but I just want to breathe a little easier, my dress feels too tight and the air too thin.

"Red," his voice sharper this time as it travels through the darkness. My feet sink into the soft muddied earth and decomposing leaves that litter the woodland floor.

I scamper between the trees, my breath short and sharp.

"Red," his voice is a silent snarl that cuts through the vast dimness of the wood. I giggle even though I know he's somewhere behind me.

Closing in.

Fear and excitement trickles inside me in slow rivulets.

My heart kicks faster and adrenaline courses through my veins demanding I run.

I hug the rough bark of a tree. My hanging breath like a smoke signal.

All I see is darkness.

I run again, my pulse throbbing.

I round a corner, the cold evening air shocking my throat and lungs as I inhale deeper, faster.

He's coming and I can't stop him.

I don't know that I want to.

"Red," his harsh whisper carries by the light breeze, sounding sinister.

I hold my breath and search the shadows.

Shivers slither up my spine as I spot him.

Wolf stalks me. He takes small quiet steps and stops to listen. I know it's him by his large silhouette and by the way he makes no sound at all.

He's quieter than me.

He's too close.

I dart from my hiding place. A twig snaps beneath me. I don't turn to look, but I can feel him behind me.

He's coming.

My thundering heart drowns out all other sound.

I see his shape scamper through the trees then vanish.

I find refuge behind a thick trunk and hold my breath. Every hair on my body stands to attention. Tension wracks up my spine.

I creep around the tree trunk, my cheek brushing along the firm bark.

But,

It's,

Too,

Late.

A chill runs down my spine and his hot breath scalds my neck a second before his giant hand grabs my shoulder and spins me around. He pushes me into the giant oak and his hand closes around my throat. My pulse ticks against his palm.

"Don't you know, little girls should not be out in the woods alone at night?" His menacing eyes glint with dark intentions. "Don't you know there are dangerous things in these woods?"

"Like what?" My heart thrashes in my chest, my stomach unravels in a slow dragging roll.

"Like me." His fingers trace my collarbone stealing my breath.

"I'm not afraid of you, Wolf."

"You should be."

I look away and his hand trails up my jaw, clasping around it and forcing my chin up to line up our faces. "Tell me, sweet Red, are you afraid I might hurt you?"

"You've already done that." My heart stings with old memories.

His face falls for a second and a slow sly smirk replaces it, "Well, then maybe you're afraid that I'm going to fuck you."

"No," I swallow hard as his grip loosens, "I'm afraid that you won't." Except that I am. Knowing how easily he can snap my heart in two.

His thumb swipes over my lips and my mouth falls open. I suck him into my mouth, and he groans as he slides out.

"I'm not a good man, Red." There's an ache in his rough voice that rips through me, but the delicate way his fingers trail my neck sparks a fierce need for me to claw at him.

"I don't believe that," I whisper as my hands creep to his waste.

"That's where you've always gone wrong."

His mouth smashes into mine in a brutal, bruising kiss that threatens to set the woods alight. His hand slides along my neck and closes around my nape as the other slithers around me and draws me into his hard body.

When his mouth leaves mine, I whimper into the dark night needing more.

The pressure on the back of my neck disappears and is replaced by Wolf's soft lips. Like a slow melting glacier, he leans in and peppers kisses on my neck and shoulders, his teeth skate along my skin leaving lasting echoes of his touch.

His free hand creeps up my torso till his fingers edge the neckline of my dress, they tickle my skin, and slither to my collar bone then curl around the fabric and tear it away unceremoniously. His hands close around my breasts and steal the air from my lungs as he groans into my neck. His cheek nuzzles my own, harsh whiskers scratch my skin. His fingers tease and pinch and roll and he whispers into my ear, "Red…" like he's praying to some unseen god. But I am the one being worshiped. His body pulses and presses against me in waves as he teases and kisses so agonisingly soft, I think I might break.

His hand leaves my aching breast which misses his touch, and heat as it slithers down my belly, he yanks up my skirt and pulls down my underwear. Cold and heat pour into me as his fingers glide along my wetness. I shiver and he lets out a tortured aching sound that threatens to wreck my insides.

His mouth finds a nipple as his fingers delicately tease me. He is everywhere and still he's not enough; I cry for more with each of my anguished moans.

Heat builds inside me, a need so severe, I ache all over. I need to be unleashed, undone, shattered, and yet he restrains his desire, fighting to remain in control when all I want is to be an animal following my instincts—savage and carnal till they devour us both.

My body tenses and sweet, fierce heat grows between my legs, the all-consuming nothing that explodes into divine sensation just out of reach as he rips his hands away and for a moment I am left unhinged, like a slave without a master. The snick of his zipper slices the night air and then just as quickly his touch is back, but this time his cock is no longer imprisoned by layers of fabric. Its big head slides along my wetness and a feral sound falls from Wolf's mouth as he plunges into me without warning.

His nails bite into my skin as his brutal hands close around me. My head whips back into the tree and I dig my fingers into his shoulders. We are nothing but a collection of hot sensations that collide in the darkness. His battering hips smash against me, again and again. His harsh pants burn my skin, and my desperate moans tear the silence. His hard body crushes mine into the harder bark and everything hurts so good.

With each thrust, he buries himself deeper and my body bends to meet him, bowing to his will until I erupt in exquisite sensation—a shattering wave of ecstasy—while Wolf growls and grunts and pumps, then savagely grips me so hard I cry as he pushes so deep it sparks intolerable pleasure everywhere.

My heart remembers its rhythm and my lungs learn to breathe again, as bit by agonising bit, we fall from the precipice and down to earth where Wolf isn't a good guy, and this is going to be nothing more than a notch in some invisible belt he hangs above his bed. The thought cripples my struggling heart as he releases me and I hang onto the tree, afraid to let go in case I might fall apart. And even with the ache inside, my mouth envies the rest of my glistening body, for it craves him like rain in the desert.

He pulls up his pants and zip and then an unbearable silence that stings more than the forming bruises on my body cloaks us.

"Fuck, Red," he finally chokes out, and the fractured pieces of my heart begins to crumble.

I say nothing.

"Just don't tell anyone." He looks around.

I search his face, but the passion from moments ago seems to fizzle into regret and a broken sound rips from my mouth. I swallow another harsh pill.

His eyes dart to mine, but I'm trying to get the dress fitted back onto my body. while fighting this heartbreak. A chaotic soup of emotions he feeds me through a straw in slow, agonising portions, till I choke on the bitterness.

"It's ripped." He swears and pulls off his jacket wrapping it around me like a substitute. "Let me get you inside to… clean up." He clears his throat. He sounds lost, like suddenly I am the predator and he is the one I hunted down.

I nod because I'm dazed—and hurt and elated—and I'm sinking in a pool of uncertain emotions.

He leads me to the edge of the woods where I grab my shoes, my muddied feet need to be washed like our dirty deed.

Wolf mumbles into the radio and nods into the night.

"This way."

He leads me around the back where a locked door flies open, and Rob stands stone faced as we walk through and Wolf leads me to a bathroom.

"Stay here." He closes the door behind him as he leaves.

The mirror isn't kind. She tells me the truth that's painted on my face. The smudged lipstick and wild hair, the limp dress and the hollow eyes staring back at me, full of unanswered questions. Long finger marks along my shoulder and harsh reddening marks that will be bruises in the morning.

I wash away the mud from my feet and wipe away the stains his brutal lips dragged across my face. Then sweep fingers through my hair. But I can't hide everything and my skin stings with reminders of him.

A soft knock on the door followed by, "It's me."

I unlock it for him, and he steps inside. His eyes slice to me then dart away, "Here."

He hands me a long red cloak with a hood.

"It's the only thing I could find that will cover everything…" he clears his throat again like he's stuck.

"Thank you." I take it from him and drape it around me.

"I, eh…" he drags a hand across his chin, "I have to go back to work, and you should get back to your party."

"Sure…"

I grab the door handle.

"You deserve better." He says it almost like an afterthought, and I can't help but scoff.

"Really? That's what you're going with?"

"Red…"

"Save it. You're a coward and a liar, and you're never going to change. You'll only ever be good at one thing … breaking my heart."

I let the door close behind me and re-join the party, knowing it will drag on forever, and I will ache and crave him till I get to go home and try to forget another night of broken promises and stupid mistakes.

As I step out of the bathroom, a pair of hands come from behind me and warp around my waste, "Sorry I'm late," Ethan whispers in my ear.

But I feel fragile, ruined, strained. I can't be held, not by him, not by anyone or I might fall apart.

"Hi." I push away from him and try for a smile, but it feels like a grimace. He takes a step back, creases mar his forehead as he examines me.

"Are you ok?"'

"Yeah, it's just been a really … stressful night."

"Well I'm here now, I can help with that."

Doubt it. *It's too late.*

Wolf

The door clicks closed behind her and I stare at myself in the mirror, gripping the basin so tightly my knuckles blanch.

Anger sweeps inside me and I know it's just masking the terror that's trying to grip me.

I'm afraid because, now that I've finally had Red, I've eradicated any doubts. I don't feel that safe indifference I usually do with other women. That certain confidence that whoever I shared myself with always wanted me more than I wanted her. Instead, I felt a want, a need so deep and strong I know it can easily grow into obsession, one that will ensure I'll take desperate measures to make her mine.

I barely make it through the rest of my shift. My body can't untangle itself from the feel of hers. Her smell is all over my jacket and drives hard nails of insanity into my heart. Like she's trying to embed her place inside it.

But I can't.

We can't, and I need to erase her before I submit to my desires.

I shrug off the jacket and throw it on the backseat. I can't go home, not when I know she'll be there. Not when all that separates us is a thin wall that I could break through. I throw Hunter some excuse about needing to think, and he smirks at me knowing what that usually means. I drive off leaving him to deal with the rest of the guys and paperwork.

The club is nearly empty at this late hour. The manager lets me in without any questions, and I sit at the bar nursing a cold beer, maybe the taste could wash away traces of Red. I spot the girl on the dance floor, cinnamon skin and glistening lips. She dances to the music.

I watch her. The way her hips ripple and move like water.

She's fluid and I wonder how she might move when she's above me.

She watches me watch her, and I can tell she's dancing just for me. I wink at her and she throws me a shy smile that makes my body sizzle. She's exactly what I need to erase any part of Red, just fuck her out of my system. I suck the rest of the beer down and stand up, giving the dancer a long look.

She gives me a timid smile and walks away coming back a minute later with a jacket and purse. I turn to leave, and we walk out into the night air. I let her into my car, and we drive to The Royal. They charge by the hour and know me well.

I park the car and she leans over, her fingers trace my jaw and her lips press against mine. My body jerks away, betraying me.

She gives me a quizzical look, "You okay?"

I clear my throat, "Yeah fine, just have to make a phone call. Go inside, room 678, start without me, I'm right behind you."

She smiles again and swipes her hand over my soft cock as she pulls away then gets out of the car. I watch her walk inside. Her ass swings and she's all curves. On any other night I would have had her half naked and barely breathing in the front seat, but as I catch a glimpse of myself in the mirror, I find a trace of her lipstick on my lips. I wipe it away.

She's the wrong shade of red.

I sit in the car for another minute then drive away.

37

TEN YEARS AGO

Wolf 18, Red 16

Red

My heart pounds so hard, I think it's going to crack a rib. I've never been so nervous. My body is in such a state of anxiety, it feels all over the place. I want to cry and laugh and sing and bounce off the walls, but all I do is check my light lipstick in the mirror for the hundredth time and go to the window.

People have started trickling in, Hunter made such a big deal of this day; I'm both delighted and annoyed.

I check my dress for the hundredth time, smoothing it along my belly.

A knock at the door brings me out of my reverie, and I turn to the door; Hunter is standing there, all smiles, "You look stunning, Red."

"Thanks." I run into his open arms, and he holds me tightly for a second then kisses the top of my head.

"Have a great time tonight." He says and my heart skips a few beats, as heat rushes to my face.

He waits for me to lead us down the stairs. Fairy lights hang along the railing and the lounge has been transformed into a dance floor by pushing all the furniture out of the way. There's a table full of alcohol I can't drink along the wall.

I know we—he—can't afford this. But he's asked me not to worry about it, and just for tonight, I don't … because I don't care. All I care about is what comes after, when *he* gets here. When he does all those things he promised. When he makes my sixteenth birthday really sweet and really unforgettable.

My cheeks flush with my thoughts as I take the last step.

The house fills up. I don't recognise most of the people, they're not my friends. But when Wolf Bennett and Hunter Evans throw a party, the whole world will show up.

The night grows rowdier. I spot Hunter with a girl. She's hanging off him and keeps kissing his neck, she reeks of desperation.

I make my way to the drinks table and sneak a beer, just to take the edge off. My body is so strained, I'm finding it hard to breathe. This party isn't really for me. It's fake, the only thing that's real is the way that Wolf makes me feel.

I grow tired of the party and I go to my room. The music vibrates through the floor and makes my bed rattle. I sit by the window like a lost girl and watch and wait as time drips by. It's nearly midnight when I finally spot him. My heart leaps from my chest.

He staggers into the back yard and high fives a few of his friends. They laugh and someone shoves a cup into his hand, he gulps it like its water.

I run to the mirror and look at myself again. I pull down on my dress, adjusting the waist, and run my hands down to flatten the crinkles. I fix my lipstick and look at myself one last time.

I suck in a galvanising breath.

This. Is. It.

I run to the window and search the garden, he's not there. I take another long sweep, but I can't spot him in the sea of unfamiliar faces. I rush downstairs and search the house, going from the kitchen and lounge looking everywhere, but I can't find him.

Wolf

I watch her from the shadows—she's sitting at the window waiting. For me. Waiting for me to keep a promise I never had any right to make and her brother is going to force me to break, breaking her with it.

I watch from my dark corner while the party is going on in full swing; she couldn't care less; she doesn't want this. She wants something else. Me.

My body caves and hollows as I take another sip of the sour whiskey I stole from my dad. I'm going to have to be really drunk to be able to put her through this.

To put myself through this.

She scours the party one more time then disappears. A few moments later she's downstairs and my breath stalls. She looks fucking stunning in a light blue dress that hugs all the slight feminine curves of her body. My own grows rigid. We're not children anymore.

She moves around the room, among strangers that don't really care about her, not the way I do. Her smile keeps falling away when she thinks no one is watching—except that I'm watching. I can't take my eyes off her. She's exquisite and my body is a war-ravaged city where two promises want to tear each other down, each more deadly and poisonous than the other. No matter whose side I chose, someone will get hurt, and I will be the big bad wolf in the middle of the bloody mess.

I swig the bottle and gulp down another sip—bravery in a bottle for a coward like me. I should go and talk to her like a man, instead I'm hiding in the shadows planning her demise. But it's not my fault, it's hers; she made me feel things I have no right to feel.

Even if I want to feel them.

I wait. I wait until I can barely stand and barely think, until I have had enough to drink to hope that some of the guilt will obliterate itself by morning—enough to help me forget what I'm about to do.

She's back at her window, her shoulders slumped. This party abandoned her long before she abandoned it. Her frantic eyes keep searching, and I'm about to show her what she wants to see.

Me.

I step out of the darkness and lunge myself at a group of familiar faces; I don't care who they are, they're standing just below her window, and they have more alcohol to help numb everything.

My stomach coils and twists as I dare to glance up and notice her window already empty.

I trudge through the group and make a beeline for Angela. She's been at me for months, begging me to have her, throwing herself at me at any given opportunity—and tonight she was going to get her wish at the cost of a splintered promise.

She smiles as she sees me coming, and I smirk at her. Her cheeks flush and I grip her wrist all the while keeping an eye out on the steps. When you're my size you'll stick out in any room, and right now I need to remain unseen.

I yank Angela with me into the kitchen and bend down to her ear, "You want me?" Bile rises in my throat.

She looks up at me, her eyes grow, pupils dilate, and her mouth spreads in a smile as she nods.

I pin her with my body, and she wraps her hands around me, prying them beneath the fabric of my shirt. I peak behind the door and spot Red again. She's standing like a perfect statue at the bottom of the stairs, her long neck craned, searching. Her beautiful face flawless and wondering and a shy smile that splits my fucking heart in two. She's devastatingly stunning and innocent, and I'm going to ruin her.

My heart falters, but I don't. I wait for her to rush to the garden then yank Angela off the wall and trudge up the stairs. She's like a rag doll being dragged behind me, and she hurries giggling.

I bypass Hunter's room and stop at Red's. I lean my forehead against the wooden door, all the muscles in my jaw dancing as I grit my teeth and steel my resolve.

I push her door open and pretend that not every single hair in my body stands with tension. She's everywhere, her sweet, delectable smell and innocent youth.

Angela runs around me and lands on the bed giggling.

Red's bed.

My eye catches the notepad on the bedside table. I pick it up. My vision blurs as I study the drawing. My breath hitches at the wolf boy looking back at me.

He has my eyes and my mouth and parts of me that seem so good, all moulded together into a wolf drawing. We are one in the same. A man and a beast. Except that once she sees me here, in her bed, she will know I'm only one of those things.

I put the pad down as Angela spreads her legs for me, "Come here big boy." I fucking hate it when people call me that. I suck in a long inhale, wishing I'd had even more to drink, then step closer to the bed.

She pulls me to her and rips at my shirt, and I let her.

Her eager mouth nips at me, and she leaves endless kisses on my neck and chest. I'm not into it; I'm barely hard, I'm barely even here, I know where I want to be.

"I've wanted this for so long," Angela's voice rips me into the past.

"I've wanted this for so long," her sweet sing song voice tugs at my heart, and her shy smile cuts into me.

"Me too."

"Fuck." I grumble as I think about Red, how her body should be the one beneath mine, how it should be her mouth I'm devouring. And I want her so badly my body wants to believe. I become so hard I'm in pain, and I deserve it except that I don't care. I tear at Angela's shirt and rip it open; her perky little tits bounce around and she squeals in surprise. Like a fucking little piglet.

Her tits feel all wrong and she tastes all wrong, and everything is all wrong and a second later Red bursts through her bedroom door and the world freezes.

"Get out." Angela screams as Red stands there. The colour draining from her beautiful face, which bends and crumples as her eyes burn so hot into mine, I feel like she's branded me.

"It's my room," she whispers a broken sound. "Get out."

Her eyes glisten with tears and her shoulders collapse while she just stands there and stares at me.

I watch her break as I stand up to my full height and loom over her. She wrenches her eyes away from mine.

"Oh, come on, don't be a baby. Let us finish." Angela is still talking as a single tear slices down Red's cheek, and it's all I can do not to take her into my arms and put her back together.

"Please just get out." Another quiet request that's worse than any other sound. I want her to scream or break something instead of just rip apart on the inside. I'm watching her destruction, the one I orchestrated, and there's not a thing I can do about it.

I grab Angela's wrist and rip her from the bed that's now rippled and ruined. Red turns sideways, and Angela giggles as she walks by her.

She just stands there, frozen in time in this moment, for all of eternity—and I know it's too late to take it all back, to resew the slash I've just ripped into her soul.

But I started and now I have to finish. The price has already been paid; the interest is just to ensure there will never be any refunds.

"Happy birthday, Red." I smirk at her as I walk out of the room, feeling like the piece of shit I am.

Angela is waiting for me, leaning against the master bedroom that's been abandoned for months. The door creaks as she opens it and giggles again, "This room is free." She steps in and I let her, while I make my way back downstairs and out the front door.

Soon enough, she will work out I'm not coming back.

My body aches, a searing devastating pain, like I've torn a giant hole inside of myself that's leaking everywhere. We were two pieces of the same cloth and now we're nothing but rags.

I shuffled home vowing to never step foot in that house again.

Red

The door closes behind them and I'm alone. Only the distant sound of music and laughter keeping me company, until even that fades away and the quiet grows longer, until I all hear is my insides snap like brittle glass, branching out inside me before imploding. The shards tear at my heart.

I stand until I feel so insignificant, I can't breathe. Till all I can see are his eyes, the way he blinked away all his emotions —all but indifference. My knees give way and I slump against my wall. My bed tainted, my room tainted, my dreams nothing but a jester's joke.

The sobs tear out of me in violent, angry cries. The tears fall through my fingers in hot desolate rivulets that smash into my dress.

Pain slices my inside as I try to find air through my ragged breaths.

I keep my eyes shut and look inside myself, searching for the chambers of my heart, watching as they beat ever slower. My heart is a deserted, old castle locking its doors for a final time, drawing down its curtains and shutting out light, where it will sit forever abandoned.

Thick thorny ivy wraps itself so tightly around it, it will be kept sealed forever, and the mere suggestion of using it will rip holes so big into my flesh, I'd know it would not be worth the pain, the agony, the anguish.

I watch my heart stop beating, knowing it will always remain empty and derelict , but will always stay safe— because no one would dare pierce that much ivy, that much growth, sustain that much damage to fill it up ever again.

When it's done, I open my eyes and water the ivy with my tears and cry until they too, turn to dust.

38

HUNTER 18, RED 16

Red

In the morning, my door creaks and I feel his presence. It's bulky and warm and I'm desperate for him to come closer and stay as far as humanly possible.

"Red?" Hunter whispers into my dark room.

"Yeah?" I whisper back, but mostly because I'm afraid that if I speak loudly, he'll hear everything I'm trying to hide.

"You awake?" I can hear the chuckle in his voice.

"No." I keep whispering, wanting all the loud noise inside my heart to die down so it could listen to my head and remember that if we just keep really still and really quiet we just might survive this.

My mattress dips with his weight as he sits on the edge of my bed. "Did you enjoy your party last night?"

"You mean your party?" I can't tame the bitterness that creeps into my voice.

He sighs. It's long and heavy and guilt stabs at my coiled stomach.

"There's something I need to tell you."

I wait.

"I'm leaving at the end of the year, with Wolf."

I suck in frozen air and wait for more.

"It's only to Southport. Wolf's parents have a house there, and it's only a twenty-minute drive to the uni…" his words drift off as a hot tear rolls free and sinks into my pillow.

"When?"

"At the end of the term. I figured I can get some summer work there. Get settled."

I nod as another tear leaks from my eyes and slides over the bridge of my nose, diving into my sheets.

"We've spoken to Wolf's mum, you can move into their house. They have heaps of space and you'll never be alone or hungry, you can finish school."

I let my eyes shut, sealing all my pain inside behind the darkness of my lids.

"Can you say something? Please?"

I don't.

I feel shredded like I've been torn to pieces; everything hurts, from the tip of my nose to my hardened nails, to my teeth and my feet and my heart. It slows, wanting to suffocate in its own misery.

Hunter sighs again and the weight disappears from my mattress. "I'm sorry Red, I just want more for myself than this."

I tip my head once hoping he'd catch the movement. He does deserve so much more, he's always given up so much, always sacrificed. I'd tell him I'm proud of him later when my heart remembers how to pump blood into my body instead of black angry ink that burns my veins and taints everything.

"I'm making breakfast," he says and then I know he's gone.

PRESENT DAY

Red

Wolf has vanished. When I get home after work, there's no sign of him and when I wake up, his door is shut. I'm not brave enough to wake him, not yet.

It's been two days since he's been inside me, since my body burned beneath his touch, and I know he's being cold.

I should have expected this.

The club is thumping, and the line is long. I cut ahead and get a bunch of filthy looks from dressed up girls that give Dean and Rob googly eyes.

"Hey Red," Rob smiles at me and cradles me in his giant arms.

"Hi." I smile at both boys, earning a few more death glares from the line of desperate women. It makes my insides glow, "I'm looking for Wolf."

They exchange a brief, well-practiced look that they think I don't notice. "He's just dealing with a situation at the moment." Dean reaches for the gold clip that holds the rope in place. The way he says it makes my stomach churn. "Want to wait inside for him? I'll get you a drink?"

"No thanks," I flash him another grateful smile. "Just tell him I stopped by."

"No problem." The boys grin at me as I walk away, feeling like one of his pathetic conquests, the one that can't let go. My stomach knits itself into twisted knots and I cringe. We both knew what it was, I should have never allowed myself to hope for more.

Wolf is nothing but a predator, whose touch and teeth and mouth crush hope to mere dust.

I call Ethan. It's time to make things right.

Wolf

The boys tell me she's been in to see me, and I feel a rush of guilt and relief. I've been avoiding her, running like a fucking coward.

I get home late, only when I'm sure she's asleep, and hide in my room till I hear her leave. I can't allow myself near her. I can't be in the same space, because if I am, I will tear her apart.

I want to mark her. Brand her like I'm marking my fucking territory. My fucking *property*. I want everyone else to smell me on her and know they need to keep their hands off—which is why, if I'm going to keep my promise to Hunter, I need to stay away—because next time we're together, I'm going to let all my barriers fall, and there's no fucking way in hell I'm stepping behind them again, not now that I've had her, tasted her, and know without a shadow of a doubt that Red belongs to me.

Red

I watch his easy smile from the other end of the table, his fingers laced in mine. He's serene. The opposite of what I am—a ball of stress and anxiety sits like a lump in my throat, and I can't seem to swallow it down.

"So, I know I've been busy lately at work, and I've let you down."

"No, it's ok." If only he knew what I'd done.

"I think I have a solution, a way for us to spend more time together."

"Oh?"

"I really like you Red, and I think we can really have something. But as long as I can't get you to myself, we will never know."

I nod. My stomach twists and churns.

It's been hard finding time to spend with Ethan, but now that Shaw has been inside me, I don't know that I want to be with anyone else. But then I think about the countless girls Shaw's been with before me and all the ones that will follow.

The pain scalds my insides.

"I want you to move in with me." He blurts it out like it's been sitting on the tip of his tongue for a while and he's finally found the courage to use the words.

I stare down into my coffee. We've only gone out a handful of times over the last two months. We haven't even slept together. Not that he hasn't tried.

"Did you hear me?" Some of his usual confidence sheds away.

"Yeah, I just…"

"It will get you away from your brother and that *friend* of yours," the word sounds hostile as it slips from his lips, "we

will have time together under our own terms, no inter-
ruptions."

He's excited, it's obvious in the way his mouth is stretched
into an eager smile and his hands squeeze mine and his eyes
are wide and glowing.

I suck in a long breath and take a sip of my coffee. It's
already too cold.

His face creases with a slight frown, and my stomach
clenches as I think about Shaw—the way he felt, the way his
lips burned my skin, the way he's been avoiding me for the
last two days.

"I know it's sudden, but we can take it slow." Ethan
pipes up.

I think about Dave and a string of other mistakes wearing
different names, there was Michael and James and Daniel.
The list goes on, the names might change but the mistakes
are always the same.

I force a smile and his mouth stretches into a thin line
when he looks at my face. "I don't think it's a good idea."

"I think you should reconsider."

I draw in a long breath and ease my hands out of his, "I
don't think I will. The job at the gallery is a great stepping-
stone for me. I've been saving and learning and soon I'll be
able to stand on my own two feet, and that's what I really
want. I want to try do this life thing on my own for a bit,
without having to rely on anyone."

"Is that what you really want? Or is this about that friend
of yours." His tone is no longer sweet.

"No. Me and him have only ever been friends and
nothing more. This is about making the right choices for
myself."

He sighs, "So where does that leave us?"

I rub my clammy hands on my thighs and look at his face.
He is lovely, but he's not Shaw.

"I see." He says, even though I'm yet to say the words, "For what it's worth, I would have given you the world, Red."

I nod as he stands and walks out of the coffee shop. The problem is, I don't want the world. I only want Shaw Bennett.

40

Red

The week slips by like water in my hands. Paperwork and acquisitions, couriers, sales and numbers, but my mind isn't where it should be. It's not with Caleb and Becca and art, it's with Wolf in the woods.

He's infected me and my days are consumed by his loss. I take him with me everywhere. His whispers haunt me in the night, and his marks decorate my body in shades of purple and yellow as my bruises heal and the long-furrowed scratches scab over.

I feel empty. And as the days scream towards my birthday, a sense of dread creeps over me.

I've hated every birthday in the last nine years. A dirty anniversary of heartbreak and pain, where I watch the ivy around my heart grow thicker and stronger and heavier with thorns and ugly things.

Caleb's voice hums in the back of my mind. The last of the paintings are getting picked up this evening and then there's money to deal with and profits to bank.

My phone rings and pierces the echoes of Wolf's voice.

"Hello?"

"Hey Red," Hunter sounds happy. It's suspicious.

"Hi?" He doesn't usually call unless he wants something, or I'm in trouble, "What's up?"

"Your birthday is on Saturday."

I shudder, "Yeah."

"We should celebrate."

"I'm not sure—"

"—Don't be daft. I've already booked a restaurant. We'll go out for dinner and after, whatever you want."

"Whatever I want?" I scoff. *I want to curl up in my bed and sleep the day away.*

"Within reason," he mocks an authoritative voice.

"Sure thing, *dad*." I can feel his grimace on the other end.

"Great. It's settled then."

"Is it? What if I've made other plans?"

He's quiet for a second, "Did you?"

Yes. With my bed, duvet, and pyjamas—and maybe a bottle of vodka. "No."

"Okay then, don't." He hangs up without another word. I hate when he does that.

"Sure, whatever you say," I mumble as I put my phone away.

Caleb is staring when I look up again. "What?"

"Was that Mr. Hot Stuff?" He wiggles his eyebrows and my stomach convulses.

"Stop calling him that!"

"Why? He is. Don't pretend you haven't noticed," he tuts at me.

"No. It was my brother. He wants to take me out on Saturday."

"Oh," His disappointment echoes my own, "that's nice," he's lost for words.

"Yeah, nice."

"You seem super excited about it."

"It's complicated."

"Dinner with your brother is complicated?"

I cover my face with my hands and groan, "It's a long story Caleb, I don't feel like getting into it."

At that he lets the papers fall from his hands and leans back into his chair, "Well now you have to tell me."

"Caleb." I whine.

He folds his arms across his chest like he didn't hear me and stares, anticipation painting his face.

I sigh, "It's my birthday."

His eyes grow large and his mouth pops open. "Your birthday? Girl, why didn't you say anything? Let's go out and paint the town, get you seen, laid even. Put a smile on that face of yours."

I grimace and my body quivers remembering Wolf's hands and lips and body imprinted on mine.

"I … I don't celebrate my birthday."

"What? Why?" His eyebrows furrow in deep lines.

"I just … Don't." I let my hands fall by my side and grip onto my jeans.

"Let's change that!"

"I have plans now."

"Cancel!"

"I can't."

"Come on Re—"

"—No. Just drop it Caleb, please "

He cocks his head for a second and glares at me then schools his face and straightens up. "Ok, let's get the courier sorted."

41

Red

For two solid days, we work on Becca's new installation and my portfolio. It's due in two weeks, and though I've chosen some of my best pieces, we both feel like it's incomplete.

Caleb riffles through my work, his face a kaleidoscope of emotions as he traces his fingers over inanimate objects sketched in dark, soft lead and brash strokes. He croons over the pieces of snatched faces, people in a crowd, a crying girl, an old toothless man, a homeless man cradling his dog, a stagnant sculpture in the park come to life on paper.

"They are incredible babe," he says, and I know he means it as his eyes linger on the boy who never grew up. He slams the portfolio shut, "But, it's still missing something, a pièce de résistance."

I nod. He's right. I need one more piece, one that conveys who I truly am as an artist, one that captures me as much as my subject.

Long walks after work have proven futile, my mind is too full by the emptiness my body feels. My heart is wounded, and my body still aches with bruises, both holding tight to the ivy that winds itself tighter inside me.

"I'll get something done," I promise Caleb, and he lets my portfolio drop to the table.

"Good. Now, let's get the rest of this installation planned."

Red

"What sort of restaurant is it?" I call out to Hunter from my room.

"One with chairs and tables, where people eat with knives and forks, and they bring the food all the way to the table."

I roll my eyes and remind myself it's only two hours with my annoying big brother and then it will be over. "But what do I wear? Casual? Smart?"

"Somewhere in between?" He calls back and I grind my teeth.

Fine. Something in between.

I grab a dress and slip it on just to see the row of bruises on my shoulders and arms. I throw it on the ground and search my cupboard. I find a short, black skirt and a long sleeve shirt that covers enough to hide the story written on my body. I pull on my Docs and brush fingers through my hair.

I'm something in between.

I walk into the lounge to find Wolf sitting on the couch.

My heart leaps to my throat, his eyes dart over me. A dark expression crosses his face. I didn't even know he was here.

He's dressed in his fitted suit pants and white button up that's rolled to the elbows, showing off his strong forearms. I wrench my gaze away as Hunter walks in. He's more casual than smart and I feel overdressed.

"Everyone's here. "

"Everyone?"

Wolf stands up.

"Yeah, Wolf is coming too."

"Why?"

Hunter shifts the weight to his other leg. "The more the merrier. Didn't think you'd mind, he's family," he shrugs and grabs his keys from the table. "Let's go." He closes the subject before I can protest.

He opens the front door and I slip through it, waiting for them to step out.

I follow Hunter to his car where he opens the back door for me. "I'm not sitting in the back," I say and get into the passenger seat before either of them can argue.

Wolf grumbles as he climbs into the back seat, and I can't help the smirk that worms its way over my face. I push my chair all the way back just for good measure.

Hunter climbs in, gives me a questioning look then takes off when I say nothing.

Wolf is almost sideways in the backseat, having no leg room.

The car is charged in an awkward silence as Hunter drives. I turn the radio on and find a tune to drown out the discomfort. With my face glued to the cold window, I watch the world flash me by.

We walk into the restaurant. Hunter should have said smart, there's nothing causal about this place. Pristine white tablecloths and silverware adorn the tables, most of which host guests dressed so elegantly they should be at a gala instead of a dinner. I grind my teeth, making a mental note to kick Hunter under the table. A multitude of eyes swing over to our party as we get shown to our table. Questioning eyes as their gazes swing from the two large men behind me and back to me. I can only imagine what they must be thinking.

We're seated and the eyes slowly fall away.

Hunter grabs a menu. "It's been forever since the three of us hung out together." He smiles and looks at his menu, missing the sharp look exchanged between me and Wolf.

Neither of us want to be here. That much is clear.

"What are you having?" Hunter asks.

"Burger." We say in unison and exchange another look.

Hunter puts his menu down, "I bring you two to this posh place for you guys to have burgers?"

We both shrug and smile, and some of the tension melts away.

The waitress comes over and her gaze boomerangs between Hunter and Wolf. Her thoughts scream loudly as she writes down our order and bites her bottom lip. I know what kind of sandwich she'd be ordering if they were on the menu.

The waitress disappears and I notice the extra swing in her ass. Hunter does too. Wolf hasn't taken his eyes off his plate since we've walked in.

Hunter wrenches his gaze away from the waitress and turns his attention back to me. "Tell me about your—" his phone interrupts mid-sentence, and he frowns when he sees the number, "Sorry, I have to get it."

He listens as a muffled voice speaks on the other end. "Now?" He's quiet for a second. "But I've…" Another pause as he nods. "Can't…" He frowns. "Okay. I'll be there soon."

He hangs up and his crestfallen face tells me all I need to know.

"It's fine," I tell him before he can speak.

"I'm so sorry, the client needs to go to Madrid."

"Now?"

He shrugs, "Guess so."

"And no one else can do it but you?"

"She asked for me by name, I can't turn down clients."

"I know."

"It's just one night, maybe two, and then I'll make it up to you." His lips stretch into a thin line.

"Sure."

"Wolf can still help you celebrate." The ivy around my heart suffocates me as it tightens, and my brother gives me a weak smile.

"Sure."

He stands up and draws me into his arms, "Happy birthday Red, I'll make it up to you."

I give him a tight smile and he hurries out of the restaurant, leaving Wolf and I in silence.

"You don't have to stay," I whisper to him.

"I want to." His gaze catches mine and holds me in place. "About the other night…"

"Not now."

"Okay," he falls quiet and nods. "Drink?"

"No. I think I just want to go."

"Red."

"Please." He grimaces for a long second.

He flags down the waitress and asks for the bill. She gives us a long sideways glance before disappearing and leaves us in a cold awkward silence.

He drops a few bills on the table and stands up, not waiting for her to come back. "Shall we?"

"Thanks," I say relieved, wanting to get out of here and away from him. This place feels suffocating and too bright, and I wish I'd never come.

Wolf pulls open the door and we step into the cold night. We join the river of humanity that flows along the bustling street, and I'm swept away by the sounds and smells of London at night. Small alleys and hundreds of expensive eateries, where street art drips over cold walls, and where the homeless eat from the palm of their hands. It's a city of contradictions and beauty, and I let it sweep me away—away from my problems and another disastrous birthday.

Wolf catches up to me and falls into step. His hand slides down mine and our fingers interlock. My skin burns with the touch and my body shivers.

"What are you doing?"

"It's still your birthday. Do you want to do anything?" he asks as we walk through throngs of smiling, happy people out for a night out, one they wouldn't want to forget but likely would.

Just like I want to forget.

I shrug and let the cold air sting my flushed cheeks, "Can we just walk for a while?"

"Sure."

He lets me lead. Our hands remain interlaced, entwined just like the ivy—I can feel it grow and tighten, wanting to protect the hollowed chambers inside.

"How's work going?" he tries for conversation.

"I don't want to talk about my work."

He frowns, "Well, what do you want to talk about?"

I stop and glare at him. The words stinging my tongue even as I bite it. I turn away, "Nothing."

He grips my shoulder and spins me, "Tell me, say what you want to say."

"Say what I want to say?" Anger rises inside me, "You fucked me in the woods and the first thing you said was not to tell anyone, like I was a mistake. Then you disappeared for a week."

"Red, you've never been a mistake."

"Well, you've always made me feel like one."

He grips the back of his neck and looks up to the dark sky for a moment before his eyes catch mine, "I'm sorry."

"It doesn't change anything."

"I'm sorry if I've made you feel that way."

"You have no idea how I feel."

"So, tell me." He leans into to me, close. Too close.

I rip away from him. "No."

"Why not?"

"Because you make me feel too vulnerable, too exposed, like I want so much more. And you—you want to have fun and the minute this gets anything other than just *fun*, you'll leave like you did before, even after we… you…" my voice drops away.

"You can't keep holding that against me, we were kids."

"I loved you, and you promised."

"I shouldn't have done that."

"There are a lot of things you shouldn't have done." I say it, even as my body floods with hot need washing away the cold lies.

He reaches out for me, but I step out of his grasp. "Red…"

"Can we just go home now?"

"No! It's your fucking birthday, and I want you to have a good night."

I scoff and turn away.

"Don't do that. Let's go do something, anything you want, come on."

"Wolf…" his name falls out in a heavy sigh. He's proven time and again that all the things I want, I can't have. Not from him.

"Come on, *anything* … a drink, a dance —"

"—will you sit for me?" The words slip out of my mouth before I can stop them, and a strange beautiful look crosses his face.

"Sit? For you?" His head cocks to the side

"Let me draw you."

"Draw?"

"For my portfolio, I need just one more piece." I bite my lower lip, thinking I've made a mistake.

"Sure," he flashes me a set of perfectly white teeth, "where?"

"Home?"

He nods and pulls out his phone, two minutes later we slide into the back seat of an Uber heading back to the apartment. His hands find mind, our fingers laced together like for some reason he has a problem letting go. I try not to think about the rush of heat that works its way through my body, the flames licking at the ivy wrapped so tightly around my heart. Instead, I concentrate on the budding, giddy excitement about drawing Wolf.

I used to know his face so well. All the chords and lines and mechanisms that made his eyes shine and his face pull, and his sadness that hid behind his slick smiles.

Now he's all sharp angles and harsh lines, a few faint scars litter his otherwise flawless skin. I want to see what lies behind his stark exterior; I want to find the strings that hold his heart and wring them till his emotions cascades out and spill onto his face so I can take them for myself and show him to the world.

The Uber pulls up and we step outside. Wolf leads me up the stairs, opens the door, ushers me inside, then seals it behind us. My stomach flutters, and somewhere, it all feels so final—like something is about to end, except I don't know what it is.

4 3

Red

"So, do I just take my clothes off now … or?" he releases my hand and takes a long step towards the couch. A slow dark smile splits his beautiful face.

"What? No." I feel the heat rush to my face as he smirks. I walk over to the kitchen and bring one of the chairs over, placing it in the middle of the room, the back faces the couch, "Sit."

He straddles the chair looking too big for it, my body stirs watching him mount it and slide forward, his hands hanging off the side.

"Rest your hands over the back and rest your chin on top." He complies easily. His dark eyes follow my movements as I grab my sketch pad and pencils and sit on the couch in front of him and allow my eyes to rake over his face.

"So, what now?"

"Now? You sit and I draw."

I bring the pencil to the paper and study Wolf's beautiful face. He has the kind of beauty that makes girls stop in their tracks. They pause as if they forget how to breathe, then turn a sharp, harsh crimson as he meets their gaze. He loves the reaction. It etches a smirk on his face and it's his first clue that they'd go with him wherever he asks. But I want to see beyond his skin and flesh, beyond his perfection, where his pain hides.

My eyes settle on his and his dark, intense expression. I bring my hand to the paper where it moves almost as if my mind is a composer and my hand is playing its symphony. My hands move on instinct.

"Can I talk? When you do this?"

I grab my 2B and shade a little as I lift my eyes from the paper back to his face, "If you must, just don't move!"

The lines around his eyes soften, "You always this bossy?"

"Only with my subjects."

He chuckles and his eyes lighten, like someone had opened a door behind them, but only halfway. His hands fall away, and he pushes one through his hair moving the strands aside, morphing the shape of his angles and shadows.

My eyes narrow and I glare at him, "I said don't move."

He barks out a small laugh and annoyance slithers under my skin. I set my pad aside and walk over to him. He stills, his gaze on my face as I thread my hands through his hair and push it back into place. He stops breathing as I touch him and steals my breath as his hands fall on my hips.

I wrench them away and rest them on the chair then angle his head once more. I bend down and look into his eyes, "Now, don't move."

As I draw the lines, they take on a life of their own. They scratch into the pad like the scratches he's left on my heart and my skin. I can see all my emotions as they blend into his face. He is my endless tormentor and my greatest desire, and I wonder if I'll ever be able to truly capture everything he's always meant to me.

Wolf

I watch the pencil roll between her lips and my body hardens, already straining under her sharp eyes, like she's looking underneath my skin searching for all my vulnerabilities. I don't want to be unravelled by her. I school my face, keeping a mask of nonchalance, but her looks are like deep tendrils that burrow inside me and search for more. I shift in my chair, my hard cock straining against my pants.

She shoots me an angry look, and I apologise for the hundredth time while my body heats under her intense gaze.

"Why did you never go to UDLA?"

She throws me a look that implies I should know and asking her was a stupid move, "You know why."

"I really don't. You could have applied for financial aid, there would have been other ways."

"Maybe," she chews on the end of her pencil, her teeth sink into the wooden rod.

"You were so talented. Are still." I smile at her.

"Stop moving, Shaw!"

"Just tell me why then."

"And then you'll sit still?" she asks over a sigh.

I shrug. I refuse to make her any more promises.

She doesn't stop drawing as she speaks and looks up only to steal snatches of my face.

"I guess I lost motivation."

"That's bullshit, Red. You're always stuck in your sketches."

She sucks in a long breath and remains silent.

"Red?"

Her eyes dart up, and for the first time I notice them glisten. I want to get up and take her in my arms, but I think she'll be more pissed at me if I move. Even if it's for the right reasons.

"I couldn't."

"Couldn't what?"

"I couldn't draw any more."

"What do you mean? You could always draw."

She scoffs a bitter, sad sound, and her eyes latch onto mine and all I can see is pain. "Do you remember the last piece I drew?"

I nod, she has no idea how much it meant to me. Half boy half-wolf. both lost, each needing each other—the boy needs the strength of the wolf and the Wolf seeks the companionship of the boy.

"Of course. It was amazing."

Her chin tips a little and her eyes latch on to the paper where her hands skillfully move around.

"After that night," the way she says it holds so much bitterness and pain, my heart clinches with guilt, "it was hard." She swallows and her eyes stay fixed on the paper, "You crushed me," her voice quivers and my insides feel like shattering, "I had to push through all that heartbreak, all that pain. I had to store it all away so I could keep breathing every day. I know it sounds dramatic now, but I was so young and so in love."

I don't miss her use of the word 'was'. It stabs deep in my gut.

"I ripped that piece in half and it ripped something inside me. Then you guys left, and I was alone. I had to survive. So, I pushed everything down, so deep down I had to make myself a rock till I felt nothing. And when you feel nothing, you can't create."

"Red —"

"Don't. Please don't apologise again, I can't fucking stand it."

Her words silence me.

"It's in the past. You guys left and Hunter's money just wasn't enough. I couldn't be a starving artist when I couldn't do art, so I got a job I hated, and a guy that wasn't who I wanted. I guess I fell into a holding pattern, where it was easier to get Hunter to bail me out than have to deal with reality."

She gives me a quick glance before concentrating on her work.

A swirl of emotion tornados through me, "But you're drawing again now?"

She nods.

"What changed?"

She sucks in a long breath and finally meets my gaze, "You're not the only one who broke my heart. I guess enough emotions managed to fill all the emptiness, and I found my creativity."

She holds my gaze for another beat before the art beckons her back.

"This is torture," I whine.

"You're a baby, I'm almost done."

"You said that half an hour ago."

"Well maybe if you stop moving, I'd be done already."

"About your birthday…" I start, even though she asked for no more apologies.

"I need to draw your mouth now, so how about you keep it closed?"

I let out a long breath as her hand goes back to the pad and her teeth sink into her bottom lip.

Fuck, she has no idea what she's doing to me.

Red

I set my pencil down and study my sketch. Wolf stares back at me from the paper, his dark tousled hair falls across his brow almost touching his melancholy eyes that contrasts his playful smile. He is a beautiful contradiction. And despite the years, I can still see the same man I knew ten years ago—his softness disguised by carelessness, his pain as nonchalance.

"I'm done," I say, and he lets out a long-suffering sigh, stands and rolls his neck.

"About time."

"Stop complaining. That didn't take that long." I look at the clock, just over an hour. I don't need him to add all the fine details and final lines. "Anyway, you said I could do anything, and this is what I wanted. Thank you."

He steps in to look at my piece and I hold it to my chest, "Not yet."

He stops and grunts then clutches the back of his neck and his fingers dig into the flesh, "I got you something."

"You did?"

He looks a little sheepish. "Yeah, it's in my room. Stay here."

He turns to leave and I follow him, I've never been very good at following the rules.

He crosses his bedroom as I cross the threshold. At his bedside table, he pulls out the drawer and takes out a thick rectangular object wrapped up in black paper and sealed with a red silky ribbon.

He turns and freezes to find me in his room.

"I told you to wait."

"I have been."

"Red," he warns but I step further into the room, "what are you doing?"

I step closer and reach for the gift in his hand, "I want my present."

"Here." He pushes it into my hand.

I let it drop on the bed and his eyes follow the gift then come back to my face, "The one you owe me."

"Fuck," he mumbles to himself, "Red —"

But I don't let him finish this time, I push myself up on my tiptoes and find his lips. Wolf's hands wrap around my waist and draw me flush against him. I tilt my head back and our lips mash together in a hungry, demanding kiss like we've both been starved for too long. My mouth opens and his tongue finds mine, and I moan into his mouth.

My nails bite into his muscular back and I reach for his shirt, tugging, tearing, desperate for his flesh against my own.

He lets me pull away the shirt and my breath stalls. On his left peck, a tattoo of a half boy, half wolf stares back at me, the haunted face ripped in two.

"Shaw… you took it?"

"You said it was for me."

"But how? I ripped it."

"I ripped us apart, and I've regretted it every day since." His confession ripples the air between us.

"Shaw…"

I trace my fingers along the delicate lines. He hisses at the touch, the haunted eyes tell a story of a broken boy, one that's now the man standing before me. I search his face, but his body is the one answering.

Wolf grabs my wrist and yanks it away from the tattoo. His lips find mine once again in a bruising demanding kiss. He lifts me up and I instinctively wrap my legs around his waist, and he clings to me with a possessive desperate hold. His kisses get deeper and needer with each swipe of his tongue. My hands wind around his neck and weave through his hair as he walks me over to the bed where I let myself untangle from him.

His big body blankets mine, his hot breath tickles my skin when his soft lips find refuge in my neck and along my jaw then fuse with my own. Every time he kisses me somewhere, the rest of my body is jealous and needy and wants to feel him just as eagerly and desperately. I inhale him, memorising every nuance of every tick of his muscles as he kisses me and exhales sharply with a groan.

My heart thrashes in my chest, as with each touch he hacks through the ivy wound tight around it. His hands rip at my shirt, tearing it away. Wolf's hands are everywhere, a long powerful waterfall that cascades in long streams down my body, he follows every curve and dip, sending shivers down my spine and a hungry need down to my core.

His fingers draw long lines into my skin, like he's marking me, branding me, making me his. All the while his lips fuse to mine, singeing me with his savage desire. He slides a finger down my throat, the nail biting into my skin, leaving a hot angry trail of memory. He grips my bra and pulls it in a harsh, demanding sweep, pulling it off my body, uncaring and desperate, leaving behind harsh marks that will stay with me long after he's gone.

"Fuck," he hisses as his dark eyes take me in, "so fucking beautiful."

His hands drag along my body, fingers feathering over my hard, aching nipples then withdraw again and again and again, till I whimper with desperation.

"Wolf, please touch me."

"I am," he teases just as he rolls his thumb over a nipple.

"Wolf," I beg, and his face splits open in a dangerous smirk that makes my body ache.

"I've waited so fucking long for this Red, I will make it last as long as I want. I'll give you your birthday present in the way I should have all those years ago. I should have taken you first." His moth twists for a second and he dips down to suck on my neck, "But, I will promise you this, this will be the last time I am this gentle and this kind." He smirks then dips his head his tongue flickers over a nipple, ripping away at my sanity.

Gentle? I shudder beneath him.

His fierce mouth closes around my nipple and I moan as

his teeth drag and tease and bite. I arch my back, wanting him to take more of me, all of me and I feel his smile curl along my skin.

His fingers slither down to my belly and tug at the fabric of my skirt and underwear, he rips it away and I am naked on Wolf's bed, caged in his arms, in the place I've always wanted to be. Light drips into my exposed heart as the ivy falls limply away, and the empty chambers begin to echo with an old forgotten beat.

His fingers creep along my thighs and he groans as he touches my wetness, the sound fills me like his fingers, and I'm already losing myself to him.

Then ever so slowly he pulls out, only to rake his finger up and down my throbbing, aching pussy. His tongue rolls over my nipples and sweat breaks across my body as I'm flooded with heat and need and a desperate ache to end this torture, which I want to endure forever.

I scratch at his back, wanting him to smother my body, to be inside me, to break me in every possible way; and still he holds himself just an inch above and lays long lingering kisses on my skin and nipples. He nips and grazes and licks and sucks till I think my body might liquefy under the pressure and soon I will be nothing but a pool of sweat and desperate unanswered need.

"Please…"

My breath comes in short, desperate pants as Wolf's fingers taunt me and his gaze burns me. He watches as I come apart with his hands all over me. I grind myself against him—wanting more, needing more—the edge is so close and then he pulls away, leaving me empty and hungry. My need unanswered. His mouth crashes against mine, stealing my desperate, disappointed moans for himself, claiming them as his.

"You are so fucking beautiful, Red," he says on a reverent breath, a sound that ripples through my body.

"Shaw…"

He pulls away from my touch and leaves a trail of kisses along my needy body, till his mouth dips between my legs and his hair tickles the inside of my thighs.

At the first flick of his tongue, I think I might explode. He groans as he tastes me and I buck as he teases my over sensitive flesh, unprepared as pleasure ratchets up my spine. He grips my thighs, his fingers dig into me, holding me in place. My fingers plunge into his hair and I rip at the strands, pulling, tugging too hard, but he doesn't care. He devours me till every sense is nothing but white light, and I am nothing but sensation and pleasure, and I scream his name till there is nothing left but my thrashing heart as I cry out and grind into his face.

I am nothing but a collection of bone and beautiful sensation when he pulls away and rips his jeans and boxers tossing them away. My gaze rakes over his beautiful features, from his face to his muscular torso partitioned by a fence of dark hair that arrows to his massive cock. It's so long and hard, the vein pulsates with gnawing need.

He blankets me with his body and his forehead falls to mine as he plunges inside me, and all reason is gone, and all doubt is gone, and we are one.

"Shaw," I whisper his name as he hisses, the muscles of his neck stretch taught. He stills in the deepest parts of me and pleasure crackles everywhere. His mouth finds mine and he pulls out then smashes inside, forcing me to break the kiss so I can gasp for air.

My fingers dig into the firm muscles of his back, which grow rigid as his hips buck and plunge into me. Deeper, harder, and still I want more, all he has to give me.

We are the current and his tide drags me along towards endless savage pleasure. His hips piston and the muscles of his back strain. He is flesh and need and he pounds into me past a point of no return till a tortured sound slips from his lips, and I am unhinged around him, pleasure spills inside me like a hot all-consuming flood, and with a final, suffocating groan, he surrenders to pleasure.

He draws me to him, driving ever deeper as his rigid body bows and breaks beneath the carnality.

He collapses, his forehead clings to mine for a second and our eyes collide. His face is painted in bliss and his lips drag a long blistering kiss from me before he rolls away, our lungs fighting for air, our bodies burning, humming flesh.

4 4

Wolf

I wake up to her hot body pressed against me. Her delicate skin burning mine, I breathe her in. She smells sweet, like fruit, and body wash, and sweat, and me. I grin and shudder at the thought. Startled at the way it takes my breath away, knowing it's not just her curves and softness I crave, but all of her. Aware that my feelings for her are already too big and too dangerous.

I stroke the length of her neck and she purrs, making my body hum with electricity as her ass rubs my groin with her movements. Her lithe body, her soft moans, the sweetness of her skin—it does things to me, filling me with a sense of urgency that rattles me, like if I don't show her how I feel, she'll slip through my fingers.

My teeth sink into her shoulder and she groans my name. I don't care, I want her to know me. I want her to know my greed, to feed my need for her.

I release her and her head slashes over her shoulder, her hungry eyes catching mine.

"Good morning," I whisper into her hair, and she squirms around me as my hands roam her naked flesh and dip between her legs, snatching her breath. I cup her chin and force her gaze to mine, I want her with me, I want to see how I affect her.

Her mouth parts and her brow furrows a little as her hips begin to move, seeking the pleasure she wants to steal from me. I snatch my hand away and roll her on her back then capture her lips in a slow drugging kiss as I slip into her. A soft cry bleeds from her lips and I start to move inside her. Slow, calm strokes that have her writhing beneath me. I press my forehead against her and drive in again, savouring how good she feels—this girl, the only one I ever wanted, the only one I've ever felt anything for, the only one I'll be willing to risk everything for.

Her breaths are sharp and hard, and her clammy skin glues to mine as I pound harder into her. Her beautiful face twists and contorts in that delicious agonised pleasure she's chasing. That only I can give her. Her nails dig long furrows into my back. I am transfixed. Her growing, desperate moans sear my soul, rip open a fierce ache to keep her clawing at me. Always.

I slam into her, meeting the desperate way that she pushes into my thrusts till her hands grip at my waist and she cries out my name, and her pussy clenches around my cock, tearing a heavy groan from me as pleasure ripples through my spine and explodes inside me in violent, splendid waves of pleasure.

I fall away catching my choppy breath and pull her to me, needing her body against mine, already aching for more of her. My need tinged with fear knowing this hungry, impatient thirst for her will never be sated, will always demand to be fed, and I realised, that for the first time in my life, I am willing to take desperate measures to not just make her mine, but keep her.

"Shaw," she snuggles around me, her limbs tangle around my body and send shivers that stir my desires.

I kiss the top of her head and pull her closer. We lay in silence. Neither one wants to fracture the moment, to ask the questions, to wonder if this will end as soon as I release her.

She pulls slightly away, and her lips brush mine in a delicate kiss that heats my skin, "Thank you for my birthday present," she whispers, and my heart threatens to buckle.

"Is that all it was?" I ask and find the long column of her neck, running my tongue along her skin then nip at her shoulder.

She sucks in a sharp breath and our eyes lock. "I need a shower."

She slips out of my touch and I let her go. I watch her lithe body move, she's delicate lines of sweetness, and I'm loath to watch her go.

She flicks me a shy smile as she closes the door behind her, and my head falls back into my pillow. I screw my eyes shut for a second and make the decision for both of us.

Red

My body hurts, but it's a good hurt; it's the kind of pain that comes from being thoroughly fucked and owned—and Shaw made me feel like he owns me, like I could be completely his. But when it comes to him, I know everything runs on a ticking clock. By tonight he'll move on and make another girl feel like she belongs only to him. So, I don't examine how my heart feels or the kind of hurt that might be inflicted on if it I think about that reality too long or too hard.

For one night he was my balm, stripping away the dead

scarred remnant of a night that burned my soul to the ground.

I step into the shower and let the hot water run along my skin, burn away the last remaining pieces of Wolf. If I keep lying to myself, maybe in the end, I'll believe that letting him go is what I really want. What we both want.

I let my head fall back and the water spill across my face when the door opens and Shaw steps into the shower with me. His beautiful face creased with emotion; his gaze ruthless, angry, full of savage desire. He cradles my face in his hands and his lips crush mine.

He breaks the kiss long enough to glare at me with a scorching look, "You don't get to wash me away," he growls.

A strangled sound falls from my lips as his smash against mine, and his body crushes me into the cold wall. His mouth hungry and bruising. My hands find his neck and slither up to his hair.

He wrenches his lips away and falls to his knees, then tucks his face between my legs. His tongue punishes me like I've done something wrong. My hands rip into his slick, wet hair and my head falls back against the wall as he inflicts his torture on me. Heat bites my body and stings my feverish skin as he keeps me on the edge. Licking over, around and below the one place I need him to, bringing me to the brink just to hold back, over and over, denying me to the point of mindlessness.

I moan in desperation and yank his hair hard—too hard—but he doesn't seem to care. Instead, I feel his smile against me. At last his talented tongue finally hits my aching clit. He holds me as I buck, gripping my thighs. His nails dig into my skin, as my bones turn to jelly and pleasure splinters across my body. I cry out his name, a reverent, broken sound. His mouth remains locked on my clit till I shudder against him. When he finally releases me, it's to stand and lift me up. My wobbly legs wrap around him in easy surrender.

He kisses my neck, and licks his way up where his gritty voice growls in my ear, "I don't just want one night with you Red."

He lines his cock up with my sensitive pussy.

"What do you want?" I ask on a shallow breath.

"More," he growls as he thrusts forcefully into me.

My breath stalls and I don't know if it's the words or the way he's pounding inside me, punishing, forceful, like he means it.

His mouth closes on my shoulder and he bites the skin, groaning as he does. His thrusts get quicker, more demanding as my hands slide along and dig into his slick, wet shoulders, fighting for grip as our bodies collide.

His fingernails bite into my hips, clinging to me in a possessive harsh hold Pleasure crackles inside me, and I cry out his name as he thrusts a final time. His body jerks, staggers, and shudders against mine as he lets out a new kind of groan, it quavers and breaks, and it's desperate and loud and echoes against the tiles as he finds his own release.

He sets me down and pulls me to him where I melt against his burning skin and his lips brush mine.

"Shaw." I give him a small smile as my heart skitters.

"I want everything," he whispers and nuzzles my neck, and I draw in a shuddering breath. My heart daring to beat a little faster at his words.

"I want that too," I try to push away, "But —"

He cuts me off with a bone melting kiss that holds too many promises I'm afraid he won't keep.

"No buts." He breaks away only to speak, then his lips are back on mine, feverish and demanding, making me his with every swipe of his tongue and stroke of his hand along my back.

"Shaw…"

"We've wasted too much time. *I've* wasted too much time."

Regret shades his eyes, "No buts, just us. You and me. I want more, Red, I want everything."

"You're selfish, you take what you want without consequences."

"I am selfish, and I want you all to myself."

"You've already broken me once."

"Then let me heal you."

I allow his mouth to claim mine, his hands to take what they want from me, and my heart to dare hope.

<hr>

He's in the kitchen, his skin flushed, his wet hair tousled in a frenzied mess. His face splits with a sexy grin as he walks towards me and hands me a cup of coffee. His lips seal on mine and he kisses me, it's tender and beautiful and my knees threaten to buckle.

He steps away and grabs something from the counter, "You still haven't opened your birthday present."

Heat stings my face as my body remembers the gift I did get. I reach for the wrapped parcel and put my coffee down.

"Thank you." I study the gift, his eyes locked on mine are coloured by anticipation.

I pull the red ribbon and strip away the gift wrap. The breath rushes from me and my gaze darts from the book to Shaw.

"First edition Count of Monte Cristo. How?"

"You seemed to really want it."

"When? I've never told you anything about that."

He shrugs and his lips tilt at the corner, "That day when you had your interview."

My brow furrows as I search for the memory.

"You stared at this book for ages."

"I could have just been looking."

"You could have, except that you have two other Alexander Dumas first editions."

"You went through my stuff?"

"Hunter mentioned it once."

"Once?"

"A few years ago." His brow digs in as if he's trying to remember.

"And you remembered?"

"Your favourite colour is blue even though most people assume it's purple. You take your coffee with a half a teaspoon of sugar and just enough milk to tame the black. You never let your guard down and you don't let anyone in, and that's probably mostly my doing. You look down when you're anxious and bite down on your lower lip when you're concentrating, and the sound of you coming on my cock is the sweetest thing I've ever heard."

I swipe at him with my hand even as a lump stretches in my throat and fire courses through my blood. Somewhere in all my anger for him I didn't realise Shaw has been storing every little bit of information he'd ever learned about me.

I gape at him with a slightly open mouth and question everything I thought I knew about him.

His arm winds around me, "I know everything about you, Red, and anything I don't, I intend on finding out."

His lips are on mine and the kiss is hard and long as my fingers weave in his hair, and my legs wrap around his waist and our coffee gets forgotten.

45

Red

Stealing time with Wolf is my new favourite obsession. It's like learning a new art form. Not just the sneaking around and hiding from the world, but learning Wolf himself. The way his body responds to mine, the way his tongue dances when he kisses me long and deep, the desperate sounds he makes when he slides his cock into me, and the way his eyes screw shut, and mouth falls slightly open when he comes.

The more I learn about him, the more I want to know. The way his low laugh rumbles through me, and how his heart speeds up when he holds me close, and the way he kisses me, like it's the last time each time he leaves my bed for his.

He is more than lines and shapes on paper, but a deep well of kindness and light he doesn't show others. Shaw, the man I used to know, the one before he became a lone wolf.

We find a dance that we master. He sneaks into my bed at night or finds me after work, where we sneak into the back alley and he fucks me like a whore while making me feel like his queen. We are shades of grey. Lack of sleep coats us as we find each other in stolen moments. But when I lie in his arms, I am wide awake pinching myself that this is my new reality.

When I am not with Shaw or at work, I sink into my art, my portfolio almost complete. The last piece done. I stare at it and my body fills with a kind of warmth I've not felt for a long time. Pride. I have captured him in a way I never thought I could. I just hope that when it's displayed everyone else can see his many faces, not the lone wolf act that he gives off so effortlessly—the cocky nonchalance—but his deep, bruising sadness and endless loyalty, his fierce protectiveness and his endless haunting love.

I'm so deep into my work it takes me a while to realise my phone has been ringing.

"Hi." I can't help the stupid grin that smears itself across my face. He makes me giddy.

"I want to take you out."

"That's a bit harsh, I thought things were good between us."

He chuckles and it makes me feel warm and fuzzy. I like that I can make him do that. "On a date."

"Date? You date?"

"I want to date *you*." He's suddenly a little sterner and butterflies swarm in my belly.

"I think I'd like that."

"I'll pick you up after work."

"I'm not really dressed—"

"—just the way I like you." He quips and hangs up on me.

I hate that I smile and melt into my chair.

"A movie?" I ask as he walks me into the theatre. I feel cheated.

"What's wrong with a movie?"

I think about all the reasons I can give him, and how I'd rather talk to him over a plate of food or a long drive. But even as I conjure up a hundred and one reasons, his lips meet mine in a long, burning kiss, and I realise any time with Shaw alone in the dark would do.

"Nothing," I shrug as he pulls away.

He smirks and leads us towards the theatre.

"Before we go inside—"

"Yeah?" he quirks a single eyebrow.

"I want to tell Hunter."

He nods, his lips stretch into a thin line and he squeezes my hand, "We will, just not yet."

"But why?"

Wolf grips the back of his neck and sighs, "It's not that simple."

"How is it not simple, you're his best friend."

"And his business partner and his housemate…" he sucks in a deep breath, "It's not the right time."

I sigh. "Okay, but we do have to tell him, soon."

He nods and smiles, and his mouth covers mine in a long warm kiss that makes my head spin and my heart flutter. "Soon, I promise."

I concede and he leads us to our seats.

The room darkens and a hush falls around us as the movie starts playing. I relax into my seat and get absorbed into the movie. And as we continue to watch, his hand slips onto my thigh and his long fingers draw slow leisurely circles on my skin. He grabs my skirt and bunches it up, pulling it up my legs with no hesitation on his part. I look around, no one is in our row, which is why I don't grab his wrist or ask him to stop as his fingers press into my underwear. When I look at his face he's staring straight ahead, as if he's completely immersed in the movie.

He doesn't look at me once as his fingers slip into my underwear. I suck in a stuttered breath and allow my head to fall against the seat, pretending to watch just like him, even as self-consciousness gnaws at my edges. Not that it matters. I stare into the big screen as Shaw's fingers taunt and tease, images on blurring into colour.

My body tenses against his fingers, my hands clutch my seat, my hips grind, seeking relief as pleasure builds inside me. He reads me, my needs, his rhythm matches mine. At last he turns to look at my face, his eyes dark and intent. My lips hurt from holding in my desperate sounds, my feet feel numb, and my hands cling to my seat as I implode with a force so intense my whimpers escape and Shaw swallows them into his mouth, silencing me. When he pulls away, he takes his fingers with him and puts them to his mouth.

"Fuck, you taste good," he says as he licks his lips and his eyes return to the screen as if he didn't just ruin me. "I can't wait to have seconds later," he growls.

"Later?" I shudder.

His gaze finds mine one once again, his face set in severe intensity, "And after that, and after that and always." He's so serious my heart forgets to beat.

"You overwhelm me Shaw," I barely manage.

"I want to overwhelm you."

And he does, later when we're alone, he shows me just how much more of him I get to enjoy.

The days keep falling away, and moments without him become almost painful till sleep becomes a memory, and every waking hour is spent kissing him and touching him and having him for myself.

Hunter

I step into the bright sunshine and squint for a second before I settle my sunnies over my tired eyes. Another long shift that ended in some girl's bedroom. I need food and sleep. I start walking towards the tube station when I hear my name. I look up and down the road till I see a blonde girl. She walks right at me and smiles.

"Hi Hunter."

I do a double take and examine her. She's slim and a little mousey but I can't seem to place her.

"Hey." I give her one of my trademark smiles and wonder if I've recently spent some time with her. She's definitely easy on the eye.

"You're looking good."

"Thanks, you too." I track her face and take her in. "Sorry I'm really trying here but I can't seem to remember where we met."

"Oh, that's because we've never met." She smiles at me, and the creep factor has just been raised by ten degrees, "I'm Wolfy's friend."

"Wolfy?"

"Yeah, I'm Jenny,"

I take a step back. And keep my face schooled. "Jenny?"

"Yeah, you've heard about me?"

"Sure."

She beams and I know I've fucked up, "My Wolfy has told you about me?"

I grimace and know I have to end this conversation right now before I give her any other wrong ideas. Wolf is going to kill me. "Hey, I have to go."

Her mouth twitches, "Well tell Wolfy I say hi. It's been a while since we spoke, I can't wait to see him again."

"Sure thing." I snap my mouth shut before I say anything stupid and take a backward step.

"Where is he working this week? I haven't seen him around for a while."

I take another step back, "He's out of town with a client."

Her face falls for a second then perks back up in a smile, "Of course, he's so big and strong and amazing at his job."

I say nothing as she looks dreamily at me.

"I'm sure he'll let me know when he's back." Her smile stretches too far across her face.

"Yeah, I bet." I take another backwards step and make a show of looking at the time, "Well, I really have to go, I have to get to work."

"Of course, you have lots of people to look after too."

A chill creeps up my spine as I force a smile.

"Don't forget to tell him to call me," she calls after me as I walk in the opposite direction to where I was going. Guess I'll have to take a long walk across town before heading home.

I feel her eyes on me for a while, and it's hard work not to keep looking over my shoulder. I take three trains, hopping on and off at random stations before I'm sure I lose her and can finally head home.

I'm going to kill Wolf.

Red

The sun feels too bright to be early. I check the time and see it's past eleven. My bed is empty, as I knew it would be. Wolf always sneaks away before Hunter gets home or gets up. My body aches. A combination of overworked muscles and weary exhaustion.

I love my time with Shaw, but the secret is gnawing at me. I've been planning on asking him again when we could tell Hunter. I understand his reluctance and yet, I feel like it's time.

I stretch and climb from the bed. I need a coffee, a shower and, if I'm lucky, a few moments with Wolf before I spend the rest of the day adding the finishing touches to my portfolio. It's due in a couple of days and excitement washes over me. I'm eager to reveal my final piece.

I make my way to the kitchen and hear them as I make my way down the corridor. They're talking in hushed voices.

"I'm telling you she fucking followed me."

"How could she have?"

"No idea she must have seen me out last night."

"Fuck." Shaw's voice is sharp and harsh. A tense silence. "Yeah I know, I know. Enough with the look."

"You need to keep your women on a leash." My heart squeezes at Hunter's words. *Women?*

"Why don't you let me worry about my women?"

"Cause obviously you can't." They both chuckle but if feels strained while my heart twists inside my rib cage. "I'll send one of the boys around to do a quick scout."

"Good idea. Fuck, and I was just getting settled. Man, I'm not ready to move again."

"Yeah," Hunter sighs.

"It was getting cramped anyway, and with Red being here and all."

There's that poignant silence again and I step away.

He wants to move out. Because of me. He has women.

Hunter catches a glimpse of me as I step out of the corridor. He falls quiet and moves the conversation onto more mundane things. Wolf tries to catch my eyes, but I avoid him, keeping a wide berth between us. My heart thunders in my chest threatening to burst open.

I want to fall apart, like a sandcastle in the tide. Instead, I fortify myself and take a deep breath. I can't believe I fell for his bullshit again. Ate up all the things he said, allowed them to feed my soul and let them tear down the ivy so securely protecting my heart.

"Morning sunshine." Hunter elbows me as I walk past. I throw him a scathing look which he doesn't deserve, and his hands pop up in the universal 'don't shoot' signal.

"Red?" Wolf tries and I walk by him, tears pooling in my eyes.

I grab my coffee and leave the kitchen. Hunter makes a comment about the wrong side of the bed. I go back to my room and slam the door behind me.

The tears slip out, rolling down my cheek in angry lines that draw pain on my face.

I swipe them away when someone knocks on my door.

"Red?" Wolf's voice calls from the other side of the door, "You okay?"

I screw my eyes shut and speak through a tight jaw, "Yeah, just not feeling great."

"Can I come in?"

"No!" I screech and the cracked open door comes to a halt.

"Okay…" he sounds confused, he shouldn't be. I just have to gather enough strength to tell him I'm done. *We're done.* Ivy tugs at my heart. "Hunter and I need to pick a client up from the Airport."

When I don't answer he steps into the room and his brow furrows, "Red?"

"Yeah, just go. I'll see you later." I throw the blanket over my head and hide beneath, shutting myself away.

I can still feel him in the room—his presence, it's overwhelming.

After a few breaths he walks out, "See you later."

When I hear the front door, I grab my phone and wait for Caleb to pick up.

"Hi Sweetie," his voice sounds way too fucking cheerful.

"Hey," I crack and sob into the phone.

"O.M.G girl, what's happened?"

"I need a place to stay." I try to sound matter-of-factly, but we both hear the desperate plea in my cracking voice.

"Of course babe," he sounds concerned.

"I'll tell you everything when I get there."

"I'll get the vodka ready."

"Thanks."

"See you soon sweetie." He hangs up, and I take a second to pull myself out of bed.

I will allow myself to be wrecked, to be broken and sad, but not yet. First, I have to get my shit and get out of here. I'll explain things to Hunter later.

I grab my suitcase and start shoving things inside. It all feels too familiar.

Except that this time I have a job and a friend. Maybe this time I can heal all on my own. Except that I don't know how I'm meant to get over Shaw a second time.

The tears keep coming like I've sprung a leak and already the ivy buds around my shattering heart.

4 8

Red

The insistent knocking on the door isn't going away, despite me ignoring it for a full five minutes. My head throbs. I've cried just enough to keep my soul alive, just enough for my tears to try and extinguish the furnace of pain burning inside me.

I open the door and am greeted by a stunning woman. Her face is slightly veiled beneath a cap that's pulled low and her long black trench coat is wound tightly around her petite figure.

"Oh, good someone's home, I was just about to give up."

The way she's standing at the door makes me feel like she wasn't. "Can I help you?"

"Yes, you can," she rips the cap off and a mane of blonde hair cascades down her shoulders, "I'm here to see Wolfy."

"Wolfy?"

"Yeah, he's my boyfriend."

"Your boyfriend?" I barely manage the question. I hear a distinct clattering noise, but it may very well be my heart falling into a dark pit and shattering into a million pieces.

"Yeah, we've been dating for almost a year."

"A year?" My stomach knots and everything hurts.

"Well, are you just going to let me stand in the street like a stranger?" She pushes past me without an invitation.

I let her barrel through me like all the emotions that blow holes into my soul, like this stranger has just held a shotgun to my heart and pulled the trigger, and now everything is leaking out of this gaping wound where my heart once was.

I suck in a frayed, broken breath as she surveys the place.

"Nice." She whispers and makes her way to the couch where she sits down and relaxes amid the cushions.

I'm still holding the door, or maybe it's holding me when she looks at me and asks, "Who are you?" I can hear the suspicion in her voice, and I clear my throat. I won't let Wolf break two hearts today.

I clear my throat, "Red, I'm Hunter's sister."

"Oh yes, I can see the resemblance." Her face visibly relaxes, and she smiles at me, "Have you been living here long?"

"No. And in fact I'm moving out this week so —"

"Oh great, there will be more room then."

She doesn't elaborate, but we both know what she means. "Guess so."

"I could use some water." She stares at me, and I finally close the door and try to shake the shock away. It's like hot glue that rolls and sticks to every surface of my skin.

"Yeah, of course." I go to the kitchen and retrieve two glasses. Nausea climbs up my throat and I bite down the urge to vomit as tears prickle my eyes. That fucking bastard, how could he? Again? And just when I was stupid enough to trust him, just when I thought he meant everything he said. I should have listened to my heart.

I let the cold water run and wash my face, erasing some of my emotion. I don't want to let this girl think anything is wrong. I fill up the glasses and walk to the lounge to find her gone.

"Hello?"

I set the glasses down and walk towards the corridor.

"Hello?"

Silence.

I knock on the toilet door but there's no answer. I walk to Wolf's room and knock, "Hello?"

I open the door to find her laying on his bed, I think she may have been smelling the pillows. I hate that she's doing that because I know how good they smell, how the fabric clings on to his musk and spice and pheromones and captivates you.

She jerks up from the bed and her eyes narrow on me, "Do you mind?"

"Erm," I try to swallow, but my mouth is a parched desert, "I think it would be better if you waited in the lounge."

She grumbles something, sighs, and reluctantly slips off his bed. She pushes by me and makes her way down the corridor. As I close the door behind me, I notice a few of his drawers are open.

She's back in the lounge and sips her water. When she sits, the trench coat slips up her legs and reveals nothing but skin. Her skirt must be very fucking short—or non-existent. Of course, just his type.

I cringe and die a little more inside as I sit next to her.

"Do you know when Wolfy will be home?"

"*Wolfy?*" I choke on the name. She glares at me like I've said something wrong, and I cough to recover, "Soon probably, they're dropping a client off at the airport."

"The airport." she whispers to herself and nods, and I start to get some very strange vibes from this girl. "Good, I can't wait to get my hands on him." Fire flashes in her eyes and I let my gaze fall to the ground so that she doesn't see the tears gathering again. Every time she opens her mouth it's like getting stabbed over and over and over again.

I hear shuffling on the outside steps then keys jangle in the door and it flies open. Wolf smiles broadly as he steps through it and a second later it falls away and the colour drains from his face as he notices his guest.

"Jenny?" he takes a tentative step inside, "What are you doing here?"

Jenny? That's her name? He dumped me for a Jenny?

"I've come to see my Wolfy."

He takes another small step and his gaze falls on me like he's assessing what state I'm in. "How…?"

Before he finishes his question, Jenny launches herself at him and wraps herself around his neck and waist then starts kissing him. He lets her as his eyes remain firmly on me.

I stand up and run to my room where I grab my backpack, then turn back to the lounge. I can get Hunter to drop the rest of my things later.

"I've missed you so much. God you feel so good," Jenny tells him as I hurry by them.

"I'm just going to let myself out." I mumble like an idiot.

Wolf says nothing as he watches me walk towards the front door.

Jenny smiles, "Nice to meet you, don't hurry back," she giggles as I let the door slam behind me.

My lips quiver as I run downstairs and into the street, and I dig into my backpack looking for my phone.

When I can't find it, I realise I left it on the kitchen counter.

"Shit!"

I do a quick, personal inventory and realise my legs still work, my tears haven't fallen yet, and my face looks intact. I can just be in and out of that house in thirty seconds flat and leave *Wolfy* and Jenny to do whatever it is they want to do.

I draw in a steeling breath and run back up the stairs.

Wolf

I watch Red walk out and breathe a sigh of relief before I let the anger wash over me. I try to pry Jenny off me but she's like an anaconda, and she's wound up tightly around me.

"What are you doing here Jenny?" I stay calm as she knits her hand into my hair.

"Oh Wolfy, I missed you so much."

"We've talked about this Jenny, you can't call me that, and you can't come near me." I keep my voice as steady and face schooled, while my insides rage.

"I know you don't mean it baby." She tries to stick her tongue in my mouth again, but I grit my teeth and deny her access. It was hard enough having to let her kiss me while Red watched. I watched her break, again. Watched her believe the lie. *Fuck.*

"Jenny."

"I love how you say my name," she purrs and bites my neck as I try to shove her hands away. "I've got a present for you."

"You know you can't be here."

As I talk, two distinct things happen; Jenny lets go of my neck with a single hand and undoes the knot of her trench coat, it falls open and she lets its slip away, at the same time I hear feet on the stairs and the jingle of keys in the lock.

Red pries the door open just as Jenny arches her back and lets the jacket fall to the ground, shoving her tits in my face.

Red's face falls but she quickly recovers, "I … I just left my phone…"

She walks by us as Jenny gyrates against me. Red's eyes latch onto mine, there's so much sadness in them that it makes my heart clench and my body ache.

"Red." I call for her as she walks by me, and Jenny jerks her head towards her.

"You need something?" Jenny's stone cold as she zeros in on Red.

"Don't worry about her, she's a no one," I say as I plunge my hands into her hair and pull her in for a kiss. I wait for Red to disappear into the corridor then grip Jenny's arms and shove. I don't like hurting girls but seeing the look on Red's face tells me I've already broken something.

"You can't be here. You're breeching your restraining order Jenny, you need to leave." I pick up her jacket and throw it at her.

"Is that because of her?" She flings her head towards the corridor, and fiddles with her coat.

My lips stretch into a grim line, "I've told you she's a no one, and I've also told you that I'm not a one-woman man, and what we had was fun but it's over."

"No, no, I know you love me Wolfy. No one makes love like you do without feeling something."

I slowly reach for the phone in my back pocket and unlock it, "We've been through this before,"

"No!" she shouts, and when she drops her jacket again, she's holding a gun. Pointing it at me with shaking hands. I assumed the weight in her jacket was a phone and wallet. I grind my teeth. *Rookie mistake!* "You love me! I know you love me."

I keep my gaze trained on Jenny and take a step towards the corridor. *Where the fuck is Red?* "Jenny put the gun down, let's talk about this."

"No more talking, Wolf. I'm starting to get the feeling that you don't appreciate everything I've been doing for you."

I keep my hands where she can see them, and my eyes stay locked on her face. I need to appease her.

"You know how much you mean to me. I've thought about you every day over the last year. The way you felt when you were inside me, how hot your breath was against my skin, how you said all those things, about how good I made you feel." Her hands shake a little, "I've stayed faithful even when I know you've strayed, and I've forgiven you— more than once. I know you keep asking me to stay away, but I also know you don't mean it."

"You've been too good to me Jenny, I really don't deserve you." I take another small step towards the corridor.

Her hands lock and she points the gun right at me, "Don't patronise me. I know what kind of man you are, how you've been with other girls while I've been so good." She whimpers a little like she's breaking inside and stitching herself together all at once.

"I'm not trying to patronise you. You're right, I've not treated like I should have."

"I mean, it's just been heartbreaking watching you from afar. You've made it so hard to get close to you."

"But you're here now." I try for a smile, but I feel the tension in my face pulling my mouth anywhere but up.

"Yes, a fresh start for us."

"Sure."

"But you've hurt me, a lot. You should be punished for that."

I run a thousand scenarios in my head, working out a way to try and get Red out of here. The fact she's not shown her face again is both frightening and comforting. "No Jenny, let's not do that, Let's just wipe the past away like you said. We can start fresh, just you and me."

"Oh god, I want to believe you," her voice quivers and the gun shakes in her hand.

I keep my eyes locked on hers, refusing to show her I'm afraid. "Believe me baby, let me take all your pain away, let me show you how much you mean to me."

"You're just saying it," she juts the gun forwards.

My hands come up automatically, "No, no, put that down. Let me show you how good we can be together." My stomach clenches and every muscle in my body is tense and alert.

"Show me."

"Come here baby."

"No! Drop your pants and show me how much you want me."

Fuck.

I'm as flaccid as soggy asparagus and nothing about this naked, crazy lady is going to get me hard.

"Come on baby, you know I can—"

"Drop. Your. Pants. And. Show. Me. Now." She's gritting her teeth, and I feel her control slipping. I can't take my pants down; I'll be more vulnerable with them around my ankles.

"Why don't you come here and take them off for me? Take me in your hands baby, come here so we can both feel better."

"Now!"

I exhale a desperate breath and reach for my jeans button, my mind races searching for anything to get me hard, anything but Red. I don't want to taint that, not any part of it. But the thought of her spreads warmth across my body, and for the first time, my cock twitches to life, like even the mere mention of her wakes all of me up.

"What just happened?"

"What do you mean?" My hands freeze on the zipper.

"Something happened to your face, you thought of something."

"Someone." I try for a smile again.

"Who?"

"Who do you think, baby?"

"Me?"

"Of course. Us, our future, our house, our kids." I wink at her.

She squeals like a toddler in a toy shop, drops the gun to the side, and in that one minuscule second, my eyes dart to the corridor before they land back on her face.

"Liar!" She screams, and her gaze boomerangs to the corridor.

She swings the gun toward the empty corridor and starts running. I beat her to the entrance but we both see Red at the same time; she's leaning against the wall, a phone in her hand.

"You bitch," Jenny screeches, "it's all your fault." She swings the gun at Red, and without hesitating, I dive—not thinking beyond making sure Red is safe.

A severe bang is followed by an explosion of pain in my shoulder that splinters and burns across my entire back and crawls up my neck with scalding pain and hot ferocity. My chest feels as if it's been ripped open, and blood pours onto the white tiles. It gushes from my wound and quickly becomes a puddle.

There's screaming somewhere—it grates against my brain, high pitched and disturbing all sliding into one sound.

"Wolfy!"

"Shaw!"

"Look what you did..."

"Oh my god, Shaw!"

"Get away from him, why are you calling him that?"

"Shaw, just hang on."

"Get away from him, why are you calling him that?"

I push myself from the floor, my bulk for once working against me, the world spinning around me. The bullet wound has rendered my right arm totally useless and my left keeps slipping in my blood. Pain slices my insides as I suck in a broken breath and reach for Red.

My hand finds only air and my body hits the floor with a thud. Pain explodes in my sides and nausea climbs up my throat. I fight the pull of darkness. It's so close and I know it will bring endless comfort, but Red is still here with Jenny and she has a gun. Every fight sensor in my overwhelmed system fires up, it clashes with the agony and queasiness ripping through me each time I move. I fall on my back, gravity pinning me down. Through the fog, I see Jenny; she's crying and screaming, and I can't work out what she's saying or how to help her. *Where the fuck is Red?*

Don't, Jenny please. I think I'm talking, but if I am, she can't hear me. There's more noise, it's fuzzy then angry and loud and a blur of colours and shapes rush by me. I think I hear another gunshot and maybe my name.

"Shaw?" A soft familiar voice slithers in my ear, and fingers tug at the strands of my hair.

Noise becomes a humming white sound that drowns away the blaring sirens, and screeching, and husky voices, until a warm darkness descends and takes away all the pain.

5 0

Red

Everything happens in slow motion. I look down the barrel, it glints with more menace than Jenny's eyes. She glares at me through narrow slits and the world falls silent. A second later there's a harsh ringing in my ears as Shaw's body moves in front of me then drops limply into the floor. He grunts in pain and his face contorts in an agonised grimace. My legs give out and I drop to the floor as a bolt of shock shoots through me.

Jenny is screaming while blood gushes out of Wolf's shoulder, painting the floor red. A hoarse pained moan rips from his lips, and my heart beats so hard I think I might pass out.

"Shaw!" I scream his name. Once, twice, endlessly.

Time is moving too fast and I can't grasp it at all. There's so much blood, too much blood, and Shaw's broken expression twisted in pain. He tries to move, his biceps straining over the effort as his shoulder lifts slightly from the floor. His lips move like he's trying to talk, but it's only a hoarse, pained whisper. He falls back down and the air rushes from my lungs, and I can't seem to pull anymore in.

"Just hang on, Shaw," I whisper to him, my eyes pooled with tears.

A crash rips through the corridor and people come running into the room. A blur of movement and noise, but all I can see is the blood as it pools around me and saturates everything. I think I can taste it.

"Red? Red?" Hands dig into my shoulders, and he shakes me from my daze.

I lift my gaze to find Hunter, concern etched deep across his brow.

"Hunter?" I feel like I'm waking up from a dream.

He pulls me into his arms then his gaze lands on Wolf. "Fuck," he mumbles and lifts me away. I protest, clawing at him, "No, I can't leave him."

"Shhh," he holds me while pulling me away, "let the paramedics work."

Strangers surround him and he's all alone, and I don't want to leave him. I rip away from Hunter's grip and fall back by Wolf's head, his glazed eyes roll to the back of his head and my trembling hands hover over him as I get snatched away.

"Let them help him," Hunter's voice tries to soothe me, but I feel like my heart is breaking all over again.

There are so many voices and so much noise, and I can't see past Shaw, past his pale face set in agony.

Hunter holds me as I follow them down to the waiting ambulance.

When they ask which one of us wants to go, Hunter releases me and says he'll meet us there.

We're moving but it feels like we're underwater and fighting a current as they work on him. I sit in the rumbling, wailing ambulance, sucking in long deep breaths and struggle not to vomit or collapse.

Wolf's strained breaths drown out all the other noise and fear saturates me like his blood, which covers half of me.

We come to an abrupt stop and then we're moving again. There's so much talking, and everyone seems so calm, too calm while all I do is want to scream. Instead my shaking fingers find his hair, and he lets out a strangled moan. I keep touching him. I keep telling myself it's to let him know he's not alone, but maybe it's just to comfort myself. I need to feel his heat, to know he's not gone.

Arms pull me away again and then he's wheeled away, and I'm left in a cold abandoned room with tears slicing my cheeks and red staining everything.

"I bought you some clean clothes," Hunter says, and I have no idea when he got here and how long he's been in the room.

He hands me a bag, but it slips out of his hand and to the floor when I fall into him and sob, all the fear and shock ebbing out of me in hot angry tears.

I want to be numb.

"You're okay Red, you're both okay," he says and crushes my head to his chest which heaves and falls as if he's reminding himself of that too.

I sling my arms around him and find comfort in his heat and strength.

"He's going to be fine, nothing keeps him down for long." I'm not sure who he's talking to. "Okay." I repeat his words in a quivering voice and let out a frayed breath.

"Red? Are you? Okay?" I can hear the strain in his voice
Not even close, "Yeah."

He kisses the top of my head and I know he doesn't believe me, but we both pretend everything is fine, just for now, just till we both get a chance to digest what happened.

"The police want to talk to you." He cocks his chin towards a uniformed policewoman standing at the door. She stands silently letting us have our moment.

I nod against his chest and mumble something, they can wait. The whole world can wait.

When I feel like I can stand on my own, I push away from him, wipe my face and stare at the red staining everything.

Hunter picks up the bag and leads me to a bathroom. The woman follows us silently. When we get to the bathroom, she holds the door open for me.

"I'm Constable Brown, I'll need to take some forensics from you." She seems kind.

I shrug. I don't know what she means. I don't care, I just want to clean up.

"I'll be right outside." Hunter kisses the top of my head.

I take him in; I've glued Wolf's blood all over him, but he's a rock—an anchor—keeping everything together.

I nod and take the bag then head into the bathroom.

My face cracks as I take myself in. Puffy eyes and blotchy skin. My jeans and shirt are ruined, painted a dark, angry crimson, my matted hair clumped together in angry knots weaved by blood.

Constable Brown is gentle when she asks me to stand against the wall. She takes pictures, my face, my hands, my body. All the blood.

I peel away the clothes, she takes them from me in her gloved hands and slips them into evidence bags. It makes everything feel dirtier, the kind that can't wash off.

I wash everything away. It doesn't help.

There are policemen, there's talking and questions, and somehow I manage to keep my tears at bay as I picture Wolf launching himself in front of me. The thundering explosion ricocheting through my heart.

Doctors check me. I tell them I'm fine. They don't believe me. They want me to sleep. To take some sedatives, I just want to be with Hunter. I know he's hurting too; Wolf has always been more than a friend—he's been part of our family for so long, they are brothers beyond blood.

51

Red

I stare at the blank white wall of the waiting room. It's the opposite of everything that's going on inside me. I'm a kaleidoscope of emotions, all crashing into one another with brutal, angry force painting my inside with anxiety and tension as guilt and anger tangles with fear and apprehension.

Hunter is pacing like a marching band without a drum major, the strain is drawn across his face and there's blood smeared along the side of his shirt.

We both jerk up any time anyone passes by, and the smell of disinfectant burns my nose.

I can't stand the empty silence broken only by his measured steps and by my uncertain heartbeat. I bolt from the uncomfortable, plastic chair, my nerves frayed. I can't take another second of this. "I need a drink."

Hunter nods like he knows what I mean, but he's a sentinel, too loyal and good to leave his post.

"They won't be done for at least an hour. And then the cops want to talk to him. Come downstairs with me."

"Red…."

"I need you." I hate throwing that in his face, but it's true.

He scrubs both hands over his face like he's trying to decide. He's torn between loyalty and his stomach. "Fine, but a quick one."

I shrug and walk out of the waiting room and along the bland corridor towards the elevator. We shuffle inside and wait in silence till we're down at the lobby. Everything feels like it's taking too long—the walk to the cafeteria, the wait in the queue, the barista making our coffee. Why do all pivotal times in my life involve a coffee?

We find a seat in the crowded cafeteria. You can tell who feels at home here and who the newbies are. The long-term family members who stick around with patients who have been in care too long greet all the staff members, they know the barista by name, and they look like the seat they've occupied has been theirs since day one. They joke and they have a version of relaxed that hides that paranoia and worry they carry with them every day. It's their normal.

Anyone else that's not a staff member is a newbie; the worry is etched so deep into their faces it's like a fresh sculpture that's not been fired yet, the worry hasn't set in, they don't know how terrible the damage is, if there a chance to walk out of here or if soon this will be their new normal.

I'm a clay sculpture, I'm waiting to enter the kiln.

"I called his mum," Hunter breaks through my thoughts and leaves my categorising unfinished, there are so many more stacks to fill.

"Good. Is she coming?"

"They'll be here tomorrow, they're vacationing in Greece."

"Oh yeah of course, I hear it's lovely this time of year." I put on my poshest accent and he cracks a quick smile.

"The best." His face falls again and he sips his coffee.

"Hey," I place my hand on his, "he's going to pull through, you said so yourself."

"I did, and he will." He clutches the back of his neck and stares at me.

"Is there something else?"

"Yeah, there is." His lips stretch into a thin line.

"What is it Hunter? You're stressing me out."

He clutches my hand and wraps his around mine. "Sometimes in life you try to do the right thing. You think that this thing is best for everyone, that it protects everyone and keeps them safe. But then you realise that that thing you did actually caused more harm than good, more damage, more pain, and you're responsible for all of it."

"What are you talking about Hunter? You're not making any sense."

"All I've ever wanted was to protect you, to make sure you were looked after."

"I know."

"I didn't want to hurt you."

I shift in my chair and a shiver slithers along my skin. "What did you do?"

He scrubs his forehead and squeezes his eyes shut, and when he opens them, they fix on mine, "Just know that I'm sorry, I thought I was doing the right thing, for all of us."

"Hunter."

"I'm the reason he's not told you how much he wants you, how much he needs you."

"What are you talking about?"

He quirks an eyebrow like we both know I'm pretending not to know who he's talking about. He draws in a long breath. "I'm the one who told Wolf not to go near you."

My mouth falls a little open and I stare at my brother. "What are you talking about?"

He swallows down a gulp of coffee and rests back into his seat, "A week before your sixteenth birthday I caught Wolf stepping out of your room. He just walked out of it like it was fine. You were fucking fifteen."

My hands tighten around my mug. "We never—"

"—it doesn't matter," he cuts me off, "I followed him outside and I went ballistic. We had plans, we had a friendship, you were my little sister, I thought he felt the same about you."

"Like I was his sister?" I say it slowly and my stomach churns.

Hunter's mouth twists in a grimace and he nods.

Eewee.

"I hit him." His eyes dart to the floor, "He let me, again and again. I was so angry, and he was so placid. He knew he'd crossed a line, with you, with me."

My heart chugs and my stomach bubbles with volcanic rage that shoots hot angry lava into my veins, "How could you?" I hiss.

"I thought I was doing the right thing."

"I loved him."

"He was a player, he would have broken your heart."

"He did that anyway." I erupt at him, "He left me so broken—"

"Red, I…"

"—but it was all you…"

"You know how it is, don't dip your pen in the company ink and all that."

"The compan—" I stand up and my chair clutters to the floor, "I can't do this right now."

I stomp away towards the exit leaving Hunter in my wake.

52

Red

A sleepy looking policeman stands outside his door. His uniform worn with too many washes and his shoes shiny. He stares at a spot on the floor, his hands fastened behind his back. He straightens up when he sees me and I muster up a brittle smile, stare at the door and give him my name. I'm listed as his next of kin, the man steps aside, pity shading his otherwise schooled expression.

Wolf lies on the bed, his eyes shut. I stop at the door, watching him. His pale face is peppered in sweat. With small steps, I edge into the room and stand by the side of the bed, uncertainty gripping me as he grimaces. The heart monitor sings the melancholy tune of his heart.

I want to soothe him. I want to take all his pain away. Guilt washes over me as my shaking fingers stroke his hair, his dazed eyes fly open.

"Red," he whispers in a strained voice. When his eyes meet mine, his features soften slightly, then fall back into a grimace as he takes a shallow breath. My heart lodges in my throat.

"Shaw..." I want to speak but I'm choking on my guilt. Tears pool in my eyes.

I sit next to the bed, my fingers trace long lines up and down his hand. His blurry eyes roll around as he struggles to stay awake. "I'm so, so sorry. I didn't know."

"Red, you're here," he whispers again and his face twists before the morphine drags him back under.

I breathe deeply to hold back my sobs. I spend the day content to stroke his fingers and brush mine through his hair as machines chirp and cry around us.

I spend two days sitting with Wolf. Stroking his hands and playing with his hair. Sometimes he opens his eyes long enough to smile and mumble. He calls my name looking dopey and heavy-lidded.

Hunter and I stand idly by the bed, things between us on ice until Wolf gets out. The doctor comes in and tells us they are planning on cutting down on his morphine so they can get him out of the ICU.

When the doctor leaves, I'm so relieved I go to the cafeteria and cry into my coffee.

That afternoon they move him to another room. When I step inside, he's sitting upright. His bristled jaw clenched tight. I freeze at the door when his gaze finds mine and his lips tug upwards.

"Red." The smile doesn't touch his eyes.

I erase the distance between us and reach for him then stop. When he smiles, I reach for his hand and lace my fingers through his. "I'm so sorry Shaw, I didn't know."

His eyes grow wide and his face colours in surprise, "Fuck Red, she almost killed you. Nothing here is your fault."

"I let her in." My eyes fall away.

"Red, look at me," he holds my gaze, and pushes up in the

bed so our eyes can be level. His jaw clamps and I see the pain and tension in his neck and shoulders, "what happened with Jenny is not your fault, it's mine. I should have never let things get as far as they did."

"Shaw—"

"She could have hurt you."

"She hurt you instead."

He sucks in a pained breath, "I would have never been able to live with myself if anything happened to you."

I screw my eyes closed, my heart finding a way to beat through the pain, "I'm sorry."

"Red."

"I believed you."

Understanding colours his face, and a smile tugs at his lips.

"I believed *her*. I believed that a leopard doesn't change its spots."

"But I'm not a leopard Red, I'm a Wolf." He gives me his slickest grin, and my stomach rolls as he grabs my wrist.

"She was the reason you wanted to move out?"

His head cocks a little, "You heard us?"

"Yes." Heat singes my cheeks.

"And that's why you were so angry?"

I nod, almost embarrassed.

"I've never been anything other than me when I've been with you. I've always told you the truth, and I always will. I should have told you about Jenny."

"But you didn't."

He sighs and lets his head fall into his pillow, "I thought I was protecting you."

"And Hunter?"

"What about Hunter?"

"He told me everything."

"He told you?" He sounds surprised.

I nod and wait for more.

The muscles of his jaw jump around before he starts speaking, "He's your big brother, my friend… he drew a line, he was trying to protect you."

"From what?"

"From me," he sighs.

"I'm so sick of the two of you thinking I need to be protected, I'm a big girl, I can make my own choices, my own damn mistakes."

He grimaces before he adds, "You have to understand, he was also protecting himself."

"Himself?"

He nods, "If we dated, and I hurt you in anyway, if we ever broke up, it would be the end of our friendship. We're brothers. It would be like losing a limb, someone like Hunter doesn't come around every day. He thought he was doing what's right for everyone."

"He never asked what I wanted."

"I don't think it mattered. Maybe you forget, but he's lost just as much as you and he made a lot of sacrifices." His face is stern as he speaks, "I guess losing me wasn't one he was willing to make." He wiggles his eyebrows letting the tension move out of his face.

His words soak into me and of the first time I can see my brother's perspective. Not that I feel like he had any right to interfere.

"I guess that's fair enough."

"Yeah. So you'll forgive him?"

"Maybe."

"And me?"

"Well, you've already been shot, so…"

He grins his beautiful smile and draws me closer.

I swipe away a strand of hair from his face and gaze into his eyes, "I don't like being lied to."

"I've never lied."

"Omission is just as bad."

He nods thinking, "Well, there has been this one thing I've wanted to tell you for a long time."

"Yeah?" I smile a little as his voice turns huskier and darker.

He gestures for me to get closer.

I move in, and his hand plunges into my hair, drawing me even closer till our breaths mingle. His lips brush mine, but before he says anything more, the door opens and a nurse walks into the room followed by Hunter. He looks her up and down, and my stomach twists in disgust.

"Seems like someone is feeling better," the nurse chirps and gives me a cold look.

What the hell is her problem?

"And yet he's still as ugly as he was when you brought him in," Hunter jabs at Wolf, who rolls his eyes.

"You're just jealous cause I'm prettier than you."

"Is that what you keep telling yourself?"

"I don't have to with—" his words die down and his eyes dart to me then to Hunter, who chuckles like an idiot.

The nurse plays around with his chart, adjusts a few tubes and touches Wolf more than I think is necessary. I see the way she looks at him, like she wants to give him a fucking sponge bath.

"Everything looks good," she chirps and gives him her best 'I would sit on your face if your girlfriend wasn't in the room,' look.

I wonder where they keep the scalpels. If I stab her, at least she'll be able to get immediate medical help.

I watch her leave. Hunter's gaze follows her, and a smirk crosses his face before he grabs Wolf's chart and pretends like he has any idea what's written on it. "You got a pen?" he turns to me."

"No, why?"

"Thought I'd ask for the results of his proctology exam, see if they found his head up there."

"You're so lame."

"So is Wolf," he chuckles, and I roll my eyes.

"At least mine will heal." Wolf says as if it's a fact.

"Pfftt," Hunter shakes his head, before his eyes zero on the two of us. "So, you two?" His demeanour suddenly changes as he and Wolf exchange and long look that I know means they will have some sort of conversation later on.

"None of your business—"

"—Yes."

We say at the same time, and my eyes flick to Wolf, who smiles like he's won some kind of prize.

Hunter nods and says nothing else for a beat, "I have to go find your nurse, there's something in my pants I need her to look at."

Wolf chuckles and I groan, "She'll need a microscope for that sort of exam."

"It's ok, it will be quick."

"So, disappointment all around?"

"Why? Is she meant to enjoy it too?" Hunter quips.

"You guys are assholes," I interject, and they both muffle a laugh as Hunter leaves the room.

"That poor nurse doesn't know what's about to hit her." Wolf says in his wake.

"Hopefully a brick in the face..." I murmur, and a smirk slithers across Wolf's face.

"Jealous?"

I huff, "Didn't like the way she touched you."

"Oh?" his smirk grows wider, "How's that?"

"Like she wanted to take what's mine."

A dark expression crosses his face and the humour falls away, "Oh?"

"Like this."

I go to the door and lock it then stalk to the end of the bed where I rip his blanket away. It falls to the floor, and I climb onto the end of the bed.

I lick my lips and his eyes zero in on my mouth. I crawl over the bed, placing my hands on each side of his torso, careful not to touch or disturb any of the tubes and machines still attached to him. I nip at his lips and a pained sound rips from his mouth. I steal it from him, kissing him hard, bruising and intoxicating. Wolf belongs to me.

When I break the kiss, I crawl back down his body and sink my hands down his boxers to find his massively hard cock.

"Red…" he growls as I squeeze lightly.

His heart monitor spikes, and the beeping becomes more frenzied as Shaw sucks in a ragged breath, and his face twists with a combination of pleasure and pain as his body tenses and his shoulder pulls.

I smile and lick my lower lip, his heart rate erratic.

There's frenzied knocking on the door, and his hooded eyes shoot to mine.

"Red." he strains as I jump off the bed, throw the cover over him and go to unlock the door.

The nurse falls inside the room, I notice her shirt is slightly out of place and her hair has been mussed. I find Hunter grinning a few steps behind her and roll my eyes. "What's going on here?"

She rushes to Wolf's bed and checks the heart rate monitor then goes on to check Wolf's blood pressure and temperature. His flushed face tells its own story as I lean against the window, smirking while she asks him a series of questions he stutters through. She double checks the heart monitor and says something about noting an elevated blood pressure. I bite down my snickers.

When she leaves, I move back to the bed and kiss Shaw.

"Fuck Red," he sucks in a gritty breath, "were you just about to—"

"Suck your cock?" I suck in my lower lip, "I was. And I

would have too, if it wasn't for your pesky heart monitor and giant hole in your shoulder."

He swallows hard, "And are you planning on doing that every time another girl looks at me?"

"I might." I wink at him and his jaw falls open for a second before a wicked smile crosses his face.

"I think I might be okay with that."

I bite my lower lip and battle a smile, "Just as long as you—"

"—I fucking love you Red." He doesn't let me finish and his lips crush mine in a bruising, bone melting kiss.

<hr>

Hunter

I manage to convince Red to go to her friend's house for a few hours and rest. I send Dylan along with her. He'll stand outside that door and bring her back to the hospital when she's ready. When I told her, she didn't even argue. I think that maybe for the first time ever she doesn't mind having a babysitter—as she calls anyone I ever asked to keep an eye on her.

When's she's gone I slink into Wolf's room. His eyes fly open when I step inside, and he pulls himself up on the bed, wincing as he does.

"Hey."

He nods in response and his pensive gaze follows me around the room.

"Saw your mum earlier."

"Yeah, she came to see I was still breathing and left. She organised some high tea with her friends while she was still in town."

"They're leaving again?"

"I'm breathing, aren't I?" He shrugs it off, but I've known

him for a long time. I know how much his parent's indifference slices his insides. The mistake they never should have made. I guess it's why we bonded the way we did, we both needed family.

"I see despite all their attempts to fix it, your face is still the same."

He smiles, "What can I say? You can't fix perfect."

I scoff at him still threading carefully around the words I want to say. "So…"

"I love her." He doesn't blurt it out or make it sound like a confession. He says it like it's fact and should be acknowledged as such, "Always have and you've always known."

I nod, "And how does she feel?"

"The same."

"Sure you're not forcing her to like you? It's hard work."

"Well, if I was forcing her, she'd be tied up and gagged in the basement right now, wondering why I haven't been back to torture and feed her for a few days."

"You feed them?" I gasp in mock horror.

"How else do you keep their energy up?"

"Mm, maybe that's where I've been going wrong."

We laugh it off and our eyes lock.

"This is not how I wanted you to find out."

"Where you going to buy me dinner first?"

"And box seats to the boxing." He wiggles his eyebrows.

"So, you and Red?"

"I love her, and I have no intention of hurting her. I'm not letting her ago again, and if you have a problem with that, then we can sort it out when I'm out of here."

I nod once. "If you hurt her…"

"—I won't, and I'm not asking your permission. Red is mine, she's always been mine."

"Spare me all the details and try to keep your hands off her when I'm around."

"Define, 'when I'm around,'" he smirks at me and I consider punching him in the shoulder.

I shot him an irritated look and he laughs.

"Relax, I know the rules."

"You already broke all of them."

"But, only for her."

I sigh. "Just…"

"I won't."

I nod just as Wolf's nurse walks into the room. Her cheeks flush red when she sees me, and I wink at her, thinking of all the things I'm about to do to her in the supply room. She checks on Wolf and gives me a lingering look before walking out.

"Seems I have somewhere to be." I smirk at him and follow her out.

5 3

Red

They release Shaw a few days later. He has to keep his wound clean and meet with a physiotherapist to build his strength back up. They keep telling him how lucky he was I was there. I don't feel the same way. Shaw reassures me Jenny has been arrested and held without bail. She's breached her restraining order one too many times, and with possession of a firearm and attempted murder charges, she will stay there for a long time. I feel safe in that knowledge.

We don't go back to the apartment. Instead, he's booked us a few nights at a hotel before his new apartment is ready. Hunter brings my suitcase, never asking why it was already packed. Maybe once everything settles, and I don't want to stab him for robbing me of years with Shaw, we could have that conversation. He doesn't stay long, he has clients and some new girl. I don't ask questions.

Shaw acts like an overgrown child, too stubborn to take things easy. His lips find mine between silences and his unin-jured hand takes leisurely journeys around my body, getting to know it all too well—driving us both crazy. I ask him to stop, he promises he will. We both suffer.

The boys help move us into the apartment. A two-bedroom unit with plenty of room. There is no history there, just a fresh start. We hold off celebrating for three agonising weeks. Movies and casual walks, the only activities he's allowed.

When we finally go to the doctor, Wolf is so anxious that he taps his leg all the way to the office and while we sit in the waiting area. He leaps out of his chair and storms into the surgeons' office as soon as they call his name.

I wait.

When he comes out, his smile is so broad and his gaze so hungry my body quivers with anticipation. He grips my wrist and rips me from my seat then stalks out. His body is a tense, muscular mountain moving with intention. He pulls me down the corridor, his grip tightening with every step.

He finds a door marked supplies and tries the knob. It falls open and his big body presses mine beyond the door and shuts it behind us. As soon as the door closes my back hits the wall and the air rushes from my lungs, as he captures my lips and lifts my legs, which automatically wrap around his waist like a belt.

"Shaw," I break the kiss, breathless as his mouth peppers a trail of kisses along my jaw and neck, "we can't..."

He steals the words from my mouth as if I didn't speak at all and rips at my shirt. It comes away with a single brutal tug and his mouth is back on mine. Impatient, hungry.

"I need you," he growls and pushes me back against the wall. His shirt vanishes, our bodies flush, and his mouth devours mine. My hands thread into his hair and as his kiss consumes us.

Intensity courses through his blood, dominating his actions and emotions. It's why he holds himself back so much, why his guard is always up, and his walls are so high, because when he falls, he falls the hardest. When it comes to Shaw, he doesn't do things half assed—especially not when it comes to me.

I reach for his jeans, pulling open the button and tugging the zip, he slides them down just enough to release his hard cock, the vein pulses along the shaft. He pushes away my skirt and rips my underwear to the side. I'm already so wet so needy. With a harsh thrust he's inside me and I bite down a cry. His face is a collection of expressions, like a hundred feelings clash all at once.

My fingers dig into his shoulders finding hot flesh to anchor myself against. I want to be gentle but he's so rough. He doesn't care about the pain, just me, just us. He pounds into me, his mouth never leaving my skin, kissing, nipping, licking at my neck and jaw and mouth—like he wants to be everywhere, making up for more lost time.

Pleasure builds inside me as Shaw keeps hitting that spot, and I move against him, needing to fall apart in his arms. He falters and stiffness and we fall. Lost to sensation, consumed by ecstasy, we are ruined, obliterated, undone.

He stills inside me, a guttural sound rips from his lips and his body tries to give out. His clammy forehead falls against mine as we gulp for air. His mouth whispers against my lips, claiming a sweet kiss before he sets me down.

"I love you, Red," his words slay me as we find our clothes and sneak out.

"I love you too."

On the way home his hands don't leave me, like he suddenly can't believe I'm here, and that I'm his.

Wolf

Red's head is on my chest, and her fingers idly run along the border of dark hair that runs down my torso from navel to chest, sending shivers up my spine. It's late, or possibly early; but after being given the green light that allows me to do more than just moderate exercise, I've finally been able to have my way with her all over this new apartment. Now that we've christened almost every surface, we can say it's really ours. I can't get over how beautiful she is, how soft, how insatiable she makes me feel and how vulnerable, like I might lose her again. Time is suddenly a commodity I couldn't take for granted.

Before Jenny, I guess I never really worried about the future, about life being so short. Before I felt like I had so much of it. I was invincible. Fuck it, I'm not even thirty yet; but when I woke up seeing Red by my bedside and cops outside my room, and felt pain slashing throughout my body, I've realised how much time I've wasted, let dissolve away like a mirage for single nights of empty orgasms instead of a life time of fulfillment with Red.

I should've never let her go, and as I stroke her hair and feel her heat against me, I know with every fibre of my being, I never will.

"I have to get up," she moans into my chest, pulling away and stretching. Her perfect fucking tits on display makes my body harden, again.

"No, you don't," I growl and pull her back, sucking on one of her delectable nipples. She screams and giggles and bats me away.

"I do," she kisses me, and I know she's loath to leave in the same way I hate to let her go, "Becca won't give me another extension and my portfolio is due today."

I release her and watch her go. The shower comes on and I force myself to stay put, knowing if I go in there with her, the only thing she will get done is me. She's worked too hard for me to ruin it for her cause my cock craves her like a sixteen-year-old teenager without any control.

She walks out with just a towel around her and proceeds to drop it, getting dresses in front of me.

"Are you trying to torture me?"

"Maybe just a little." She winks.

"I've been up all night, I've worked hard, and I am one hungry fucking Wolf. Don't tempt me Red, I'm not sure I keep my hands to myself much longer."

A sly smile creeps onto her face, "Once I'm done with Becca, you can show me your very big hands."

I clench fistfuls of the sheet and our eyes lock, "The better to feel you with."

"And your very big mouth," she steps forwards her voice husky.

"The better to taste you with." I lick my bottom lip, my cock harder than a desert rock.

"And your massive cock." She straddles me.

I groan desperately as she grinds against me. "The better to fuck you with."

I snatch her mouth and kiss her brutally. She wrenches away breathless and climbs off.

"Later," she croaks, and I know if she doesn't leave now, there will not be a later.

She exits the room and I fall back onto the bed, sucking in all the air in the room. It doesn't help, her smell is soaked into every surface. I let out a hungry groan and go take a cold shower.

<hr>

Red

"These are beautiful," Becca smiles at me and it's all I can do not to evaporate into a self-satisfied fog.

"Thank you." I hope she knows how much I mean it.

"You are very talented Red." She beams at me, "I'll make some phone calls, I'm sure a few of my friends would love to display your work in their galleries.'

"Really?" It's hard to stay composed when I want to squeal and jump out of my skin.

She puts down my work and sighs, "Guess I'll just have to find myself another trainee."

The way she says it leaves no questions; she believes in me.

"I can't thank you enough, for everything," I'm giddy, "but I'd like to stay as long as you'll have me. I know I still have a lot to learn, and Caleb would be miserable without me."

"Well, no one wants that." She winks at me.

We sit for a while longer and discuss my future and everything it might hold, before I leave she draws me into a warm hug and tells me how proud she is. My eyes sting with tears and my heart with pride.

I want to run all the way home. I'm a ball of excited energy when I burst through the door and search for Wolf. I find him in the bed, looking only half awake. His mouth splits into a panty melting smile when his gaze latches on to mine, and my fingers itch to run through his mussy hair.

"Hey."

"Hi. How did it go?"

"Amazing!" I let out my excitement in a too high-pitched scream and launch myself onto the bed where he chuckles at my joy.

"Amazing?" He pulls himself up on an elbow and the sheet falls away from him, showing off his sculpted torso.

I fill him in on my meeting with Becca and he grabs me onto him, our lips crash together.

"I'm proud of you," he murmurs against my mouth, and I pull at the sheet that covers him. He's still naked, and just my eyes on him makes his cock swell and harden.

I grip his cock in my hand and squeeze lightly. He hisses and I squeeze a little harder as his mouth collides with mine.

"Red," he growls, as my hands pumps his hardening cock, "you're fucking amazing."

I don't answer but rather pull away, slide down the bed, dip my head, and lick the tip of his cock. He hisses, his head falls back into the pillow, and his hand sinks into my hair, fisting the strands. I take him into my mouth, and his purr ripples through me.

He sucks his lower lip into his mouth and his eyes screw shut as I lick and suck and flick just the tip of his cock, while my hand glides up and down his shaft. His hips buck as he grows even harder in my mouth, wanting to force his way inside.

"Red," his voice cracks with warning and desperation; it's a delicious mix that trickles through my body. I close my mouth around his shaft and glide down along it. His body goes rigid and an agonised sound tumbles from his mouth.

I torment him, keeping an uneven pace. He growls and grumbles, needing his release. I love watching his pleasure build, the way his stomach clenches and face twists and breath falls from him in short, sharp pants.

When I reach for his balls I think he's about to rip the sheet in half. His hands clutch at the fabric, his knuckles white, "Fuck Red," he groans and everything inside me lights up. I always want him to call my name like this.

I line up and suck him deep then glide up and down, quickening my pace till his body jerks and his hand rips into my hair. "I'm going to come," he warns, but I don't pull back. His eyes squeeze shut, jaw slightly parted. He gasps and his release spills down the back of my throat.

When he's done, I let him fall from my mouth and give him a beat to catch his breath.

"Fuck Red…" he sucks in a gritty breath, "will you do that every time you get a gallery to show your stuff?"

"Probably." I wink at him and his jaw falls open for a second before a wicked smile crosses his face.

"I think I might be okay with that."

I bite my lower lip and battle a smile, "You seem to be

okay with anything where my mouth is wrapped around you c—"

"—I fucking love you Red" he doesn't let me finish and his lips crush mine in a bruising, bone melting kiss that promises our happily ever after.

T he end.
    The beginning…

Please consider leaving a review on Amazon and Goodreads to tell everyone how much you loved Wolf.

ACKNOWLEDGMENTS

A Word from Jane

I would like to start by thanking you the reader, so much for reading! If you enjoyed the story, please leave a review and recommend the book to any friend you think would love Wolf and Red's story. You will have my eternal love and gratitude.

Even a few short words go a long way.

As always, I would love to thank my wonderful friend and beta Dawn, her enthusiasm knows no boundaries, her genuine love for books reading and helping authors is contagious and humbling. I have loved having her in my corner. Thank you.

To my amazing editor and friend Sarah, you're inspirational and you have all the right words to say when I'm feeling like mine aren't sufficient.

To Kirsty, you know how much you mean to me, thank you for everything little thing you do.

To the ghost man who haunts me, this book wouldn't exist without you. Without your input, feedback, motivational techniques and nights full of laugher I would have never got this done. Sometimes when you're not the worst, you're the best. Thank you x.

To all my other betas and C/Ps your input and critiques have been invaluable without you Wolf would never have been.

Jane Wynters doesn't quite know how to answer the question of "where are you from?" She's moved from place to place like a snowflake on the wind always searching for a safe place to land. She loves meeting new people and exploring new places. She loves reading, writing and conjuring new worlds from her imagination. Coffee is at the top of her food pyramid and she is fluent in three languages and sarcasm.

Want to know more about the author and keep in touch? get snippets of up coming books and have a bit of twisted fun?
Come join me in Wonderland…